RUN

RUN

By

Darleen Innis

1

Sheila Harper, office clerk of the county highway department, leaned over her counter as far as possible to whisper. She was in secret communication with Avery Underwood, the highway department's assistant engineer, and the only other female on staff. "Do you *really* plan to tell him now?"

A confrontation awaited Avery inside the office of Jasper Hollister, chief county engineer.

Avery looked more like a boy than a girl, the complete opposite of her friend and confidant, Sheila. Avery always wore jeans, a long-sleeved tee, and her work boots, scuffed and worn by years of trudging through dirt, gravel, and asphalt. Sheila, on the other hand, was never without makeup and always wore a skirt and blouse. The blouse was, more often than not, some pastel shade, lavender today.

"I have to, Sheila. I don't think trying to unseat him is something I can hide. Do you?"

"God, I hope you own a helmet and a Kevlar vest. I need to be somewhere else or an itty bitty fly on the wall when the-you-know-what hits the fan."

Avery arched her eyebrows in lieu of a shrug. She was trying to keep the topic of their conversation concealed from Hollister, who was sitting in a separate office only fifty feet from Sheila's counter. His door stood slightly ajar. Avery adjusted her glasses and shuffled papers on the counter in a series of useless motions. "I have to tell him soon. Maybe today, since I don't have to track him down. For once, he's here in the office instead of out who knows where." Avery stole a glance toward Hollister's office door but made no move toward it. She felt a sudden nervousness about what she had to say regarding her decision to run for his job as county engineer in the fall.

She absent-mindedly played with a metal box on the counter. It was an aluminum storage clipboard that Hollister always took with him whenever he left the office. It was a rare occasion for it, and her boss, to be in the highway department's office. Avery lifted the top of the box and peered inside. Gas receipts lay inside, along with ballpoint pens, mechanical pencils, and a county gas card.

"Why don't I get a gas card?" Avery asked.

"You drive your own vehicle. You fill out the travel reports. I reimburse you per mile. Jasper never uses his own car. He always takes a county truck. He even takes one home every night. Justifies 'in case I have to leave for a road emergency,'" she said, quietly mocking Hollister's gravelly voice.

"He *always* takes this with him?"

"Yes. Why?"

"I don't know. No reason," Avery said. She closed the top and straightened the box. The work order clipped inside was not something he needed since he had assigned the task to her. She wondered if the paperwork was just a ruse, something to make him look busy should anybody ask. Her mind soon jumped from the bridge paperwork back to her present problem.

"We're the same party, he and I. I'm not likely to beat him in a primary, anyway."

"Maybe you should hold off saying anything to Jasper just yet," Sheila said.

"I feel like I'm being dishonest if I don't speak up soon about my intentions."

"Don't feel that way," Sheila said. "Politics is not about honesty. You take your time. Lay low. He doesn't owe you a thing, and he doesn't *own you*. You do know he was pressured to hire you by the commissioners, don't you?"

Avery looked at Sheila in surprise.

"They don't have any control over what he does, but the majority are also democrats. They convinced him that you'd be an asset to this office. I was in the commissioners' office and overheard. They loved your resume over all the others when he presented several for approval last year after that storm emergency. He resisted. He knew then you were better qualified for the job, even better qualified for *his job*! I think he was scared of you, your credentials, I mean. He was stalling on hiring you, but they pressured him. Besides, the county needed people fast because of all the damage from the derecho. You just keep doing your job," she paused. "Keep doing *his job* the best you can. Say nothing now. Please. He'll ride my butt the moment he hears what you plan to do."

"Why you?" Avery asked, perplexed.

"Because we're *w-o-m-e-n*. He'll take some of his attitude out on me because I'm sitting right here in harm's way. I can't get away from this desk. I'll be collateral damage."

"Oh. I'm sorry. Really? He'd make your life miserable because of me?"

"In a heartbeat. You watch. That's what I meant when I suggested you wear body armor when you do tell him. Your life here will become Hell after he hears your news. I've seen how he's treated others who dared go up against him, and they were *men*."

In his office, unaware of anything else happening around him, Jasper Hollister bent over his computer keyboard, drafting a letter to a pal living in Montana. His friend had promised Hollister a place to stay if he ever traveled out to join him for some big game hunting. Jasper was counting on an uncontested win at the polls come November. He figured he could spare a week, maybe even two, in the fall. A trip to the Rockies would let him escape the local press, which, in his opinion, always seemed to have some axe to grind. He could go away, have a good time, and hunt elk rather than chase down votes.

Hollister looked up from the screen with annoyance when Avery knocked on the door frame.

He assumed his assistant had some irritating little detail to run past him, probably related to a personnel issue among the road crew. He'd instructed her to take care of all those kinds of irksome duties herself as part of her job. He hated personnel problems. There is always too much paperwork.

Jasper wrinkled up his nose at the thought. A vast amount of Jasper's paperwork had never been filed properly before Avery arrived. Since he'd hired her, Jasper took full advantage of her presence to disappear "out on the road" as far from his job, paperwork, and especially this woman as he could get. She could sign all the damn forms herself. The woman was a workaholic, in his opinion.

"What now?" he asked curtly, rolling his chair back from his desk.

Warned to be on guard, she sensed Hollister seemed to be in one of his foul moods. As a precaution, Avery remained standing in the open doorway. She shoved her hands deep into the pockets of her jeans. From the scowl on his face, she thought maybe this was indeed the wrong day to announce her plans. She took a deep breath.

"I thought you'd better hear it from me first, not get blindsided by anyone else," she began.

She paused to be sure he was listening. Most of the time, Hollister ignored her. She suspected his poor hearing was intentional. Maybe she was lucky to have caught him in the office. Maybe not. In the past, she'd wasted untold work hours hunting for him because he'd be out. He always seemed to be hiding in the farthest corners of the county when she needed him. She cleared her throat and bluntly made her announcement.

"I've decided to run for office this fall."

Jasper paused. He was about to return to the keyboard. He blinked, still not tuned in to the specific meaning of her announcement. "What? Whatever *kind of office would you run for*?"

Avery took another breath. "I plan to run for county engineer."

Jasper thought Underwood was trying to make a joke, a poor joke at that. He imagined this female upstart standing there in his doorway that day, even thinking of trying to oust anyone, him in particular, from any office. He began to laugh at the absurdity. A smirk became a chuckle and then a bellowing, sarcastic laugh that eventually forced him to double over in a coughing fit. A tear began to stream down his red cheek. Then, his brain, which had been slow to process possible adverse ramifications of her announcement, brought him to reason and anger.

"What the hell?" he finally muttered once he'd regained the ability to breathe. "Are you… have you gone completely mad? Do you think you… a *woman*… could unseat *me* or anyone in an election in this county? You *are* mad. What on God's green earth made you think you could try? I gave you this job. This is how you repay me? You…"

Hollister's tone had turned in a matter of seconds from hysteria to fury. Avery was prepared for the outburst. She held her ground, not moving, hands still shoved deep into her pockets, trembling slightly but well hidden from Jasper's view. She breathed slowly to calm her nerves before speaking.

"I do realize that this presents some problems for us," she began.

"Problems? *Problems?* Like Hell it does. I don't have problems, girl. But you do!" Hollister's voice bellowed beyond the confines of his office walls. Three of the road crew who had just entered the outer office to speak to Sheila could hear his every word clearly. They paused from their initial mission to huddle around Sheila's counter, remaining silent. Listening.

"You can just get your ass out of my sight, out of my office, and out of this job right now."

"Are you trying to fire me?" Avery asked with a degree of indignation in her voice.

"I don't need to fire you, you stupid twit. You can't work for me if you want to run for this office! See? You don't know the first thing about about politics. You can't work for the county *and* run for county office at the same time. You're a God dammed classified civil servant employee. A bad one at that."

"Exactly, I have certain job protections under civil service regs," Avery began to argue. "I can't be let go unless I've done something wrong, and I've done nothing to merit dismissal."

"Just how thick is that numb skull of yours?" Hollister yelled, rising abruptly. His office chair rolled backward on its casters until it slammed against the wall. "Civil servants aren't *allowed to run for public office*! So get your ass down to the courthouse and fill out the damn paperwork to *quit*. You're done here. And don't you ever, ever, show your face around here again. Don't take anything with you, either. I want you out of this office, *now!*"

"Sheila? Sheila!" Hollister yelled, charging toward the doorway where Avery stood on his way toward Sheila's counter, not bothering to wait for his clerk to respond.

Avery's jaw had gone slack. She had not expected this. She did expect Hollister to be surprised at her announcement. Angry maybe. Probably, according to Sheila. But she did not expect to lose her job over a plan to run for public office. *What is this regulation he spouts? Is there even such a rule?* She immediately felt determined to verify Hollister's assertion. But where to start?

The guys who had popped into the outer office abruptly slipped back out the door before the boss could see they'd overheard his rampage. Hollister was so angry he could barely see straight anyway. Sheila's shoulders drooped, watching them escape, leaving her alone to deal with Hollister, who was stomping toward her workspace. She rolled her eyes before turning to face him directly.

Nora Radnor removed and began to polish her large red-rimmed eyeglasses. She returned a special cloth for that purpose to the pocket of her linen suit, then placed the glasses back on her face. Stepping back, she paused to observe her handiwork. The little kitchenette of the Tea Basket Quilters hall shined spotlessly. This place, the women who filled it with laughter and fabric, humming sewing machines and chatter, was her reason for getting up every morning. This was her domain, the place where she happily made everyone feel at home. Nora's hospitality extended to all the Tea Basket members as well as to the Shining Star guild members who shared their building. She also welcomed any visitors or guests who happened by. She prepared a pot of coffee every day for all who entered. It was easy enough and a task she enjoyed. This sunny and warm early spring morning was no exception. Coffee was brewed, and the kitchen was tidy.

Nora had always been the first to arrive since the guild had acquired the building some years back, often unlocking the front door before eight. She lived nearby, so this simple duty seemed only natural to her, even before falling into her new role as Tea Basket president earlier in the year. She had reluctantly accepted the office, feeling unsure of her ability to lead a large group, considering her advanced age. Nora was in her nineties.

The wood frame building that served as the permanent home of the Tea Basket Quilters stood at the corner of Shannon and Morris streets thanks to the bequest from a founding member who deeded the building in her will, along with a sizeable trust fund for its upkeep. Tea Basket members used the open first floor for meetings and classes. In the back, they added the little kitchenette where Nora always kept the coffee pot perking. To the side, they installed a small bathroom. Up the stairway were several smaller rooms for members' use. In the largest of those rooms, a long-arm quilting machine was installed. White carpet covering one wall in the big room served as a design wall.

Nora scanned the empty hall this morning. She saw several six-foot white folding tables arranged around the hall in short rows with two chairs per table for sewers. The day before, a class on the disappearing hourglass block had filled the space with women, sewing machines, chatter, and laughter. Nora thought someone should remove them in readiness for their upcoming meeting. Usually, only chairs would be arranged for business meetings. Members would line up a few rows facing a single table in the front reserved for the president, secretary, and treasurer. Nora decided she would ask more able-bodied members who popped in today to do the honors of folding the legs on the long tables, take them down, and haul them out to the storage garage in the rear of their lot. Her thoughts then jumped ahead to the meeting that she would chair and what she had put on her agenda.

Just then, the front door opened, and her counterpart in the Shining Star guild, Lois Caldwell, walked in. Lois, a large woman clad in a billowing pale blue cotton dress covered in white polka dots, entered, her arms laden with tote bags. Lois barely managed to catch the door with her shoe. She then deftly shoved it closed on her way in. Lois was both a member of the Tea Baskets as well as the appointed president of the newer Shining Star guild.

"Hey-dee-ho, Nora," Lois said as she lumbered under her weight and that of the bundles she carried.

"Good morning, Lois. Here, let me help. What is all this?" Nora rushed forward to remove some of the heavy tote bags from her friend's arms.

"Hens are in full production this week. I thought I'd bring in some eggs for ladies to take home. You know how expensive they've become. As usual, they can leave their money in the jar by the fridge. I'm not raisin' my prices, though. Still three dollars a dozen. I've some extra fabric, too, if ladies want to take some. And I have papers for the Shinin' Star members. It's a little table topper pattern they voted to try as a group."

Lois began to distribute her tote bags. She then dropped a stack of patterns from one overburdened hand. The patterns landed on a small table beside the stair steps leading up to the second floor. She then made her way with some difficulty to the kitchenette. There, she carefully unpacked and shuffled several cartons of eggs into the refrigerator.

Nora remained busy unloading a bushel of fabric onto one of the tables. Seeing so much tumble out of the shopping bags, Nora changed her mind at once about taking this particular table down. She saw that Lois had brought a vast quantity and variety of cotton fabrics that now covered the entire table top. Her mind started thinking; perhaps this fabric should be spread out for display and a small sign posted.

"Do you want this fabric reserved for Shining Star members?" Nora asked.

"No, no. It's free for anybody who wants it," Lois explained as she stacked the final carton of eggs into the refrigerator and closed the door. Guild members were all willing to share their knowledge of quilting as well as extra fabrics. Sharing was a perk for being a member of their collective of like-minded enthusiasts of the craft.

"One of my grange ladies is movin' out of state. She didn't want to take all that fabric with her. She's downsizin', movin' into a little condo down in Florida. Anyway, she said for me to find homes for her fat quarters. Might even be some half and one-yard cuts in there, too. She thought maybe she'd buy new stuff once she's settled." Lois chuckled, "Wouldn't find me living in a tiny little place down south. No, siree, not for a million bucks. Too many hurricanes for my comfort."

"And besides," Nora added, "Where would you keep chickens and cattle, and how would you grow hay in all that hot sand?"

The two laughed. Lois was a former farm wife turned widowed farmer. The sixty-something kept a small herd of Highland beef and a flock of Rhode Island Reds and helped the young men she hired each summer put up hay off her fields for the cattle. "When she had time," as she was known to remark, she pieced quilts. She had made time recently to preside over the Shining Star guild. By special arrangement, her guild used the Tea Basket hall with all of its amenities. Many, if not most, of her members, including Lois, were also tea baskets. But unlike the majority of Tea Baskets, her Shining Stars were relatively new to the craft. They greatly benefited from meeting at the hall, mixing with more experienced quilters, and picking up tips and techniques.

"Do you want me to sort this fabric?" Nora asked, still picking over the pile of colorful cottons.

"If you want to. It's not necessary, though. I'm goin' to have a cup of coffee. You made some, right?"

"Of course."

While Nora began to shuffle and sort fabric by color, Lois selected a large coffee mug from the cabinet and poured herself a cup. "You want some?" she yelled.

"Love a cup. Small one, please," Nora said.

Lois joined Nora at the table, which was now littered with a variety of cotton fabrics arranged more or less from light shades to dark by her elder friend.

"I've a problem I wanted to talk to you about," Lois said as she handed Nora a small delicate china cup. She pulled back one of the chairs at the table and lowered herself onto the seat. Her voluminous polka dot dress billowed around her, completely covering her lap and the chair, the hem falling all the way to the floor. She took a sip of the hot beverage, then lowered the cup.

"Oh, sounds serious," Nora said, pulling out a chair for herself and sitting down beside Lois. Nora crossed her legs and smoothed her crisply pressed gray linen slacks. Her lips were painted this morning a pale pink to match her pink silk blouse. She puckered those pink lips and gently touched the rim of the cup to take a sip of her coffee. She approved of the taste. She was pleased with herself, knowing she always made a good cup of coffee. She then looked to Lois, waiting for an explanation to follow.

"Well, as you know, my gals aren't ready to tackle somethin' big or complicated. Not yet. They just don't have confidence or skill. But they agree that our guild should have a charity project. Now, unlike us Tea Baskets, who change our charity from year to year, I been thinkin' us Shinin' Stars need one long-term project, a project that runs for more than one year. Not all of them can accomplish tasks quite a fast as Tea Baskets, you know. I don't know what to suggest. I do know they aren't ready to make a raffle quilt together. Shoot, a few of them still haven't got the knack of the quarter inch seam. Sure as shootin' if all those gals tried to make blocks for one quilt, too many of their blocks would have to be ripped out and completely redone. None of the blocks would end up the same size."

Nora smiled and nodded her head in agreement. The quarter-inch seam was the first and most basic lesson to learn for any piecer worth her salt.

"So, what you want is one project, but not necessarily *one thing* to achieve that goal. Right?"

"Right. And the project, or projects, have to be fairly simple to complete. Whatever they make, they should be able to produce that *somethin'* on an individual basis. Maybe we should make lots of the same thing, in other words. But what, and for who? Or should I have said, for whom?"

"Well, that is a problem," Nora agreed. "You need to give me some time to think about that." Nora took another sip, satisfied she had made a really good coffee this morning, having used a different and new-to-her brand.

"Don't think too long. I'd like to present an idea at our meetin' next week," Lois said.

The door to the hall opened just then to admit Avery Underwood, another member of both guilds. The tall, lanky woman wore a face that seemed unusually dejected. Clad in her usual attire of jeans, work boots, and long-sleeve tee, Avery, who looked more like a tall boy, took no notice of the colorful fabrics spread over the table between her friends. She barely smiled as she approached her friends.

"Ladies. I need to talk to someone."

"Well, here's the place to share your troubles," Nora said. "Grab a cup of coffee and join us. Tell us what you need. Lois here is looking for an easy charity project for you Shining Star gals."

Quite at home in the Tea Basket hall, Avery went straight to the cupboard herself as Lois had done, retrieved her favorite mug, and poured herself a cup. She had joined the Tea Basket guild when she first arrived back in Athens a year earlier, between jobs and looking to reconnect with the people of the community where she had gone to college. That was months before taking on a leadership role in the Shining Star guild. She had been initially appointed the Shining Star's first vice president by its organizer. She'd only held the office a short time before she had been offered her job as the assistant county highway engineer following a disastrous storm. The new job had forced her to resign from her guild office to take on the workload as the county's number two engineer.

Lois Caldwell was suddenly promoted into Avery's vacant position as a result of Avery's departure. She nervously became the Shining Star vice president and, soon after that, found herself their new president. A storm disaster threw the community into temporary chaos and their founding president out on the street, homeless.

Demands for the new job had ended most of Avery's guild-related activities. She often worked twelve-hour days for the county. She supervised road crews. Took care of Jasper Hollister's neglected paperwork and dealt with disciplinary issues for the department. That left little free time to enjoy the company of her quilt-making friends. But as busy as Avery was, she tried to stop by the hall as often as her schedule allowed, just to share a cup of Nora's coffee and chat with her friends.

Today, the look on her face was serious. She pulled out a chair and sat down at the table heaped with fabric.

"Well?" Lois said, not being as patient as Nora to hear Avery's concern. "Tell us. What's wrong? Nora here can fix just about anythin': seams, mitered corners, even machines."

Nora grinned and scoffed. "Ha, ha," she mockingly said.

Avery took a deep breath, letting the air out slowly. "I've decided to run for political office… for County Engineer."

Nora and Lois looked at one another in stunned silence, jaws agape. This was not the kind of help either of them could offer their younger friend.

"And Hollister informs me that because of my decision, I have to quit my job."

2

Nora nearly choked on a sip of coffee. "Well, well!" she said, recovering quickly, dabbing her lips with a tissue. "You mean to oppose your boss? You're going to run against Jasper Hollister for county engineer?"

"I am. Or I was," Avery replied, her secret definitely out by telling Nora. Nora was well-known for sharing the latest news about her Tea Basket friends. For months, Avery had been bottling up the idea, telling no one until this day. Having revealed her plan to Hollister, it now looked like she was either going to eat crow or be unemployed. Neither of those consequences had ever occurred to her, and neither sat well with her.

"I've never campaigned for any office, not in high school, not in college. I've been anxious just thinking about campaigning. Now it seems all my concerns, how to get votes, how to get funding, were all just a waste of time and energy. I never once imagined my decision would cost me my job."

Nora leaned over to pat Avery on the knee with a look of concern on her face. "Worry is always a waste of time, child." Nora felt it was her privilege to refer to almost everyone as 'child.'

Avery sighed. She looked down into the cup of coffee in her hands. "I just came from Hollister's office. He practically threw me out. Thought I'd stop to share my troubles before I go over to the courthouse to process paperwork and resign. Does anyone have some kind words of comfort?"

"Well, girl," Lois said, "you're goin' to have an uphill battle with ol' Jasper. He's been county engineer for decades. Probably ain't nobody qualified 'round here to run against him until you arrived. Sounds like he's not takin' kindly to one of his own, and a qualified woman at that, challengin' the ol' boy. Better brace yourself for more backlash." Lois sat with her arms across her ample chest. Made of sterner stuff than most of her friends imagined, Lois could be a formidable foe when the need arose. "Stand your ground," she advised. She would. "You have friends here who'll have yer back."

"I thought I was ready for whatever he had to throw at me. I'm sure I have the required credentials. I checked the ORC on that. But what I don't understand is why I have to quit."

"ORC?" Nora asked.

"Ohio Revised Code. It's published online. Lists the requirements for any civil service or public office job."

"Oh, I see."

"What's your first step?" Lois asked. "It sure seems like it shouldn't be quittin'."

"Well, Hollister said I can't run for public office and hold a civil service job simultaneously. I'll have to go to the courthouse and pick up a petition form from the board of elections office. Then guess I'd better talk to the commissioners about resigning."

Nora knew that Avery was a democrat. The two had discussed politics a few times while doing menial tasks together in the hall. "Don't be so hasty," Nora warned, "You should talk to the party chair first. That would be Joe O'Feeny. He's our county prosecutor. Handles legal stuff for the county in his role as chief prosecutor. Joe will know why Hollister told you to resign, or he might even have a solution."

Avery took a sip of her coffee and shrugged her shoulders with little enthusiasm.

"Never take 'no' for an answer, child," Nora said. "While I wish you well in this endeavor, I think Jasper Hollister might not be one hundred percent truthful about you having to quit. I'm sure you'll do a fine job if you're elected come this fall. But it does seem premature for you to quit your job before you're even on the primary ticket this spring."

Avery sighed. "Fall elections seem like such a long way off now that I'm about to be unemployed. Have to get through those primaries first. I'll need to find a civilian job if I hope to survive financially for all the months ahead," Avery had quit her last engineering job over continued harassment. She was reluctant to return to the private sector for that reason. Working for the county had certain protections in that area, and she found she got along well with most of the crew at the engineer's office. Hollister was the exception. He was curt and surly with her most of the time and a devil of a hard person to find when she needed his signature.

As Avery huddled over her coffee cup, imagining herself begging on a street corner for living expenses, the door to the Tea Basket Hall opened once again. This time, another woman entered. She was different as anyone could be from the three seated around the table. She was handsomely dressed with dark hair styled in a French twist, followed by an equally dapper-looking man in a sports coat politely holding the door open for her.

"Oh, my!" Nora said. "If it isn't our honeymooners!"

"Hello, Nora, Lois, Avery. Yes, we're back!" Simone Beck, formerly Simone LeBlanc, said, greeting her friends as she embraced each one in turn. "You all remember Kyle, my new significant other from the wedding, don't you?" she joked.

"Of course we do," said Nora. "Coach Beck. Hello. Welcome to Tea Basket Hall."

The couple who entered were both smartly dressed. Beck wore a navy blue sports coat over a casual polo shirt. His dark hair was just beginning to show gray at the temples. His wife was dressed in a coral linen suit that hugged her form as if made for her. They looked like a movie star couple who were stepping out for a springtime luncheon.

"Ladies," Kyle Beck said. He held each woman's hand briefly, giving each a gentle shake, starting with Nora's. "It's nice to see you all in a less formal setting. I had no idea my bride had so many friends in the community. Our reception line was longer than a football field. I only recognized half the guests, and those were my own team players. I think my little Simone could start her own team or fan club."

"I know she could," Nora said with pride. She'd known Simone for years and always liked her.

"I want to be on her team," said Lois.

Everyone except Kyle chuckled.

In the past, Lois Caldwell had held a reputation as being a shy person. She did for others without fanfare, preferring to remain in the background. She never sought recognition for the week she single-handedly cooked and fed women temporarily housed in the Tea Basket Hall, where they had taken refuge after being displaced by a severe storm. More recently though, Lois had blossomed into a more outgoing person. She was gaining confidence in part thanks to a fast rise from secretary to president of the newly formed Shining Star guild. She was proving to herself and others that she was a competent leader. She was finding her voice after a lifetime of standing quietly in the shadows.

"Simone has quite an extraordinary group of friends," Beck said with a forced smile.

The three women received his comment well. Simone beamed with pride.

Nora was the first to spread Avery's news. "Avery here is going to run for county engineer this fall."

Beck turned his head and looked skeptical.

"Oh, Avery," Simone said, giving the woman a hug around the neck. "You'll be great! That current engineer lets the roads degrade so badly! I can't stand the condition they're in. When I drive my car to Ximi's, I need a tire alignment afterward because of all the potholes. Maybe I'll help your campaign, girlfriend. And I'll ask Ximi to help, too!"

Avery thanked her bubbling friend with a smile, but in her own mind, that future was looking bleak. "Well, we'll see if it comes to pass."

"I have faith in you. I know you'll win. Won't she, Kyle?"

Beck smiled thinly again and nodded.

Simone had met Coach Beck at a university reception only last fall. The administration held the event to thank financial supporters of the football team. Simone had been a long-time donor. She had written modest one hundred dollar checks each year for more than thirty years. Those donations earned her an invitation to the annual reception of private backers, where she could rub shoulders with other more generous donors, the team, the coaching staff, and university administrators from the sports department. She enjoyed talking to the players, some of whom she tutored privately in English literature.

After dinner and speeches, while everyone else milled about introducing themselves and talking, Simone did her best to put on a brave face apart from most of them. Mixing in a room full of strangers was the most uncomfortable part of her evening. Simone decided to take refuge behind a glass of wine in the darkest corner near the open bar. That's where Kyle Beck saw her. She was holding a glass of Chardonnay to her lips, standing beside a potted palm branch, which provided limited cover.

"Where's your husband?" he had asked her. "Why did he abandon such a beautiful creature as you?"

That was the opening for his pursuit of Simone, which was soon to follow.

Simone blushed in spite of her fifty years. She explained politely, "I'm not married. Have never been married. When I'm at large functions like this, I prefer simply to people watch."

What she did not say was that she could hide amid the foliage of potted plants surrounding the banquet hall and thereby keep a watchful eye out for any man on the prowl. Still, Coach Beck was a popular and indeed handsome man. He was tall with an athletic build and his dark brown hair was just beginning to show some gray. She was flattered that he, the person of the moment, was taking an interest and actually speaking to her.

Beck was taken with Simone's beauty and elegant appearance. She wore her auburn hair in a French twist at the back of her head that day, as she did every day. It was her signature style. She wore a suit of pale blue linen, which fitted her slender form as if tailored for her. She radiated a certain mature elegance, which Beck appreciated. He also liked that this woman appeared to be of a similar age to himself. He sensed an awkwardness in her standing in his presence. This he chalked up to his status and popularity and possessed no discomfort at all to engage her or anyone in conversation.

Because he was one of the stars of the evening's program, he couldn't keep her in conversation long. He pulled out a business card from his jacket pocket and gently put the card into her hand, not holding a wine glass. He apologized for his forwardness but asked her to call him next week, after the game, of course. He wanted to take her to dinner, a nice place, somewhere quiet, to an establishment where no fans would be milling about expecting him to be attentive to them as well. There were always fans, of course.

His charisma and manners instantly attracted Simone and, of course, Beck's good looks. She felt flattered. She assumed he probably didn't even know her name. That he wanted her to go on a date with him made her heart skip as if she were once again a teenage school girl.

That particular evening, however, was not the right place or time to devote his attention exclusively to her. "I'm usually in my office by 6:30 every morning. I take my lunch from eleven to noon. You can reach me on my cell number listed on the card. If you call the college number while I'm working, a staffer will pick up. I prefer not to share you with my greedy and equally handsome assistant." He laughed.

His laugh was disarming.

He took her hand that evening, just as he was doing this day with the Tea Basket quilters, and looked directly into her eyes and said, "You're the most beautiful creature in this room. I've got to make you mine."

Simone LeBlanc was smitten. End of story.

"We only stopped to thank you for the lovely Noritake China personally," Simone said to her friends. "I love the Rothschild pattern. Not once did I imagine anyone would get us the entire fifty-piece place setting! I mean, when I registered, I thought maybe we'd get a gravy bowl, but not *every piece.* Thank you so much."

"We were very happy to do it, child," Nora said. You've done your share for the guild over the years. Taking up a collection for a wedding gift was a pleasure for everyone. We hope you use and enjoy that china for years to come."

"The pattern looked like you," Lois said. "I'm an ironstone kinda gal, myself. But the floral pattern was perfect for you. Elegant and refined."

Kyle Beck took Simone by the arm to usher her away. "Ladies, my new bride and I must depart. I have to see to some problems at the university, and Simone needs to unpack that China you so generously gave. She's eager to display all those pieces in the hutch. I look forward to visiting with you all at some other time,"

"I'll be back soon," Simone promised her friends as Kyle led her toward the door. "I have a top to finish quilting for Ximi at the shop. After I finish, I'll bring it here for her to pick up." She was barely able to finish her sentence before her new husband had whisked her out the door.

Ximi Ling was Simone's best friend. Lately, they hadn't seen much of each other since Simone's preoccupation with romance and subsequent engagement to Coach Beck. Simone had promised she'd quilt Ximi's last top at the Thimble and Chatelaine quilt shop before she left on her honeymoon. Unfortunately, Kyle had kept her jumping from one event to another related to his role as head football coach, so Simone had not kept her word. That failure ate away at her conscience. Simone believed that one gave their word with conviction, just like saying wedding vows, "Till death do us part."

Kyle still had Simone's arm in his grip as the pair walked down the sidewalk away from the hall. As soon as they reached his Mercedes, he muttered, "That Lois friend of yours must weigh as much as my linebackers."

Simone was stunned by such a callous and shallow remark about a woman, especially about someone she especially liked. In spite of her slim figure and excellent fitness level, Simone never criticized others for weight issues. Not everyone needed to be Hollywood's ideal, and body shaming was wrong. In her opinion, Lois had a big, kind heart. It needed a bigger body simply to hold it. Kyle obviously wasn't aware of Lois' generosity or her limitless kindness toward others. Those were the qualities that mattered more to Simone than exterior illusions. No one should be judged on their size. Realizing, suddenly, this difference in their perceptions of others gave Simone a moment of hesitation. His comment stung.

Nora had risen from her chair to walk to one of the windows that flanked the hall door to watch the couple walk toward their car. "Seems like Simone found herself a nice man," she observed. "Some of us have been blessed like that." She looked back toward Lois, who was finishing her mug of coffee still perched beside Avery at the table. Lois had been widowed after a marriage lasting nearly thirty years. The farm couple had married right out of high school. The young pair made their home on a little farm and started to make their living off the land, working together as a team.

Nora knew they were a well-respected couple in the farming community. They had raised one child rather late in life, a daughter. Lois called her a "change of life baby." And change their lives she did. She resented and rejected their simple lifestyle in the country, bolting on some misplaced adventurous life in a city far away as soon as she was old enough to fledge. Nora knew Lois ached for her daughter, who rarely made contact with her mother since the death of Lois' husband. Lois would never share such personal sorrow except to a very few close friends like herself. Nora felt honored to be counted among them and kept the information to herself.

"How about you, Avery? Anyone special in your life?" Nora asked as she returned to the table.

Avery had risen and walked to the hall's kitchenette, where she was rinsing out her cup.

"No, Nora. I've never been much for dating. Never been serious about anyone. Guess I'm too focused on work. Now, this run for office will probably consume me. Speaking of which, I'm off to the court house to get started or ended. Whichever happens, happens. I'll talk to you later."

"Now you stop by the prosecutor's office and ask questions before you up and quit," Nora scolded. "Don't jump because Jasper Hollister says you should."

"I'm with Nora," Lois added.

Avery nodded with a weak grin, then headed for the door. Once outside, she decided to leave her big Ford 350 pickup truck parked in front of the hall. She thought the hike of a few blocks up to the center of town might give her mood a boost. Finding an empty parking space this hour for her long vehicle would prove difficult, if not impossible, anyway.

The sun was warm, and the air was sweet, with the scent of daffodils in bloom. Neither sun nor blooms had any cheering effect on Avery Underwood. Her mood was bleak as a rainy November at best. *Maybe there is something in what Nora says about not obeying Hollister. Maybe I shouldn't quit right away. Get that second opinion from that O'Feeny. Still, Hollister does know more about running for office than I do.* She had never had any reason to speak to this county prosecutor Nora mentioned. Nor had she ever seen the guy. *Maybe, probably, it would be a good idea to touch base since he is the party chair.* She doubted he'd be of much help regarding the end of her assistant engineering job. As she walked through residential streets toward the business center of town she failed to notice trees just beginning to show buds, their beauty lost on her. Avery's mind was following a different path toward depleted savings and uncertainty about her future as a public official.

The hike from Shannon Street up to the court house took Avery no more than twenty minutes. Like Athens, Greece, the town center of Athens, Ohio, sat elevated above most of the residential areas. The county court house dominated one corner of the downtown business district. Commercial businesses comprised only three or four square blocks. Court Street catered mostly to students, offering multiple bars and fast food establishments since two sides of the town were hemmed in by the sprawling university. Avery ascended the gentle incline effortlessly on her way to the courthouse, her long legs keeping the same pace as they had on the flat through neighborhoods. She put one boot in front of the other in a march toward the unknown.

A deputy directed Avery to exit the court house immediately upon her arrival. The board of elections office was housed in the court house annex next door, not connected by any door or hallway to or from the old courthouse. The broad-shouldered deputy-turned-security-guard standing duty just inside the old court house entrance explained this to her. Since 9/11, his job had been to confiscate weapons before they are brought into the government building or to stop a terrorist attack at the door. The big guy was fully armed with a standard-issue pistol, a Taser on his hips, a radio mic on his shoulder, and a pair of shiny cuffs dangling from the back of his belt. His duty station more often called for him to serve as an information clerk than a deterrent to violence in the small town.

Avery retreated outside and turned west only a few steps to the annex door. An old yellow cat lay napping on the sill inside the window near the door. Once within, she found a staff of women busy with paperwork seated at old desks. One of them rose upon her entering and walked up to a tall counter that separated them from customers.

Avery stammered as she began, "Ah, is this where a person starts a mission to run for public office?"

The elections office employee smiled and nodded. "Yes. Yes, it is."

Avery explained, "I intend to run for County Highway Engineer in the fall. Can you get me started on the steps and forms I need to get my name on the primary ballot?" She was pleasantly surprised to find the office staff eager to help. The clerk supplied her with the necessary paperwork to be completed and returned for processing and added a brochure printed by the Secretary of State's office for potential candidates like herself. There seemed to be much paperwork. Avery was confident she could complete the task without much trouble. At first glance, it seemed to her way of thinking that writing a grant proposal for bridge replacement with ODOT required much more documentation than running for public office. But then she was dismayed to see that the deadline for the primary election was only a few weeks away.

Avery thanked the clerk, then left the board of elections office with her bundle of papers to backtrack past the sleeping cat and out the door back toward the courthouse to once again engage in conversation with the deputy. This time, she wanted to talk to the prosecutor. She dropped her papers and emptied her pockets into his tray so he could see her possessions and confirm she carried no weapons as she stepped through the scanner. Nothing in the bin posed a threat. Avery's pockets, like her life, were plain for all to see.

"Where do I find the prosecutor's office?" she asked him.

He pointed to a door down the hall.

Avery pocketed her meager belongings: a small wallet, a few coins, a notepad, a mechanical pencil, and keys to the big Ford. She scooped up her board of elections documents and left the deputy standing guard behind his scanner. When she arrived at the ancient wooden door, she stopped and knocked.

A voice within, female by the tone, called out, "Come in. It's open."

Avery entered to see what appeared to be a secretarial pool. Three desks of similar vintage to those she had seen at the board of elections were arranged so that each secretary had space for her swivel chair, a computer screen, and a keyboard on each desk with a short filing cabinet alongside. Each woman was typing rapidly at her station. They had appropriated a long shelf to one end of the room lined with indoor plants that required no natural light to survive. One plant, Avery thought might have been called devil's ivy, thrived in this basement environment lit from above by several banks of harsh florescent lights. The green vine with variegated leaves had grown to an enormous length, covering the entire shelf nearly twenty feet long. The plant, and probably these women, had been here a long time. Everyone was firmly entrenched, just like Hollister, she thought.

"Can I help you?" one of the clerks asked, standing up and approaching.

"Yes. May I speak to Joe O'Feeny?"

"May I tell him your name and your business?"

Avery gave her name. "I'd like to run for public office. I just came from the board of elections."

"Of course. Just a moment." The clerk picked up a phone sitting on the edge of her desk and placed the receiver to her ear. She punched a button, then waited. Soon, her call was answered. The clerk repeated Avery's name and the topic of her visit. "Yes, she's here now. Uh-huh, she'd like to speak to you."

The clerk hung up and tipped her head to one side opposite that of the devil's ivy, indicating another office door. "Mr. O'Feeny will see you." His door stood slightly ajar. A pane of frosted glass on the top half of the door was painted with black lettering trimmed in gold in an arch that read, "County Prosecutor."

3

Joe O'Feeny had arrived early that morning to catch up on a few details before his day began in earnest. O'Feeny often worked long hours, putting in extra time as the county's only prosecuting attorney. This day, however, was a rare and welcome departure from most.

O'Feeny had won a burglary conviction on Wednesday. Then, at the preliminary hearing, a local well-known villain pleaded guilty to possession with intent to sell. The guy had been caught by a pair of baby-faced undercover detectives from the sheriff's office posing as high school seniors looking to buy. Their sting was recorded with both audio and video. So overwhelming was the evidence they'd gathered that O'Feeny told the defense attorney that his client should not bother trying to BS his way out of a jail sentence to a jury of his peers. This guy had no peers, in Joe's opinion. Nobody was as dirty as he was. No one could stoop so low as to sell tier-one drugs to kids. All that remained for O'Feeny to do was to urge a long, long sentence for the scumbag at the sentencing hearing that would be scheduled later in the month if there was no trial. He made a mental note when in front of the judge to be sure he listed every past offense this guy had. The list was long. O'Feeny smiled, remembering how he had joked with the defense attorney, suggesting that his client would likely never pay any attorney fees. Bad news for that lawyer, who was not a member of O'Feeny's political party. The defense was not likely to relish taking on pro bono work by default. But, for O'Feeny, it had indeed been a good week for a small county prosecutor.

He yawned, stretched, and then headed for the coffee maker on the far side of his staff's outer office. He checked the water level in the reservoir, selected a single serving pod from the tray, and installed his selection. Caffeine did not keep him awake at night. He slept very well. In no time, he had a hot cup of vanilla hazelnut in hand. Caffeine did, however, start the day off on the right note. He returned to the silent interior of his private office carrying the steaming mug. His small but well-appointed room was located behind a door that almost always stood ajar. If he could keep his record of successful indictments and convictions going, he'd be a shoo-in for prosecutor once again. This, however, was not his year to run for reelection. This year, the county engineer's office and one of the county commissioner seats would be contested. O'Feeny could continue to rack up convictions for two more years before he had to mount another campaign. Instead of running for office himself, he would use the time as chair to support his party's incumbents.

O'Feeny set his coffee mug on the big desk and slipped off his jacket, draping it neatly across the back of his leather chair. He retrieved a legal folder from the bottom drawer of a file cabinet, dropped the file onto his desk, and took his seat. He took a sip of the hot liquid, then opened the file to scan what he already knew by heart. He did this task at least once every month. Beyond his door, he could hear the sounds of his law clerks, who were just beginning to arrive.

Color photographs of a woman lay on the top of the folder's contents. The glossies had been taken by investigators at the local hospital where the victim had been transported for treatment. Her face was battered and swollen. A large bloody gash sliced across her forehead. Her brunette hair was a mess. Another picture showed a lacerated forearm. Others revealed tattered and torn clothing barely clinging to her frame. Additional photos from officers attending her call for help revealed the alleged scene of the attack. They showed a kitchen in disarray, with a broken stool littering the floor and shopping bags spilling garments across the tiles.

O'Feeny flipped through the photographs quickly, taking another sip. This was a case his predecessor had not presented to a grand jury. Therefore, it was ancient history, too old for Joe to present. Closed case. A situation that greatly irritated Joe because O'Feeny disliked public office holders not doing their jobs fully. Joe O'Feeny liked criminal convictions nearly as much as he disliked slackers.

In O'Feeny's gut, he believed the woman's story. He knew she had been honest about her attacker. Joe enjoyed prosecuting cases he knew he could win. This could have been one of them —probably—with more work. It only needed a bit of pressure on one witness for the perp's alibi to fall apart. About this, he felt confident. This repeated lack of effort by the previous prosecutor was the main reason O'Feeny had won his race against the man. The prosecutor then was weak, easily intimidated by political pressure, and downright lazy. This case had been one of several the office chose to ignore back then. So, no charges had been brought before a grand jury. None. Not one single charge. Why? Because the attacker was a very popular local personality. The victim had been his girlfriend. Someone without public appeal. He said. She said. That was the lame excuse for not going forward with charges. But the photos told a more gruesome truth. The pressure against the weak prosecutor to cover it up must have been intense. O'Feeny shook his head and slammed the file closed. He felt strongly that this woman deserved some kind of justice. He reopened the folder, this time rereading her written statement from the first word to the last, just as he had done many times before, doing so even now as if he had never read it.

"I got home late. Later than I should have. I knew he'd be upset. He's been upset with me before when I've come home too late. But this time, he really exploded.

He likes his dinner on time, and I wasn't home to make it. The girls and I went shopping, you see. We went to Parkersburg. To the mall. They kept me away from home longer than I should have been gone. I didn't drive. No car of my own. When I did get home, he was waiting, of course. He didn't say a word at first, so I knew he was really mad.

He asked me where I'd been. I told him. He wanted to know e-x-a-c-t-l-y where. So I told him; to all three big department stores and several dress shops in the mall. He asked me if I spent any of his money. I had. I told him everything I bought. How much I spent. I even pointed out I bought clothes he said I should have, things he liked to see me wear. I offered to show him the receipts, and the clothes.

He stood up from his chair, and that's when he jerked the shopping bags from my hands in a rage. He didn't want to see. He threw them across the room. One of the bags hit the dog's bowl and spilled water everywhere. My new clothes got soaked.

I tried to rescue them. I begged him to stop destroying my things. That's when he shoved me from behind. I think I hit the wall or maybe the counter. He's strong, you know.

Anyway, I lost my footing on the wet floor and fell. He grabbed my shirt, pulled me up off the floor, and slapped me hard across the face. I fell again into the counter. He picked up a bar stool and slammed it down on me. I ducked. Most of it hit the counter. A broken leg sliced my arm.

I begged him again to stop.

He accused me of being out with lesbian girlfriends, buying stuff only they liked. He told me I dressed like a slut after I go shopping with them. Said he hated everything I wore. Said he hated me.

I was crying by then. I didn't hear everything he said after that. But that's the gist of it. Then he kicked me. Twice. And left the house.

I was dazed. I didn't know what to do at first. I finally dialed 911. Eventually, the deputies arrived. The squad took me to the hospital."

O'Feeny flipped to the next sheet of paper in the file. He read an investigating officer's report. The deputy sheriff chronicled the scene.

O'Feeny quickly flipped through the report, stopping to read a follow-up filed by another officer, a city police officer this time, who had located the woman's fiancé inside a local brewpub.

The officer noted that the man seemed very concerned when he learned of his fiancé's attack. He was surprised and doubtful that his fiancé had been attacked. He said she was known to drink heavily at times, and mixed them with her medication. She often got confused about details. He denied being her attacker.

"I've been here since late afternoon, enjoying the company of my friends. She told me she was going shopping, so I had no reason to rush home after work."

Observed two empty bottles and newspapers open on the table in front of him. The man appeared to have been reading. The bartender corroborated his statement. Said the man came in at five thirty, ordered beers, and had not left.

O'Feeny shuffled all the papers and photos back into a neat pile inside the folder, then pressed a button on his desk phone to listen to a saved voice mail message from the day before.

"Mr. O'Feeny. It's Debbie Taylor. I've dropped my land line. Too many robocalls. All I have now is this cell phone." She recited her new number.

O'Feeny took a pen off his desk to copy the number, then pressed the phone button again to confirm he had written it down correctly. He deleted the voice mail and crossed off the old number written inside the folder. He closed the file folder, sat back, and took another sip of coffee, which was now bitter and cold.

Good as her word, the victim, Debbie Taylor, who had moved out of the county soon after the attack, was keeping him informed on how he could reach her. She, too, had little faith in the previous prosecutor's ability or willingness to follow through. O'Feeny wanted to prove beyond a shadow of a doubt that the fiancé was her attacker. He wanted to twist that alibi from the bartender into a tangled knot and hang the guy up for all to see. Get him on the stand. Make him commit perjury and prove he had. But not now, the statute of limitations on the crime against Debbie had long passed. But next time… next time, O'Feeny would get the man on the stand, along with this lying bartender. There was no doubt in O'Feeny's mind that the perp had paid or promised to pay for that alibi.

O'Feeny believed Debbie. He told her so the first day he called her after reading over her file shortly after he'd taken office. He explained to her the statute of limitations on her assault. Debbie Taylor understood. She was still willing to testify against her ex-fiancé if ever there was another case against him. She'd draw a picture of the man's past behavior should that man ever attack another woman again. She wanted to testify, no matter when. She swore she would. Both Debbie Taylor and Joe O'Feeny were convinced that one day, in the future, this man would repeat his attack on some other woman.

O'Feeny also believed the old saying that leopards don't change their spots. Abusive men don't suddenly become kind old souls willingly. One day, this guy was going to explode and strike another woman. He'd gotten away with it at least once. He would surely do so again. When he did, Joe O'Feeny planned to do everything in his legal power and ability to clasp the man in stocks. He'd have Debbie's hammer and nails to see they never released him. Until then, Joe O'Feeny was watching and waiting.

O'Feeny's phone rang. Obviously, his staff had already found work for the county prosecutor this morning. His day was about to start in earnest. He was pleasantly surprised to hear that a Ms. Avery Underwood wanted to speak to him about running for office against ol' Jasper Hollister. *Interesting way to start the day*, he decided. He was looking forward to meeting this woman.

"Send her in."

O'Feeny was a tall man, in excess of six feet, dressed in a long sleeve white shirt with a blue and red striped tie pulled loosely around the collar. His long stride took him quickly to his door that was ajar. He opened it wide to admit Avery. Avery, to his surprise, was nearly the same height as himself. He looked directly into her eyes with a bit of amusement in his own and offed an outstretched hand.

"So, you want to run for office?" he asked. "Please, come in. We can talk in here."

O'Feeny led Avery inside his private office, which looked orderly yet busy. Several legal briefs were scattered over the top of a credenza. On his desk, a pencil holder held center stage. Yellow #2 pencils of varying lengths leaned around the rim. Attached to the desk was a lower work surface holding a keyboard and a computer screen turned on to a word processing program waiting for his return. A file cabinet door hung ajar. A multiline phone occupied the other side of his desk. The arrangement suggested that O'Feeny was an organized person who was able to get work done.

Avery took a seat in one of two guest chairs in front of his desk and squared up the forms in her lap.

"The board of elections and a friend sent me over. They said I should talk to you before I file my candidacy." She failed to mention that her old friend, Nora Radnor, had also insisted on making inquiries as to Hollister's statement that she must quit.

"I see," O'Feeny said as he smoothed down his tie and sat, swiveling his chair around to close the gap between the two of them. Only his desk separated them. He touched a key on the keyboard, thereby minimizing the documents on his computer screen. "I assume you want to run for office as a democrat since I'm the chair and you came here specifically.

I don't know anything about you. Please, tell me about yourself and how you think I can help you run for…?"

Avery looked O'Feeny in the eye and matter-of-factly announced, "County engineer."

O'Feeny's bushy red eyebrows arched in mock surprise. To Avery's thinking, those eyebrows were the only part of O'Feeny's appearance that seemed unkempt on his otherwise crisp and tidy business appearance. They were wild, hinting of an ancestry of forefathers who might have survived harsh winters on the North Sea.

"County engineer?" O'Feeny repeated as if he was trying to understand words not spoken in his native tongue. "Well, now, that presents a bit of a problem, Ms. Underwood."

"How so?" Avery asked.

"We have an incumbent holding that office. I don't think it's going to be possible for me to endorse you since you'd have to oppose him during our primaries, which are coming up fast. I don't think you have time to meet that deadline."

"Oh, I see," Avery said somewhat quietly.

"So then, you *are* a democrat?" O'Feeny repeated as if confirming what he knew.

"Yes."

"What kind of experience do you have that makes you think you can unseat our incumbent, Jasper?" O'Feeny folded his hands atop his desk, waiting for her answer.

Avery straightened up. She had nothing to lose. Obvious to her, this trip into the party chair's office was going nowhere. She assumed she would have to form some alternative plan than seek help from any local officials like this O'Feeny guy. She decided to be blunt about Jasper Hollister.

"I already do Hollister's job for him while he goes fishing, plays golf, and dines out with his cronies. I'm his assistant engineer. I hold every credential necessary for the position and then some. I've been performing most of his duties for months since I was hired. I think it's about time I get the pay and the title, even if I have to quit like he tells me I have to. I also think it's time the voters get to know how little work Hollister actually does for this county."

O'Feeny smiled and tried to stifle a chuckle. "Jasper's a character. I've known him for a long time. I don't doubt what you say about his work ethic. He always was one to put his own pleasure before hard work, any work, actually. Been like that since high school. He's one of the few people in the world I know who can literally consistently con the public about what a great job he does. But you must understand, my hands as party chair are tied. He is our incumbent. As such, the democratic committee will stand behind him during the primaries and, of course, endorse him during the general election this fall."

"I see," Avery said. "So, do you have any suggestions at all for a misguided neophyte like myself?"

"I do have," he said. "Don't bother. You'll never get the democratic party to back you."

O'Feeny punched a button on his phone and spoke aloud to the microphone. "Yvonne, can you bring a cup of coffee in here for our guest?"

He turned to Avery. "Do you like flavored coffee or plain?"

Avery was puzzled by this sudden act of hospitality to someone who had just announced that he had no intentions of endorsing her. "Plain. Black, I guess."

"Regular, please, Yvonne, if you don't mind."

O'Feeny released the button on the phone and waited. Soon, a woman, probably Yvonne, entered carrying a piping hot coffee mug, which she placed on the prosecutor's desk in front of Avery. She smiled at Avery and quickly departed, closing the prosecutor's door behind her.

O'Feeny nodded toward the cup. "Best coffee in town except for Donkey Coffee."

Avery picked up the cup and sipped gingerly. It was indeed hot, the aroma hinting of a robust blend. She set the cup back down on the edge of his desk to cool off. She'd already had Nora's coffee. In spite of Joe O'Feeny's claim, this coffee was just so-so. Nora's was infinitely better.

"So why this," she asked, indicating the cup, "If you can't help me?" Avery asked.

"Who said I couldn't help you? I said I couldn't *endorse you* as a democratic candidate, not that I couldn't help. Now tell me this BS from Jasper about you having to quit?"

4

Kyle's comment about Lois' size sent subtle alarm signals through Simone's chest, a twinge of pain she had never felt before. She liked Lois, admired the woman for her strength and generosity, and how she ran a farm successfully, a woman alone. Kyle's words gnawed at and settled uneasily in a deep corner of her heart.

In spite of the hurt she felt, Simone remained silent, saying nothing and very little else on the drive home. By the time she walked through the door of their house and inhaled deeply the mixed scents of new carpet and musty air, she had almost forgotten the hurt. Like her wedding vows, something old and something new, she wondered if Kyle's comments were just something new. Or were they something, some part of him she had missed during their whirlwind courtship? She walked to the wall and turned on the air conditioning. The air would rid the house of stale odors even though the day was mild, and cooling the house was unnecessary. Her thoughts returned to her new husband's cutting remark.

Silly me, she thought, *he meant nothing by it. I'm sure.*

She and Kyle had jointly purchased the house one week before their wedding. The split-level was only a few streets from the mall, less than a mile away. If she chose to walk to the store on a beautiful day such as this, the distance would take only half an hour at most. Simone liked the location. It was on a quiet street off a main artery that headed east.

Simone sold her condo using the profits for a down payment. Kyle moved all his things out of a deluxe apartment near campus and into the house on the day of closing. He agreed to make the mortgage payments. Every room remained exactly as it had on that day they left Athens, Ohio, on their honeymoon, every room a cluttered mess to Simone's OCD sense of tidiness.

Gifts, still wrapped in white or silver paper, were spread across and piled high on the dining room table. A few chairs supported smaller gift boxes and cards as well. A new hutch Simone purchased to store the China from her guild sisters had been delivered and stood awkwardly blocking the center of the entry hall. The store had delivered it, just. Stacked against and nearby the new hutch, several unopened boxes wrapped in exactly the same paper, ribbon, and bows cluttered the floor. These were the assembled Noritake china pieces from her guild sisters, generous gifts given from the heart. Simone knew what was inside because she had opened only one box wrapped up in the same paper before they'd left for New York. She recognized the beautiful handwriting on the card. It was from her best friend, Ximi Ling. That box alone revealed to Simone what the contents of all the others would be. Ximi's gift was an expensive China tea pot she had registered for in the Noritake pattern. Suddenly, seeing the tea pot nestled inside the open box and all the other unopened gifts made Simone miss having Ximi nearby to share in the joy and excitement of opening the boxes and writing thank you notes to all those who thought so much of her.

Kyle hauled suitcases noisily from the car into the hall and deposited them just inside the front door, adding to the clutter of her new home.

"I'm going to the office. You can get this put away, right?" He yelled from the doorway.

Simone turned and looked at him and then down at the pile of luggage, several soft-sided suitcases, and a couple of overnight bags. She sighed. "What's going on that you have to rush off?" she asked, thinking Kyle could remain home together, opening presents, putting away travel items, just being together. He wasn't due back to his coaching job for a few more days.

"Don't concern yourself. I'll be back by five. Can you have dinner ready?"

"Why leave now? We just got home, and you haven't even changed clothes."

"It's the job!"

His tone was a bit harsh. Once again this morning she felt a twinge in her chest. "Sorry," Simone said. "Yes, I'll take care of the luggage, and I'll have dinner ready. Of course, I will."

Kyle smiled at her, showing a row of perfect white teeth. Simone loved the way his smile seemed to embrace her.

Instead of leaving, he approached his bride and gave her a hug. "I'm sorry. I'm just being a jerk. I didn't mean to hurt you. I do have to go to the office, but I'll be back and give you a hand with some of these presents. You said you wanted to write thank-you notes when we unwrapped gifts. I'll help.

Might even bring you another gift when I get back if you'll be good."

Simone returned his smile and nodded. "Yes, I'd like that." *I'd like to share our time together doing things, anything really, now that we're married. Normal. Almost. Too old to have children of our own. I so long to enjoy every single day with you, just doing things together and growing gray.* She let out a sigh.

"Good. Now I'm off. Let's have roast beef."

Kyle closed the front door behind him, not waiting for a response, leaving Simone alone.

Roast Beef? Simone sighed again. *So this is what being the wife of a coach is really going to be like. Just great.* She grabbed and extended the handle of the largest suitcase and climbed the carpeted stairway to their bedroom. The case made a muffled thunk, thunk noise as she ascended, dragging it up the steps behind her.

Once in the bedroom, Simone tossed the heavy bag onto the bed. She observed that at least she'd thought to make the bed before they left. One less chore to attend to today. She sighed again. Turning away, she picked up the phone on a night stand and dialed Ximi's cell.

"Ximi, hi! Simone here… yeah, we just got back… about an hour ago… great, how about you? Want to meet me at the grocery store? I have a million things to do before five, and one of them is to buy food for dinner. We can meet over a coffee, and you can show me where the store has moved everything since I've been away… They did? I was joking… They really did *what* to the front of the store? Oh my. I'm sure now I *really* need your help. Can you meet me there in twenty minutes? Great. I can't wait to see you. Bye."

Simone spotted Ximi's dark gray Maxima circle the parking lot three times. Her friend finally settled on a space being vacated near the front door by someone leaving. Ximi jogged across the lot dodging cars, her jet black hair cut chin length flying back in the breeze. As usual, Ximi was chewing a wad of bubble gum, her only vice. Simone watched her friend coming through the front doors of the store along with other shoppers, even though Ximi was petite, barely five feet.

Ximi spotted Simone standing by the coffee shop, holding out a cup.

"Ah, you remembered."

The friends embraced. Simone stood a foot taller than Ximi.

"Of course! Oh, it's good to see you," Simone said.

"Good to see you, too. I was beginning to think you deserted me *f-o-r-e-v-e-r*." Ximi said, mocking the tone of a valley girl and popping a bubble of gum inside her mouth.

"Never. I'm so sorry that I didn't have an opportunity to say good-bye to you. But I'm back now. I think I can fix that. So, good bye. And hello. And thank you for the wonderful tea pot!"

"Welcome back. Maybe we can spend some time together now. You look good. Was your trip lovely?"

"I had a wonderful time. Kyle has been so sweet. We're back a day early, though. I guess he has problems to solve at the university. Not sure what, but he dashed off and left me with his dinner order."

"His dinner order? Gads. That sounds like you're his chef or waitress. I don't take well to any guy ordering me around. My older brothers used to order me around. They would threaten to make me do stuff like their chores, 'or else.' They took martial arts classes for years, you know, before I was born. Threatened me with their moves." Ximi raised a knee and held out her coffee in a mimed Karate chop. "So I begged my parents until they caved in and finally let me take lessons, too. It wasn't long before I was able to clean my brothers' clocks after I got pretty good. After that, no more getting bossed around by brothers... or anybody."

Simone chuckled quietly. "I never knew you had wimpy brothers! I didn't mean Kyle ordered me around. Kyle just likes to keep his life on a schedule, like dinner. Dinner at five.

"Three of them."

"What?"

"I have three brothers. And know what? Each one now teaches martial arts. And still, not one of them will challenge me to this day. I'm that good!"

"Oh, have gossip. Must share even though Kyle asked me not to repeat this, but I must share it with you. So please, don't repeat this to anyone else. Please. He'd hate it if it ever got out. Did I ever tell you about a woman he almost married?"

Ximi shook her head, tossed her wad of bubble gum in a nearby trash bin, took a sip of her coffee, and looked at her friend with eagerness. Simone had not shared much information at all about Kyle other than he was "the one" while they were dating. She explained early in their relationship that the coach liked his privacy and preferred she not talk about him publicly. Ximi knew very little about Kyle Beck other than what she read in the local sports pages, and that wasn't saying much. Ximi wasn't into football, basketball, or baseball, so she rarely read sports news, even local stories. Those three sports and car racing were about the only sports that seemed worthy of coverage in the local paper. Never was there any story about martial arts. Simone's guy, now husband and the famous coach of the college football team, was a mystery to her.

"Rumors get started. Stories have a way of getting muddled, and false information makes its way around. That sort of thing," Simone said. "But I must share this. Please keep it to yourself."

Ximi was more than eager to hear any and all details of this mysterious past love life. "Cross my heart. Tell me everything as we shop. Where's your list? Good. Give it to me. I'll lead the way down the aisles of where-did-they-move-that-to here at our favorite ever-changing grocery store."

Ximi sipped the latte offered by her best friend while looking over Simone's list. "Produce first," she announced."

Simone pushed the shopping cart and talked as the two friends walked side by side. "White or yellow?" Ximi asked as they approached onions.

"Yellow, Simone said. "Kyle was engaged once before. Some time ago, as I understand it. Don't know the date. He's never gotten over the trauma of that breakup and has had a very hard time trusting any woman ever since," She began. "Turns out she was a closet lesbian. Really hurt his feelings."

"No! Meat counter dead ahead. Four pound beef roast?"

"Yes. Four to five pounds. He was so blindly in love with her that he never realized her sexual peculiarities, I guess. Funny she didn't tell him. Turns out she was quite selfish, too, and self-centered. She always spent tons of his money on clothes for herself. Drained their joint bank account one time while he was on the road with his team."

Ximi listened to Simone. She found every detail about the affair fascinating. She wondered when Simone had learned about this past love of his. *And yes, why didn't this woman disclose her diverse sexual preferences? She'd agreed to marry him, after all. Maybe she was bisexual.* Ximi's thoughts were interrupted by Simone.

"He was an assistant coach back then, touring somewhere in another state. Almost cost him his job he told me. He went to pay for a meal with his debit card, but it was declined. He was mortified. Think of the embarrassment! Just think of it! He had to apologize and ask his boss to pick up the tab. She'd used up all their money on frivolous clothes and 'girly things' he called them."

The two were making their way around another aisle, with Simone still talking about Kyle's former lover. Ximi felt sympathetic for Kyle. *Poor man probably didn't expect to lose all of his money to the fiancé, especially when he was way out of town. What a piece of work that woman must have been.*

"And then when he got back home, tired after being on the road, she comes waltzing in laden down with bulging shopping bags containing more new clothes. Can you believe it? Then she had the nerve to tell him she was a lesbian. She flaunts the news. That ended the affair right then and there."

"So that's when they broke off their engagement? Did he press charges since she took his money?" Ximi asked.

"Yes. And no. They were soon to be married. So yes, he broke it off. Press charges? How could he? He's just too kind-hearted. Ever since that woman hurt him, he's been leery of entering into another long-term relationship. He's been so kind to me that I can't imagine what pain he must have gone through, Ximi. He's so generous and smart and, of course, good-looking."

Not so smart for being generous with his bank account, Ximi thought. *Would any guy share his funds with a woman before they were married? After the wedding, sure. But before? I dunno.*

"I'm lucky to find such a nice guy this late in my life. Did you know he asked me to marry him on our very first date? Yeah. Said he could tell that I was different from all the other women he'd ever known, especially her. I was more mature, more capable, brighter, and, well, more beautiful. He's a dream come true. Well, of course, I told him I needed to spend a lot more time with him before I could ever consider marriage. There had to be a lot between our first dinner together and a marriage proposal! But here I am, the new Mrs. Kyle Beck."

Simone giggled.

"You've told me your proposal story many times, girlfriend," Ximi said. "But this is some story about his ex-fiancé."

While Simone had been relaying Kyle's tale of woe, Ximi, saying little else, had been pulling items off shelves from Simone's list, filling up the shopping cart as they walked. She knew her friend wasn't easily bamboozled, but her fiancé's story didn't seem logical as she thought about it. Ximi wasn't aware of any lesbians she knew of, nor what shopping habits other people had. Were all women clothes horses? She doubted it. She wasn't. Ximi was dressed in a Browns athletic tee over black Under Armor leggings and running shoes.

Stereotyping. Bad. Wouldn't a man know if his girlfriend, his fiancé, was really a lesbian? Wouldn't he? If they were to be married, might the topic of sex or children or even past lovers have come up at some point? Hadn't the two ever engaged in sex with each other? Or talked about sex? Was Kyle one of those extremely rare males who "saved himself" for his intended on their wedding night? Was the subject of sex taboo to him?

Ximi had doubts about Kyle's chastity, given his gender and age. But her curiosity was piqued about this period in his past. She made a mental note to engage in some recreational investigative work on Kyle Beck. *At the time this failed affair took place, he was an assistant coach. Shouldn't be too hard to find out where he'd worked.* She regretted now having been so indifferent to local sports facts.

A place to start her inquiries would be to Google Kyle Beck's name. His current position as head coach of a college team would surely produce some sort of biographical information and subsequent clues.

It wasn't long before Ximi had exhausted her thoughts about Kyle Beck and had found everything on Simone's grocery list. The shopping cart was full. The lattes were finished, and they had encircled the entire circumference of the store and down nearly every aisle in pursuit of Simone's groceries.

"If you need help at home, I can be counted on. Just say the word," Ximi said as Simone paid the cashier, and the two watched a teen drop her heavy paper bags haphazardly back into their cart.

"Thanks, but today I'll manage fine. Kyle's agreed to help me start thank you notes after he gets home. I so love the tea pot you gave me. Yours will be the first note of thanks that I write. I still can't get over the fact that the guild bought so many of the place settings and serving pieces I wanted. That was such a wonderful surprise."

"We all care for you. Besides, Nora told us you'd probably be entertaining after you became the wife of a college football coach. Who can argue with Nora's advice?"

The two friends left the busy grocery store together. Ximi went to her car, planning to head back to her home office to work on an architectural drawing needed by the end of the month. Simone pushed the cart to her Subaru Outback and unloaded the grocery bags into the back. She had a stack of suitcases to unpack, dirty clothes to wash, and dinner to prepare. She had a pot roast recipe in mind that was absolutely delicious. She was sure Kyle would love it.

Kyle walked through the front door minutes shy of five o'clock. Simone had dinner ready and steaming hot, and the kitchen table was set. The hum of the dryer joined the rattle of the washing machine in a nearby utility room. On the table, a gleaming Noritake platter in the Rothschild pattern held a roast beef surrounded by potatoes and carrots. Simone had unpacked and cleaned two place settings from the gift boxes. She found a small vase for daffodils picked from their back yard as a centerpiece.

Kyle looked appreciative. He took his place at the head of the table, opened the bottle of wine Simone had set out, and poured them each a glass. Simone joined him at the table for their first meal together as husband and wife in their new home.

"A toast?" she asked.

"Absolutely," Kyle agreed. "To a long, happy life together as husband and wife."

They touched glasses and sipped their wine.

Kyle reached into his jacket pocket and retrieved a small box. He handed it to Simone.

Simone took the velvet box, slowly opening the lid. Inside, she found a sparkling cocktail ring set with small diamonds and an evening emerald.

"The green stone is a peridot," Kyle explained. "The jeweler said this gem has healing properties. I hope this ring heals your heart, which I did not mean to break today. The stone is also said to protect the wearer from nightmares and ensure peace and happiness. I want us to have all the happiness we each deserve."

Simone was speechless. She leaned over and kissed Kyle and whispered in his ear, "I love it, and you."

Kyle smiled that big smile of his, rubbed his hands together and said, "Smells great. Shall we eat?"

"I hope you like this. I used my mother's recipe for pot roast."

"Oh?" He sounded a little surprised. "I'm used to roasts coming out of an oven, not out of a pot."

"Oh, you'll like this one. I used a cinnamon stick, sugar, beef bouillon, red wine, and soy sauce. The soy sauce gives the potatoes and carrots a lovely color, don't you think?"

Kyle carefully tested the flavor of the meat. He arched an eyebrow. Nodded approvingly. Then he tried a piece of potato. Those, too, passed his inspection. But when he tried one of the carrots, he wrinkled up his nose.

"Augh, too soft. You cooked the carrots way too long. Next time… the next time you make this dish, use the oven and watch how long you let the carrots cook. I don't like carrots soft like this."

After that, Kyle launched into a soliloquy about his staff. He had signed off on renewed contacts for most of them, ordered some changes to the weight room, and told her how much the school was planning to spend on the football program come fall. He remarked about how he appreciated being allowed to park close to the stadium in a space reserved just for him. Kyle devoured seconds on the roast, cleaned up all the potatoes but left every carrot on the new platter. At no time did Kyle talk about any problem that he had been so eager to address when he had dashed out the door that morning.

Kyle rose from his seat, leaving the kitchen to catch the evening news on TV. Simone was left alone with a sparkling ring to wear while clearing the table and washing up dirty dishes.

5

The following day, Simone drove to her part-time job at the Thimble and Chatelaine quilt shop. The little shop, located in the small village of Shade, was only a few miles south of Athens. She arrived shortly after the owner, Molly Menear, had unlocked the front door and flipped over the open sign on the door. The sign still swayed as Simone touched the handle.

Simone was intent on finishing Ximi's Sunbonnet Sue as soon as possible. She planned to work eight hours at the quilting machine if she had to in order to finish. She had promised to have the top done before leaving on her honeymoon. That promise went by-the-bye with too many excuses: accompanying her fiancé to spring sports award banquets and faculty dinners, accepting invitations to various fundraising events, and finally, preparing for the wedding.

She had also allowed many of her own priorities to fall away over the past few months. Now that she was home, the wedding and the honeymoon over, she felt obliged to resume some of those neglected responsibilities. Chief among them was being Molly's long-arm free-hand quilter at the Thimble and Chatelaine. Simone also felt compelled to prove she was a good partner on the home front, infinitely better than the former spendthrift and callous woman of Kyle's past. She was determined to make every effort to give more of herself than she took. The question in her mind was how to balance those two demands. *Wasn't that the problem every new bride faced?*

The new Gammil at the shop allowed owner, Molly, to quilt a top unattended while she busied herself with other duties. The computerized programs provided a feature that Molly demanded based on her own limitations. Molly was no good at free-hand quilting. She admitted that to everyone. The fact that the machine could also be manually operated was a plus. Someone with talent and skill could create freehand designs across the sandwich of backing, batting, and pieced top. It was freehand that was Simone's forte, not Molly's. With only minimal practice on Molly's old Gammil, which was housed in the Tea Basket Hall, she quickly discovered Simone possessed a talent to create superb quilting patterns with it.

Molly's old Gammil had been awarded to the Tea Basket guild after the women of the guild raised thousands of dollars for Molly's 5K team to benefit breast cancer research. Fitted only with a stitch regulator, Simone's work on the old Gammil was nearly indistinguishable from that of a computerized program on Molly's new Gammil at the shop. The difference existed in Simone's creativity. A computer repeated identical and perfect patterns within a designated area. Simone was not limited by artificial borders. Simone could produce variations and subtleties that encompassed the nuances of the entire quilt top's design. She had become an artist. Molly needed such skills at her shop.

Molly often visited the Tea Basket hall. She found any excuse to visit just to gaze upon her old long-arm machine, remembering her late sister, Orpha, who had once been its sole operator. Molly would chat with guild members over a cup of Nora's coffee and share funny or disastrous quilting stories. On several occasions, she had the opportunity to watch Simone stand at the controls just as her sister had once done. She noticed the accuracy of Simone's feather stitches and how precise her board and battens looked and realized Simone had a definite flair for creativity. Watching Simone stirred happy memories of Orpha. On one such visit to the hall, Molly asked Simone to come to the shop sometime to ostensibly chat about a new line of fabric she might order. That chat turned out to be a job interview, where Simone found herself hired on the spot as The Thimble and Chatelaine's new freehand longarm quilter.

"Welcome home, *Mrs. Beck,*" said Molly as Simone joined her boss in the shop. "It's good to see you. How was your holiday, or honeymoon, I should say, with Coach Beck?"

Simone smiled broadly. "Simply wonderful. We went upstate New York and then into New York City. Ate out all the time. Saw a Broadway play and the amazing sights of the city. Just enjoyed ourselves completely. And yesterday, for no reason, Kyle gave me this." Simone extended her hand so that Molly could see the new green peridot and diamond ring.

"Beautiful, Simone. Simply stunning. Isn't he the generous one? And for no reason? You're so fortunate to have him."

"I am."

"And your honeymoon also sounds lovely. So, you're home now? Ready to get back into your traces?"

"I am indeed. I'm so sorry to have left Ximi Ling's quilt in the machine and tied things up so you couldn't quilt. However, I plan to finish the job today. I promised her I'd have that thing finished a week ago."

"You have at it, then. I took in four more tops for you while you were away. You're gaining a following. Ladies are starting to request you by name. That suits me, Simone. The more quilting you do, the less I have to do. I can run the shop if you do all the quilting service."

"I'm glad if you are. I don't want to step on your toes. If you need the machine, you should tell me. The thing is yours, after all."

"No. No. We'll keep to the schedule policy as is. Everyone gets in the queue, and every top is quilted in the order received, no matter which operator is requested. That always worked for me and Orpha. It will continue to work for me and you. Ladies know they have to queue up. They don't mind. And to be honest, if there's a customer who absolutely, positively cannot wait her turn, she's free to put her name on someone else's waiting list. Maybe you should think of starting a list of your own at the guild hall."

Simone grinned but shook her head at the thought. "Oh, I don't think that would go over well with our members. All

Tea Baskets are supposed to have a turn on your old Gammil. We keep track of the rotations so nobody like me can hog the machine's time. Besides, I like working here with you. When I quit retail long ago for a college job, I thought I'd never want to return to the private sector. I enjoyed teaching literature and tutoring for a while, but this job is different. I don't feel like I'm working at all. Does that make sense to you?"

"It does," Molly said. "You're being creative. Creating something that will last for years. That's not work. Not at all."

Just then, several women entered the shop, all talking at the same time. They greeted Molly and Simone with waves and more simultaneous conversations. Molly turned her attention to the shoppers while Simone pulled a sheet off Ximi's unfinished Sunbonnet Sue. The sheet kept the quilt clean while thrown over the idle frame. She folded and set it aside, then closely examined the stitches that she had already completed. Her mind soon blocked out the noisy shoppers milling about the store. She ran her fingertips across the Sunbonnet Sue as she began to recall details of her design for Ximi's quilt top. Her examination revealed what remained to be done: echo quilting around the Sues, tiny cables in the sashing, and something very special, McTavish, planned for the border. Simone turned on the machine with the flip of a switch, then took the handlebars in hand and pulled the trigger. The motor hummed. The needle rose and fell. Soon, Simone settled into a rhythm and blocked out all else happening beyond the borders of Ximi's Sunbonnet Sue.

Robin Prescott walked into the kitchenette at the Tea Basket hall where Nora was at work cleaning out coffee pots. Nora turned and was pleasantly surprised. Her eyes told her that the woman standing before her was her friend, Phoebe Prescott. But Phoebe, she knew, was in Cleveland for an extended visit with her beau. The woman standing before her was, therefore, not Phoebe. Something struck Nora as different about this woman. Same height. Same dark complexion. Same overall petite size. Nora adjusted her red-rimmed glasses and realized that this woman's hair was nearly all gray. Phoebe's hair was salt and pepper, and she did not wear glasses.

Nora adjusted her own oversized glasses one more time to be sure that the person before her was truly *not* Phoebe.

"Goodness, you look almost exactly like…."

"My sister, Phoebe?"

Nora caught her breath. "Are you? Wait a minute. You're Phoebe's older sister, Robin."

"Oh, I do not like to hear the words *older*. I think I prefer to be known as Phoebe's *nicer* sister. Or maybe her *smarter* sister. Or you could even say her *better* sister. I do not like to be reminded that I am the *elder* sister in our family." She smiled. "You must be Nora Radnor."

Robin reached out with a smile and hand to take Nora's hand.

Instead of shaking it, Nora pulled Robin in for a hug.

"You look so much like her. I thought at first you were Phoebe. Only by your hair and glasses did I finally realize who you were. Have you seen or spoken to her lately?"

"Phoebe's fine. Happy fine. After all these years, she's now in love. Silly, isn't it? Spending the season with your old almost-but-not-quite-beau-from-college. I'm happy for her."

"I assume you're staying in her cabin while she's in Cleveland. She said you might be up from Florida to watch over things during her absence."

"She told me once I settled in, I was to visit the hall to look you up. She said you'd probably be here."

"She was right. I come in most mornings to make a pot of coffee for the girls who want to come in and work. I go upstairs and do a bit of sewing myself nearly every morning. The girls elected me president this term. Now I actually have to work. But truth be known, I don't work very hard. At my age, I'm wise enough to get younger gals to do most of the heavy lifting and the paperwork. I simply preside over very short meetings. Committees really do the work in this guild."

Nora led Robin by the hand and up the stairs. "I have girls I want you to meet. They will be so surprised when they see you."

"Haven't they seen black women before?"

"Oh shoot. You are a stinker. Phoebe said you were. No dear. They'll be just as surprised as I am to see that Phoebe has an old…," Nora caught herself, paused to correct words, and said, "*Better* sister who could pass as her twin."

Nora led Robin on tour into and around each of the workrooms on the second floor of the Tea Basket hall. She introduced Robin to several members along the way. Robin was forced to endure further remarks about her uncanny resemblance to Phoebe. Robin smiled and took all their comments well. Once Nora's tour of the facility was complete, she led Robin back into the room for handpieces, where several overstuffed chairs and a couch offered comfortable seating. She motioned for Robin to take a seat.

"Now, tell me what I can do for you during your stay in Athens County?" Nora asked.

"I'm actually quite self-sufficient, Nora. Phoebe's cabin has everything I need. I located the local grocery store, so starving won't be an issue. And I actually stumbled onto a part-time job in town. I saw an ad for a social worker in the paper and applied. Phoebe didn't even cancel her subscription to the paper. Job seemed like a good fit. I interviewed. They liked me, and I liked them, so I was hired. I'll drive into town a few hours on days needed, some weekends, maybe evenings, too."

"Oh, my. That sounds like full-time work. Where is this job?"

"I'll work for the new shelter for battered women. I'm not at liberty to disclose exactly where the shelter's located, for security reasons, of course. But it's called Harbor House. The house offers comfortable housing for women who need emergency shelter due to abuse. Children are permitted to accompany them, so that can make the place quite lively at times. I'll be helping victims obtain resources to sustain them financially, emotionally, and physically during their transition to independence or their eventual return to…"

Robin's voice trailed off momentarily as she thought about how many times victims have returned to the arms of their abusers and how many of those women, as a result, faced repeated assaults. She blocked the thought from her mind and returned to Nora.

"I'll conduct educational programming one-on-one or in small groups. We'll see. The shelter is new, and the staff is building a program as needs present themselves."

"Phoebe told me you were a social worker down in Florida. I would imagine coming up to Ohio is quite a change from the Sunshine State. Where's your home down there, if I may ask?"

"I have a condo in Tampa. I think I'm going to love experiencing the changing seasons here in Ohio."

"Oh, just wait for August, girl. It was dreadfully humid last year."

"Can't be much worse than Tampa."

"No sea breezes to enjoy here in the foothills, Robin. No lovely sea breezes at all." Nora recalled the destructive derecho that blew across Athens the previous year, flattening houses, trees, and buildings on its drive eastward into West Virginia, Pennsylvania, and beyond. She shuddered at the memory.

"Well, Phoebe's cabin has air conditioning, as does my condo back in Tampa. While I'm up here house-sitting for her, my condo is getting an overall facelift. My place is old, and the time was right for major updating. The cost is outrageous, but at my age, I thought I'd better have the work done now or never. When Phoebe asked me if I'd like to house-sit, I thought the timing was perfect. So, I have a free place to stay as long as I keep her cabin clean and forward her mail. And now I have a temporary job to help pay off my renovation loan."

"Sounds like everything is working out well. Will you stay here with us for a while today? Are you, like your sister, a quilter?"

"Thank you, Nora. No. I can't stay. I've got to make some stops for the shelter. But I will stop by on occasion. I promise. Phoebe's the quilter in the family. Quilting isn't my thing. I prefer knitting. This room looks like a good spot to bring a project should I have the need for conversation and company. Do you allow knitters?"

"Oh poo. Of course. You just tell anybody that you're Phoebe's sister *as if they need to be told*, and you make yourself right at home. Coffee's always on. Maybe we'll infect you with the quilting bug. Once caught, never cured."

Simone's determination paid off with big dividends. She had finished Ximi's quilt top by mid-afternoon and, by five, had completed a small lap quilt next in the queue. Simone updated the waiting list and then noted the quilting fees due to Molly for Ximi's project and the lap quilt.

"Molly, I'm going to take Ximi's quilt to the Tea Basket Hall on my way home so she can pick it up there. I've just sent her and the other customer texts to tell them what they owe the shop."

"Thank you, Simone. You've certainly put in a full day's work today. Are you finished?"

"Yes. I'm going to be late getting home, but I think Kyle will understand," she said as she rushed for the door laden with Ximi's bulky quilt. "See you tomorrow."

But Kyle was not understanding. He was seated at their kitchen table, eating alone, when Simone came through the front door. He glowered at her from his place at the head of the table.

"You found my note about the leftovers, I see," she said, noticing his plate of half-eaten beef. She quickly averted direct eye contact, sensing a tension building in the room.

"Yes," he said curtly, "I found a note telling me where to find my food and your orders to microwave the stuff since you'd be working late."

Simone attempted to offer a positive defense. "I finished quilting Ximi's top, which I promised I'd do before our wedding. It took most of the day. She'll be so happy to have it back. Molly has several more tops waiting for me. She said customers are asking for me by name. Isn't that great?"

Kyle grunted. "Maybe. But don't you think your first priority should be your responsibilities here, in the home, as my wife?"

Simone looked up from the platter where she was carving a portion of beef for herself to place in the microwave. An inner radar pinged in her gut. It reminded her of the unease she felt when Kyle made that nasty comment about Lois' size. Her senses went on alert. She started to question her judgment about working as long as she had that day.

Have I failed in my responsibilities already? No. I have been 'responsible.' I prepared the potatoes ahead. I left a note where Kyle could find them and the leftover beef. He could eat dinner at five, and I could get my work done at the Thimble and Chatelaine. What's the big deal?

"What do you mean, dear? Dinner *was ready*, just not hot, waiting for you in the fridge. I knew I might be late. I had everything ready for you. You hold an advanced degree, so surely you know how to operate a microwave from all those years of school."

"That's not the point," he said, putting down his fork abruptly and shoving the plate away.

The microwave pinged with Simone's dinner.

Simone removed her plate of hot food and sat down at her place beside him.

"You need to be home when I get here," he said, jamming a finger down on the table for emphasis. "The table needs to be set. I shouldn't have to heat up leftovers after my day at work. I want you here, with me, when I get home." He punctuated each sentence with a stab of his index finger on the tabletop.

"*I miss you*," he whined. "You don't need to be working down in Shade. That town's a dump. And you watch, that woman you work for will slowly start piling on more and more little things for you to do until there's no *you* left for *me*."

In that moment of silence that passed between them, Simone's mind flashed to an image of the other woman from his past.

"Okay, look, I'm truly sorry. I didn't realize that you wanted *me* as much as you wanted dinner. I promise. I'll do my best to always be home when you arrive. Okay? I'll tell Molly I have to quit no later than four. I'm sure she'll be agreeable as long as quilts don't back up. This marriage is a learning experience for me, Kyle. I've never been married before."

Simone looked over to her pouting husband. She placed her hand over his. She was wearing the new ring he had given her and waggled her fingers to draw his attention to it.

He grinned and eventually shrugged. "Sounds like you have a plan. Just don't let your work interfere with our relationship. Okay?"

"Deal," she said, pulling his hand to her lips and kissing the back of his fingers.

Kyle smiled with satisfaction. "Can you warm this up? It's gone cold." He shoved his plate her way.

Simone looked down at his half-eaten meal, her mind beginning to question how best to tread this tightrope between her old job and new marriage.

6

Nora rapped her wooden gavel gingerly on the tabletop. She was now and would forever remain uneasy with any act of force, even that of gavel pounding. "Meeting adjourned," she announced.

The Tea Basket hall erupted with the usual clamor of chairs scraping over wooden floorboards mingled with the din of female voices, everyone rising to their feet at once. Friends conversed in small groups, their laughter joining the cacophony. Women queued up for a fresh cup of coffee in the hall's little kitchenette or a turn in the lavatory. Others ascended the stairs to work on waiting projects.

Nora stood a while by the front table, gavel still in hand, relieved that the monthly business meeting had concluded quickly. She was still uncomfortable in her role as president and her new perspective standing up in front of her group. She had come to notice from that perspective that very few members seemed interested in the details of their budget. A few whispered asides; others stared somewhat blankly toward the floor or ceiling. Fortunately, the treasurer had been brief and to the point. After all, the Tea Baskets would continue to remain solvent thanks to a deceased member, who had long ago endowed them with both their building and the means to sustain it for many years.

Once in a while, a topic would seem interesting to all her members. They had received a copy of the year's program back in January, so no one expected changes. Today's only piece of business was the announcement finalizing this year's long-term charity project. That brought several comments of approval from the floor. The program committee had selected the Broken Dishes pattern for a charity quilt. Fabrics for the project were to be donated from members' scraps using a wide variety of solid or tiny cotton prints. These would be pieced together by the group on one or two sew days, then bordered with white cotton that the program committee would purchase from the Thimble and Chatelaine. This was the only committee report received with enthusiasm. Everyone agreed that, when finished, guild officers and members of the program committee would present the quilt to the local chapter of the American Red Cross. The Red Cross, not Tea Basket members, would determine how best to raise money using the quilt for their local needs. The program committee assumed Red Cross volunteers would hold a raffle. The Tea Baskets had only to make and deliver the quilt to them by the end of the year.

The program chair asked all members to report for an all-day work session on the third Saturday in May. Some would sort and select fabrics from among the donations. Others would cut pieces to size. Others would strip-sew blocks together. Irons and pressers would be needed to press seams. And, of course, a small crew should bring their favorite rippers to remove any unsatisfactory quarter-inch seams. The committee posted a sign-up sheet at the door for members to note their preferred tasks before leaving. The committee would then review the sign-up list and assign people as needed for anyone with no preference. An email or phone call would soon follow. Those unable to attend the May work session were to sign in the column marked "unavailable."

Nora sighed with relief, knowing her guild presidential duty was now at an end for another month. She met up with Lois in the kitchenette, where her friend was enjoying a snack plate piled high with potato chips. Potatoes of any kind were a weakness and love of Lois. She nodded and grinned at Nora as she munched on chips. Nora shuffled her gavel and three-ring binder of official papers to one arm, then snatched one of Lois' chips off the plate with her free hand.

"Did you hear that our Avery is going to run for County Engineer?" Nor asked.

Lois stopped chewing. "No. *Really?*"

"Yes, she told me herself."

"Nora, I was *here* when she told us!"

"What? Oh, good grief. I'm losing my memory. Do you think I'm coming down with early-onset Alzheimer's?"

"*Early onset?*" Lois snorted, "Not unless 'early onset' hits people in their nineties."

Nora pondered a moment, then let out a snort herself. She rolled her eyes at her own remark. "You'll have to forgive me. I'm getting senile."

"Not hardly. Just stressed. Bein' in charge of a meetin' will do that. I know. It's not easy for me to stand up in front of the Shinin' Star gals. Even though I think of them as friends, I go through the agenda with my nerves on edge, just tryin' not to make a mistake speakin' in public. I'm so exhausted after I finish a meetin' that I have to go home and relax for a while."

"What do you do to relax?" Nora asked.

"Eat." Lois grinned, grabbing a hand full of belly fat as evidence.

Nora and her friend laughed at Lois' self-deprecation. "OK then, let me ask you this. Did you know that Phoebe's sister has arrived from Florida? She looks just like her sister."

This was news to Lois. She had gotten to know Phoebe over the years and liked the woman. Both were long-time members of the Tea Basket guild. Lois looked forward to meeting this Robin. "So's she stayin' at Phoebe's?" Lois wondered aloud.

Nora nodded.

Lois had originally been reticent to strike up a conversation with Phoebe Prescott, who she heard from other members had been a college instructor. Lois was habitually quiet and shy around almost everyone. She herself had barely finished high school before getting married. Her school years gave way to her role as a farm wife, a role that lasted four decades. She had a child, a daughter, to raise more than a decade after their wedding. Her circle of friends was small before she joined the Tea Basket guild. She felt insecure in the presence of others, knowing most of them did not share her rural lifestyle. Some, she imagined, scoffed at her lack of formal education. Her own daughter had been chief among those who addressed this fault. Sensitive to any form of criticism, even these years later, Lois never thought that just managing her little farm as a widow was a job to merit any kind of status. But she had slowly come out of her solitary shell once she had been forced to do so. Taking over the farm following her husband's death was the first hurdle. Managing their farm on her own was not a choice. What else could she do? That was a necessity. She still needed money to live on and support herself, and the farm was her only source of income. Presiding over a guild of friendly women, though stressful, was something new and frightening, too. But time spent in that role gave her even more confidence.

Lois finished off her plate of chips, wiped her fingers with a paper napkin then retrieved her cell from the pocket of her dress. She punched up the numbers for Phoebe Prescott's cabin. Lois wanted to greet Robin Prescott, welcome her to the community, and invite her out to the farm for a meal. Her call went to voice mail.

"Well, I s'pect she's out and about. No answer," Lois said to Nora.

Disappointed, Lois left a message for Robin, reciting her own number. She told Robin she was welcome to call any time.

"I think she's probably at the women's shelter," Nora said.

"Women's shelter? I didn't know we had a women's shelter," Lois said.

"Me neither 'till Robin told me. That's where she got a job. I suspect there's a need if we have one. Awful to think about, isn't it? Robin's going to do part-time social work for them. Though the way she explained, I think she'll come into town most days. Maybe we should ask Robin to come talk to our guilds about that shelter. That would be an unusual program, wouldn't it?"

"Sounds good, but Tea Basket's program's set for the year. How 'bout I see if Robin can talk to us, Shinin' Stars? If she'll talk to us, I'll invite all the Tea Baskets to join us."

"Oh, that sounds perfect, Lois. I like the way you think. You're getting good at this president thing," Nora patted her friend's shoulder.

Lois felt awkwardly pleased. She felt her cheeks growing warm.

Later that day, as Lois was shoveling cow manure out of the corners of a stall in her barn, her cell phone, now tucked in a coverall pocket, sounded the opening bars of *Evil Woman,* a cue that her friend, Phoebe, was calling. But of course, the call would not be Phoebe.

"Hi, Lois? This is Robin Prescott returning your call."

"Hey-dee-ho. I wanted to invite you to my place sometime for a meal and chat. Me an' your sister have been good friends since the day she helped me repair fence. She's a fast learner. Not afraid to get her hands dirty or an old shirt torn up by barbed wire."

"Thanks, Lois. I'll take you up on that offer. Phoebe told me all about you. Said you were the 'lady on the farm with a big heart and lots of work to do.' I guess you really got a full day's work out of her on that fence. She enjoyed helping. Said you've helped a lot of people over the years. She was happy to return some of it your way for a change."

"Yeah, I taught her the joy of fence repairs."

"She always was a fast learner. Got her PhD at age twenty-four. She's the type who loves learning."

Eventually, Lois turned to another topic. "Do you think you could pick a date to come to my place? I'll fix us a good meal, lunch, or dinner." Then Lois asked, "Would you be able to give the Shinin' Stars a talk about that new women's shelter where Nora told me you work?"

Robin agreed at once to both invitations. "Lunch or dinner sounds great," she said. "I'll check with my supervisor about speaking to your guild. I'm confident a presentation to a room full of women will be seen as a good outreach event. I could include a brief account of what signs to look for in abusive partners. I'm certain someone in your group will recognize a friend or relative who's being abused. You know, Lois, simply being aware of the signs is helpful. When might you want me to present?"

Lois had already jammed her pitchfork into a pile of manure and straw and was walking toward her house. She had some difficulty at the boot jack beside her front door. She asked Robin to "Hold on a sec. I'll get my calendar and give you some dates." Her big black rubber barn boots were encrusted with mud and manure from her work in the stall. Once she had them off, she left them on the porch and walked into the house just far enough in her stocking feet to pull a small binder off a tabletop near the door. Flipping to her guild's schedule of activities, she saw many dates that were wide open. She relayed the openings to Robin, and the two settled on a tentative date.

Sheila Harper leaned over her counter as far as she could to whisper to Avery. Staying quiet had now become standard practice between them since Avery's announcement.

Avery had returned to the engineer's office on the advice of Joe O'Feeny. Just because Avery had announced her intention to run for County Engineer didn't mean she was qualified yet to be on the ballot and campaign. As a result, she did not have to quit her job, as Hollister had led her to believe. O'Feeny advised her to confront Hollister with the news and share the fact that she had been in consultation with him. She was in no violation of any civil service regulation by simply announcing an intent to run.

"*Now?*"

"Once again, Sheila, I feel like I have to."

Avery absent-mindedly played with the aluminum storage clipboard on the counter. Jasper had once again left the box on the counter when he came back into the office.

"Since we're the same party, he and I, I'm not likely to beat him in the primary. Not even the party chair would endorse me. I asked Joe O'Feeny. He said he has to back the incumbent, loyalty or something like that. He sent me back to the board of elections to file as an independent. They told me I didn't need to file anything before the primaries. Running as an independent seems to be my one and only option. I don't know who'd support an independent in this county. Do you? But I'm going to tell him, and I'm going to keep doing my job here as long as I can, whether he likes it or not."

"Maybe you should hold off saying anything to Jasper about that independent run," Sheila whispered. "You've got enough to hit him with coming back here against his wishes. Wait until after the primaries. Wait as long as possible. Have a backup plan in case he goes ballistic again, 'cause he certainly will."

Just then, Hollister pulled open his door and walked out of his office, cell phone in hand. When he saw Avery, his face reddened. He bellied up to Sheila's counter beside Avery and shook his phone in her face. "What the hell are you doing back here? I thought I told you to get out of here and quit."

Avery mustered all the nerve she could to stand up to the man who was her boss. "I'm not going anywhere," she said. "I spoke to Joe O'Feeny. As long as I'm not approved by the Board of Elections to be on the fall ballot, I'm guaranteed my right to continue working as a county civil servant. You have no authority to fire me or to keep me from doing what I was hired to do. I have no obligation to quit just because you want me to."

By now, Jasper Hollister was in a right rigid state. His face redder than ever, his posture one of defiance and his loss for words palpable. He knew his ploy had failed to rid him of Underwood. He felt genuinely threatened by her. His tack had been one of aggression, thinking he could gain an upper hand to scare her off and rid himself of her. But knowing she had been to the courthouse and had spoken to O'Feeny, his party chair, he was now unable to make more demands.

"Then, if that's so, get back to work! You're not hired to stand around chit-chattin.' Don't you have somewhere else to be?"

It was but a momentary stalemate in his mind.

But Avery had just won a small victory for her livelihood.

Hollister turned his back abruptly on Avery and bellowed instead toward his clerk. "Sheila, Give me those bridge specs for Road 75!"

"Yes, sir," Sheila said, shuffling through a stack until she found the right folder. She then handed the papers over the counter to him.

Hollister slammed his phone on the counter and opened the file. He continued to ignore Avery as if she wasn't standing beside him. Instead, he scanned the papers, grumbling about the cost of three culverts. "That damn road," he muttered, turning away, carrying the file back into this office and slamming the door behind him. No more than 30 seconds passed before he was yelling from his office.

"Sheila! Have you seen my damn phone?"

The two women looked at each other, then at his cell phone on the counter. It was a habit of Hollister to misplace his cell phone multiple times every day.

"You left it out here, sir," she yelled back.

With a disgruntled look on his face, he retrieved it and stomped back into his office, slamming the door shut once again.

Avery took Sheila's suggestion. Difficult as it was, she kept mum on the subject of her political aspirations as an independent. She went about the rest of that day and weeks to follow tending to all the supervisory tasks that fell to her, all neglected by her boss.

One such onerous task involved a grader operator, Pat, who was caught tipping a bottle of Jack Daniels while on the job. This was Pat's second such offense involving alcohol. She handed the guy a three-day suspension, warning him that the next infraction would likely be a permanent release from the job. She explained to him that if it happened one more time, she would have to schedule a disciplinary hearing with a department head outside the highway department if he was found to be drinking on the job one more time. He would likely be fired because of this repeated habit. His future employment, therefore, depended on his behavior. She ordered him to undergo substance abuse awareness counseling during his suspension. He needed to provide documentation that he'd been in attendance before she'd allow him back behind the wheel of one of the county's graders. No proof of program participation. No driving. No job.

Avery doubted anything Pat heard in those sessions was likely to stick in his alcohol-soaked brain. The unsavory task of suspending Pat forced her to process disciplinary paperwork for his personnel file. She really needed to be out on worksites. Her main crew was repairing a road slip north of Athens along the Hocking River. Another crew was repaving a worn-out stretch to the east of the county. That morning, she'd dispatched a small team of new employees out to cut and haul away a fallen tree lying across the

Hockhocking Adena bike path up near Hamley Run. She needed to visit all those sites to oversee their conclusion and sign off on the jobs. But instead, she was writing up a report. She understood why Hollister hated paperwork and always left the task to her.

After she finished and handed her paperwork to Sheila to file at the courthouse, she drove to each of the work sites. Worry crept into her thoughts about how Jasper Hollister was going to take the news when she finally did tell him she was going to campaign as an independent. She was sure Sheila's warning would prove correct. Work would only get worse once he knew. As if it could get any colder than it already was. Though it pained her to keep her secret, she followed Sheila's advice and kept this new plan to herself.

7

At the next Shining Star meeting, Lois announced the addition of a program. Robin Prescott had agreed to present a talk related to the new women's shelter at their next meeting. Lois's announcement ensured the program change would be included in the minutes emailed to anyone absent. She asked the secretary to write an official invitation to the Tea Baskets. Robin, she explained, wanted to reach as many women as possible, so Tea Basket members would be welcome to attend. Because the Shining Star guild met weekly in the Tea Basket Hall, there was no confusion as to the place.

Nora arrived earlier than usual at the hall on the morning Robin was to speak. She busied herself making two forty-cup urns of coffee, one pot of regular, and one decaff. The hall was soon abuzz with members from both guilds arriving to claim a seat, a cup of coffee, and a cookie. Lois asked that the first two rows of chairs be reserved for Shining Star members as this was their meeting. Everyone complied.

When Robin Prescott arrived she was greeted by a circle of women professing friendship with her sister. She had not met some of them on her first tour of the facility with Nora. But it seemed to her that each new face remarked on her uncanny resemblance to her sister Phoebe. Lois stood quietly by her side and beamed with pleasure.

Ximi Ling shook Robin's hand, welcoming her to the neighborhood. Ximi's best friend, Simone Beck, shook her hand, too, offering her own words of welcome. Ximi and Simone rattled on pleasantly that they were members of both guilds and looked forward to sitting in the front row. Everyone present, they explained, belonged to one big quilting family. Robin, they urged, should join the clan and take up quilting.

Others followed. By the time of her presentation, Robin felt as if she had known some of the women for years. It seemed like the older members could certainly rattle on for hours with Phoebe's stories. She felt Lois tap her shoulder who then walked off toward the front of the assembly. This was her cue to politely break away. She excused herself from the last group of talkative admirers and moved to stand at a spot between the officers' table and the rows of chairs where most of the guild members had already seated themselves.

Lois wrapped her gavel boldly on the table for order. Unlike Nora, Lois treated her gavel like a hammer pounding nails on a fence post. Anyone still milling about quickly found a seat and settled down to hear their guest speaker.

Lois made no lengthy introduction. She simply opened her arms wide to welcome Robin into the fold and to the front of the group. "Ladies, this is Robin Prescott, 'n case you haven't met her. Think you all know who she's related to."

There were grins and happy chuckles from many.

"Welcome, Robin. We're all ready and interested in hearin' from you 'bout this new women's shelter called Harbor House."

"Thank you, "Robin began. "Thanks, everyone, for coming in today to hear what I have to say. A special thanks to Lois for inviting me to talk about Harbor House, our new shelter for battered women, and to talk to you all about the subject of spousal abuse."

Robin nodded to Ximi, who had taken a seat at the end of the front row beside Simone. Ximi stood. She had been recruited to distribute a stack of brochures.

"I assume you have many stories about quilt retreats. Women, usually, go to a secluded place to piece quilt tops unencumbered by the distractions of the normal day. They enjoy each other's company. Lots of talking. Lots of laughter. Lots of eating, I understand. Sometimes folks even have time to complete an entire project."

Chuckles could be heard from many corners of the room.

"Abuse is not a subject that often comes up over dinner, at guild meetings, or on retreat. Is it?"

A general low rumble from many in the audience concurred.

"But that's what I'm here today to talk about. Spousal or partner abuse. You're each receiving a brochure for Harbor House, which contains a phone number, though not the address. Keep in mind that women staying in our shelter need a place of refuge out of necessity, not out of pleasure. Residents of Harbor House retreat to us for safety reasons. There, they begin to patch together the shattered pieces of their lives. Nothing gets finished at Harbor House for these women. But we hope it's a place for a new beginning. Their well-being and safety are our prime concerns.

The only way a woman reaches our shelter is by the personal escort of local law enforcement officers or an agency social worker, or by a staff member of Harbor House."

Robin paused a moment while brochures continued to travel across rows in the rear of the hall. Ximi, at last, returned to her seat up front next to Simone. When satisfied that everyone had a brochure in hand, Robin continued.

"I'm new to the area, having just arrived from Florida. I'm a social worker for Harbor House. I'm also the sister of your guild member, Phoebe Prescott, who at this moment is enjoying a carefree life with her beau while I get to enjoy the delights of living in her cabin in this beautiful part of Ohio." She looked across the spectrum of faces seated in the hall. Several were acknowledging her with smiles.

"Harbor House," she continued, "is a new shelter designed to house women who need a safe place to live, safely away from an abusive partner. County adult protective services, local law enforcement, and the court system have identified and often rescued our residents from life-threatening situations, sometimes accompanied by their children. These victims come to us oftentimes with battered bodies and broken bones. All of them need time to heal from their physical injuries. It will take years for them to recover from the emotional trauma they've endured. Harbor House is a place where they can begin that process of healing."

"One of my jobs at Harbor House is to educate our residents and the community. I'm also there to support those abused women who sometimes cannot admit to themselves that they have been victims of abuse."

"Up until the moment she's been rescued, and even then, a victim may remain in denial. She's spent months, sometimes years, trying to figure out what's wrong with *her*, not what is wrong with her *abuser*. Putting herself first is not something she's had the privilege of doing. It takes great effort on her part to adjust her way of thinking, to find value once again in herself."

"Literature on the subject points out that a victim of abuse will have spent much of her time being obsessed with ways to please her impossible-to-please abuser. She will have struggled constantly to keep him from hurting her again and again. She will have wracked her brain to discover what it is that *she does* that makes him so angry."

"To these victims, who cater to their abuser's demands, nothing seems to satisfy. In fact, the more she gives in to his demands, the more he will demand. In this confusing cycle of self-blame and constant abuse, these women are in extreme emotional pain and confusion. Many of them have lost all their freedoms. They have been forced to give up all their rights, even denied the right to feel anger at their treatment. They wrongly turn inward toward an obsession of self-blame. The worst part for them, they live lives in constant fear. What this all adds up to are women who have come to believe *they* are the crazy ones."

Robin paused to pick up a glass of water thoughtfully left on the table for her by Nora. She took a sip before she continued. She hoped in the pause that her description of victims was clear.

"So who are these ogres, these abusive partners? Well, they're our next-door neighbor. They might even be a relative. An abuser can be young, middle-aged, or old. Often, it's a male. He can be rich or poor. These abusers don't reside in one neighborhood or belong to one socioeconomic group. You might even know this person as the funny guest at your backyard barbecue who's always quick with a joke. He might be kind and warm in your presence. Often, he's successful. Sometimes not. But if he's your friend, you think he's a great guy. He might seem generous in the eyes of the partner he secretly abuses. He might shower her with gifts, which is part of his public persona. He's charming. Even the victim has told you herself, perhaps repeatedly, just how wonderful he is."

"Does this sound like anyone you know? Of course. But not everyone who's nice publicly is a closet abuser. What, then, is abuse? Simply put, it's disrespect. Abuse includes coercion. Abuse is delivered as insults. Abusers devalue their partners. Abuse itself can span the spectrum from mental cruelty all the way to physical assault. An abusive situation that finally escalates into assault is, sadly, the one act which most often brings women into our shelter."

"A victim doesn't usually go around talking about how bad her life is at home. No. Not at all. You might not know anything is wrong because she hasn't told you anything is wrong. Remember, she's trying hard to come to terms with what's wrong with herself. She might, therefore, feel shame. She might even fear you will criticize her for not having left at the first sign of abuse."

"What has she been dealing with in her silence? Perhaps I can explain. The disrespect probably started with a single verbal barb. Maybe he said something nasty about one of her friends. She probably let the comment slide. After all, she loves him. He is her ideal. It's early in her relationship with this person. Perhaps he has told her that she's the only woman to treat him right. She's not like *all the others*. She's *different*; somehow, she's *better*. In this scenario, as the wronged fellow, he paints for her a sad past, his wounded image, and his story, which plays on her sympathy and compassion. However, his disrespect gradually increases. The barbs will eventually be aimed at her. How she dresses. How she speaks. What she says. Maybe he'll point out her lack of skill in some area."

Simone, sitting attentively next to Ximi, shifted slightly in her seat as if the chair was a little uncomfortable.

"Slowly, he begins to assert control over her. He might start to tell her what to think. The putdowns escalate. Once a generous, loving partner, now begins to turn selfish. Should she dare air a grievance with him about his actions, her complaint will be turned around that his behavior is a result of *her doing*. How dare she question *him*? He might even begin to tell other people that she has a mental problem. He might abruptly cut her off in their private conversations. He may issue rules for her to follow in public as well as in private. She must wear the clothes he selects. She must not speak to others without his permission. He may criticize the food she prepares or the condition of their home. He'll order her around as if she's a servant. Whatever *he needs* becomes *her responsibility* to provide. His opinions are the only correct ones. He is above all criticism. Oh, watch out if she chooses unwisely to disagree with him."

"That's when the physical abuse begins to play out. Up to that point, he's been using mind games on her. His mood might change suddenly. He might grow increasingly quiet or withdrawn at first. His sulking might be followed by screaming and yelling, all directed at her. He might show signs of jealousy and accuse her of the most ridiculous behavior. She is, of course, innocent. Truth plays no role in his performance around her.

He might begin to punish her. Maybe he will destroy things, her things, not his. He might hide her things and then put them back to make her think she's losing her mind. Eventually, he will physically assault her. Slap her around. Push her. And sadly, the assaults can escalate to extreme levels. The worst physical attacks happen if she should ever attempt to leave him."

Some of the Shining Stars and Tea Baskets, who had once been staring down into their laps scanning brochures, were now focused intently on Robin's words. Most of them had given no thought to what abused women faced on a day-to-day basis. The pictures now playing out in their minds made some of them uneasy. A few shifted uncomfortably in their seats. Simone Beck glanced first at the brochure and then gazed over briefly to see if Ximi was looking at her.

Ximi was not looking her way but laser-focused on Robin Prescott standing in front of the room. Ximi had already pegged Kyle Beck as the principal subject of Robin's presentation. As Robin resumed her presentation, Ximi stole a quick glance toward her friend. Just for a moment, their eyes met. Just as fast, they redirected their attention back to Robin.

"Watch for the signs. If you notice a relationship that seems just a tad out of step, be aware and on alert. Above all, be supportive of the woman. She's suffering in silence. Perhaps you could casually mention to her when she's alone that there is help, a shelter at Harbor House available for battered women.

After all, you're hearing this news yourself today, so please do share what you learn with all the women in your circle. Remember that your friend or relative, whom you suspect might be a victim, is struggling with confusion, fear, shame, and all sorts of emotions of which you cannot possibly be aware."

"I caution you, do not encourage her to stand up to her abuser."

"No. Absolutely not. That could place her in danger. She just needs to know that when the time and circumstances are right for her when she has found an appropriate time and way to escape, there is a place for her to run to. Let her know you would offer your support to aid her. But be honest, don't say you'd help if you don't mean to. One day, or late one night, you might get a desperate phone call to back up your words… with action.”

With that, Robin concluded her talk. She was rewarded with a round of applause. She held up both hands to quiet the assembly, then asked if anyone had questions.

“How many women really need shelter? I mean, c’mon, I don’t read that much in the paper about abused women,” asked one of the Shining Stars in the second row.

“You aren’t reading about every case of abuse in the paper because victims often won’t report abuse. You’ll only read about the truly sensational events that involved police intervention. Reporters listen to police scanners. They don’t hang around the waiting rooms of agencies where these women must run for aid. You don’t see reporters shoving microphones into the faces of women bearing black eyes and toting a screaming baby up to some receptionist at the welfare department in order to apply for help putting down a deposit on an apartment or asking for monthly benefits.”

As usual, there were quiet comments among this group of women who all knew each other well. A few nodded their heads in agreement with the information they had just received. A couple were shaking their heads in disbelief. They were the fortunate ones who had never had to witness any kind of abuse toward anyone they knew or had ever been the target of abuse themselves.

After Robin had answered a few more questions, she concluded her presentation.

Lois rose with difficulty from her place at the head table to announce that the meeting was adjourned and everyone was welcome to refreshments. She invited Robin to join them.

"Later," Lois said, "After everyone's gone, I need to ask you somethin."

"Sure, anything," Robin said.

The din of the group breaking up lasted only a few minutes. By the time several trays of homemade cookies held nothing but crumbs, most of the women had moved on. As usual, those with projects waiting upstairs in the workrooms had traveled up the steps. The ones interested in lunch with friends had departed. Eventually, Lois found the opportunity to talk to Robin alone.

"Would you be able to get me a meetin' with your director? I'm tryin' to come up with a charity project for these girls, and I have an idea that might also benefit your Harbor House."

"Why sure. I'd be happy to introduce you."

"You said your place is secret, so maybe your director would rather talk to me here."

"I think I can arrange a visit for you to the house if that would be helpful."

Lois was surprised to hear this. "Really? Oh yes, that would be. I'd like to see how your guests live. I'm particularly interested in your sleepin' arrangements. Do you really think I can get a tour?"

"I know a tour would be possible. I'll set it up. Any particular day better for you?"

"No, no. I can meet anytime." Lois thanked her guest speaker as they both walked out the door together.

Simone and Ximi said goodbye to Robin as they passed each other on the front steps of the hall. They had been stacking chairs and moving tables out to their storage shed in the rear of the lot. "I had no idea that an abused woman felt it was her fault," Ximi said to Simone as they resumed collecting more chairs to move out. "Did you?"

"No. Me neither," agreed Simone. "But really, don't all couples argue? That's not abuse."

"Didn't sound to me like abuse is just arguments. Sounded like it kinda grows from a little irritation, like a fungus or cancer. Like a victim doesn't even know anything's wrong at first. She just feels something's off, but that any wrongness is within her. You ever feel that way about Kyle?"

"No!" Simone said rather quickly, then fell silent. She continued to stack chairs and forced herself to think about something pleasant. Once or twice, her new ring caught a ray of light. She smiled. "Everything's OK with me and Kyle. Don't go reading anything into that silly remark I made about him wanting dinner on time. You hear me, girlfriend?"

"Yeah, I hear you," Ximi replied. But Ximi didn't believe everything was okay between Simone and Kyle. The youngest member of both guilds, Ximi could read others' characters better than most people twice her age and experience.

Simone had little more to say as she helped Ximi move the last of the chairs into the garage behind the Tea Basket hall. Robin Prescott's words kept replaying in her mind. *Surely, I'm not one of those women. Kyle's no abuser.*

Several times more, she caught the glint of light off diamonds encircling the peridot on her finger. Secretly, she resented what Robin said. She was hurt that Ximi would even suggest all was not right and good between her and her new husband. *Kyle is just a man who likes structure in his busy life. That's all. Having dinner on time, with me, well, that's something I can do without becoming some sort of victim. It's no big deal. And his previous fiancé was awful.*

Simone arrived home that afternoon with ample time to set the table for her husband and have their dinner ready at the appointed hour of five. She made herself busy experimenting with a new recipe she hoped Kyle liked. Turkey tetrazzini. No carrots. She set out the Rothschild pattern china she so adored, arranged a small centerpiece of spring lilacs from the bush in her backyard, and even found a CD of quiet music to play on their sound system. She had just finished making the sauce when Kyle arrived. She heard his keys drop onto a small table by the door.

He smiled broadly at her as he came into the kitchen, his nose in the air, catching the aroma of something spicy, anticipating what was to follow. He gave Simone a quick kiss on the cheek where she stood at the stove then took his place at the head of their table.

"Grab me a beer, will ya, hon?"

Simone poured sauce from the pan over the pasta and placed the serving dish on the table near Kyle; she then retrieved a cold can from the refrigerator.

"Bad day on the gridiron?" she asked, placing the beer in front of him and taking her own seat at the table.

Kyle tipped the kitchen chair back, balancing it on two back legs. "Just the usual," he said, then took a long gulp. "We have to attend a dinner at the President's house tomorrow." He lowered the chair and stared admiringly at the frosty can in his hand.

"We? 'We' meaning your staff? Or 'we' meaning you and I?" she asked.

"We, as in us, doofus," he said, taking another sip of beer. "I want you to wear something business-like but sharp. Nothing that's too revealing. Sometimes you can dress like a slut, you know."

Simone felt a severe pang in her chest. She protested. "Kyle! I've worn the same clothes that I've owned since before we married. You told me back then you liked what I wore. What's changed? And I do not dress like a street walker, thank you."

"Like hell. I'll tell you what's changed," he barked. The look in his eyes was warning Simone not to take her contradictions any further. "We're married now. You need to look the part of a coach's wife. We're going to the president's house. That's what's changed. We're not going out to some nightclub. There'll be members of the board of regents present, the upper echelon of the university, all the people I have to appease and impress. I do not want any of them to say my wife is anything less than perfect."

Simone remained silent through their meal as Kyle rattled on, presenting a chronicle of his coaching day. She passed her husband the serving platter when she saw his plate was empty. She refilled his water glass. Once, she got up to replace his empty beer can with a full one. She took away dishes. She waitressed. But she offered no remarks about the day she had experienced. All the while they ate, the image of Robin Prescott kept lurking in her mind and whispering most annoyingly in her inner ear. It took all her strength to chase back tears and fight off the urge to scream at Robin for planting such nonsense inside her brain.

The following day, Simone tormented herself with what to wear that evening. She made an appointment with the hairdresser for a French twist to her auburn hair. Simone had a natural glow about her; however, this day, she took inventory of her makeup, which she rarely bothered to wear. She was worried. Perhaps something more than natural good looks would be necessary. This evening, she would dab just a bit of shadow on her eyelids. On the way home from the salon, she stopped to buy a new pair of pantyhose, just in case. In fact, Simone spent most of the day imagining what perfection should look like.

She pulled three potential outfits out of her closet and spread them over their bed. She chose a linen pantsuit in black. She felt that black was always perfect for any occasion. Then, she laid out a turquoise suit of boucle fabric. Prettier than black, but still classic in design. Not at all revealing, as if. And finally, she removed an olive green dress with long sleeves that might work. She decided Kyle could say exactly which outfit he preferred. She would wear the one he thought best and thereby avoid any unpleasantness over her attire for the evening.

When she asked, Kyle pointed to the green dress. She was relieved it was suitable and reassured when Kyle selected the same one she had imagined he would. He said it would match her eyes and "go well with that expensive cocktail ring I bought." She dressed, then met him waiting impatiently for her at their front door. He did not open the door at once but kept a hand on the knob, and the door closed. He had something obviously very serious to say to her.

"I know how opinionated you can be. But tonight, I need you to be agreeable. Do not argue with these people. Got it? Whatever they say, just bob your head and agree. Don't go on and on about your quilt buddies, either. These folks don't care to hear about your little club activities. I'll have to leave you while I rub shoulders with these people, so don't disappoint me. Remember, my job depends on your good behavior. So. Ready to go?"

Simone resented this little lecture and his tone of voice. It made her feel like a mischievous child about to be ushered reluctantly into the adult world where she might be wantonly destructive. Wasn't she herself an educated adult woman? She could converse intelligently about more than guild meetings and her work at the Thimble and Chatelaine. She held a degree in literature with a minor in art history. Surely, he hadn't forgotten. She could carry on a decent conversation with others in the learned community, including college administrators and their spouses. She'd been to enough of these functions with him to have already met most of them anyway, even members of the board. She was very much aware she would see familiar faces and know what *they* liked to discuss. She knew how not to embarrass him. Her frustration must have shown on her face.

"What's that look?" Kyle asked.

"Nothing. Nothing at all, Kyle. I'm just surprised you would think I'd embarrass you."

"Good. Then, don't."

Though they arrived together at the president's house that evening, Kyle promptly abandoned her to mingle with others. Simone took a glass of white wine from a passing waiter and then looked around for a familiar and friendly face. She spotted an old professor from the English department looking her way. She smiled at him and took a sip of her Moscato.

"Mrs. Beck," the bearded Dr. Mortimer Mathias said as he walked over to stand beside her. He looked characteristically professorial in every way, including in his wool tweed jacket and blue bow tie. He approached and offered his hand. "Nice to see you again. Love these shindigs, don't you?"

Simone wasn't sure if he was being honest or just kidding. She furrowed her brow in puzzlement. But she could see the slightest gleam in his eye and, finally, the impish grin behind his salt-and-pepper beard.

"Oh, you know, all the schmoozing with everyone trying to be the most up-to-date on whatever topic surfaces or the latest in print. The race to know the best people to solve a current social or political issue. One-upmanship to the nth degree. It's all a dance of peacocks if you ask me."

Simone could not stop herself from smiling broadly. She watched her own handsome peacock across the room, strutting from one VIP to the next. He was standing amid a crowd of admirers, themselves obviously on full-tail feather display. Two of the regents soon joined his flock.

"Couldn't agree with you more, Dr. Mathias. It's nice to find you here."

"I hope you don't mind me standing in your shadow," the old professor said. "You're by far the prettiest tree in this desert of old prickly palms. Coach Beck is lucky to have you. I'm positive that you feel the same about him. He's well-liked by everyone here on campus, and not because of his winning record, either." The old professor clinked his wine glass to hers with a smile and a wink.

The two discussed an article on Shakespeare's sonnets and the Bard's view of the world stage. Eventually, both sought out a second glass of wine.

"Shall we go schmoozing ourselves?" Simone asked the professor. "Let's be selective, though, as to whom we allow to grace us with their wisdom."

"Lead on, m' lady. I am but your servant."

With nearly every new encounter, Simone was showered with words of praise for Coach Beck. Some told her how dedicated he was in his role as coach. Some gushed over his good looks. Others mentioned his charisma. Everyone told her how lucky she was to be his bride. Her affable companion would chuckle a little, then chime in with his own opinion, wholly in agreement with theirs. Simone's head started to swirl with all the praise. It seemed everyone thought highly of her husband. None had anything bad to say. She was surely at fault. *I should not be critical of his actions in the privacy of our home. Obviously, I've been at fault, not Kyle, if we have issues. That comment about Lois was nothing I should concern myself over. I'm just being hypersensitive to his observations.* Add to that, she was simply being silly to think anything wrong about Kyle wanting her to behave well.

Kyle did not join his wife until a bell announced dinner was served. He located her, took her by the arm, and escorted her to their seats at the long table in a great dining room in the old president's mansion. In spite of her earlier frustration at the front door of their home, Simone had enjoyed her evening with old Dr. Mathias. She enjoyed meeting and talking to all those who so respected Kyle. By the end of the dessert, she was confident that she had not embarrassed Coach Beck, not one iota. She had been *perfect*.

8

As they had agreed, Robin picked up Lois from the Tea Basket hall then drove to Harbor House. An escort with Robin was the one way Lois would gain admittance into the shelter. Lois watched the town pass by the car window and rattled on about her farm to fill dead air. Robin picked up on the woman's unease.

"You seem tense," Robin said.

"Never been to a shelter," Lois admitted. "Never seen battered women. Don't know what to expect."

Robin smiled. She reached over, patting Lois on the arm. "You'll find it cozy and comfortable. And you'll love the women, both staff and residents. I've heard how you care for others. Folks at Harbor House are the same."

The shelter house was an imposing three-story Victorian with an adjacent garage, probably added much later. It had a large fenced-in back yard surrounded by a stockade fence for privacy and, Lois imagined, a means to keep wife beaters from gaining access. Each window had wooden shutters to increase the privacy and security of its residents. The front yard had been recently mowed. A lilac was just budding up, promising to bear the sweet fragrance that Lois loved. But there was no sign, no indication of the building's purpose.

Lois, whose whole life had been spent among friends with a loving husband of many decades, was more than a little uneasy about venturing inside. Mostly, she feared seeing the physical effects that battering probably left. Her imagination was running wild. Too much TV. But upon their arrival, she lumbered out of Robin's car, determined to press on with her mission in spite of her unease. She wanted to identify something for her inexperienced guild members to do as part of a long-term charity project. She had an idea in mind, but first, she needed to see for herself if her idea was remotely suitable, or welcome, for that matter. Talking with the director and completing a tour might answer all her questions.

Robin led Lois inside through a set of oaken front doors into an entryway tiled with little squares of marble. The walls were covered part way up in wainscot of polished oak, now darkened with age. A large chandelier hanging above a sturdy oaken table cast a cheerful light on an enormous floral arrangement in the center of the room.

Robin and Lois entered an office just to the left of the front door. The tiny space had barely enough room to hold a desk and two guest chairs. Perhaps it had been a spacious coat room in the early years of the old house. Lois was surprised to see someone so young seated behind the desk. She stood up as Lois arrived, a tall, thin woman still in her twenties by Lois' estimate.

"Lois Caldwell, may I present the director of Harbor House, Brigitta Johansson."

A remarkably young woman, in Lois' opinion, came around her desk to take Lois' hand. Lois accepted. The girl's grip was strong but gentle. Brigitta Johansson wore a light yellow oxford shirt tucked into blue jeans. Lois saw no raggedy holes glaring back at her on this girl's knees, which seemed so popular with young women these days. She herself would never get caught wearing such rags, not even on her barn dungarees. Everyone would think she had no money at all and couldn't afford to buy nice clothes. Or worse yet, that she had no ability to repair her clothing. Brigitta wore expensive running shoes. A single strand of small colorful beads hung around her neck under the shirt. They barely peeked out between the open labels of her blouse as she moved. Her blonde hair, cut off at the top of the collar, as well as her name made Lois assume she was from Scandinavia.

"Lois, I'm so pleased to meet ya," Brigitta Johansson said in an accent hinting at someone who grew up in Kentucky. "Robin tells me you're the president of a quilt guild and that you're seeking a charity project. I'm very excited to hear what you have to say. Welcome to Harbor House."

Behind the girl's desk hung three college diplomas framed in black. Several certificates also adorned the wall. But from her perspective across the room, Lois couldn't read what they had been awarded for. There were no photographs of a boyfriend, a husband, or children. Lois guessed this: Brigitta Johansson was probably not yet old enough to marry.

Lois forced a smile and stammered. "I'm surprised to see, ah, someone so young as a shelter director."

Brigitta laughed with ease. "That's because PhDs like me are as plentiful as geese on the Hocking River in this town. Our board hired me on the cheap. Somebody with years of experience and gray hair to prove it would have been beyond their budget. They took a chance on someone just out of grad school who happened to have written her dissertation on the ramifications of spousal abuse and the need for community shelters."

"You sound like you're from around these parts," Lois said, catching a bit of southern twang in the woman's voice.

"I grew up in Portsmouth."

"Really? I think Roy Rogers lived in Portsmouth at one time. I have a friend who used to live there. She started college at the branch. She's much older than you, my age, actually. So you wouldn't know her or Roy Rogers. He's long dead. My friend's on a world cruise."

Brigitta Johansson smiled kindly, listening to Lois' ramble. "Robin tells me you'd like a tour of our facility. Would you like to get started?"

"Oh, yes, if that's okay with you."

"Absolutely. Robin will show you around. Afterward, please come back, and we'll talk."

"Thank you," said Lois, who then turned to Robin still standing in the doorway.

"If you follow me, Lois, we'll start in the kitchen and move on to our communal living room."

Lois grinned. No doubt Phoebe had told Robin that Lois' favorite room in any house was always the kitchen.

The aroma of baking bread reached Lois as soon as she entered the kitchen through a sliding pocket doorway. Aluminum pots hung like large ornaments from a hanger over a centrally located stainless steel prep table. A woman even larger than Lois was stirring an enormous pot of soup on an eight-burner stainless steel commercial gas stove. Someone, Lois assumed the cook, stirring the soup, had already prepared a salad which lay on the table. The greens glistened in a bowl the size of a bird bath. Lois' thoughts turned to the residents she had not yet met. Were they starving women who hadn't had a good meal in days? The thought tugged at her heart.

"Bonnie, I'd like to introduce Lois Caldwell from the Shining Star quilt guild. She's taking a tour today," Robin announced to the cook. "Lois, this is Bonnie Forrester."

Bonnie turned away from the stove. She smiled and waved a white towel at Lois with one hand while she continued to stir the large pot with the other hand. "I heard we'd have a guest today. Nice to meet ya, Lois. Lunch will be served soon. You'll join us."

Bonnie spoke as if it were an order more than an invitation. Lois thought maybe Bonnie Forrester was the real boss around the shelter rather than that girl with the PhD. *Cooks rule.*

As they continued on with the tour, Lois learned that Harbor House possessed a modest library located on the first floor just off the kitchen. The room was carpeted and, therefore, quiet. Early afternoon sun filled the space with light from a pair of windows flanking empty bookshelves along the opposite wall. Additional shelves around two adjacent walls held a small collection of books. Wood-framed chairs with padded seats were shoved in around a used matching dining room table that occupied the center of the room. The table was adorned with a single centerpiece of artificial flowers. There were no readers present that morning. *Maybe they're all too injured. Maybe they read in bed, trying to recuperate from their attackers,* Lois imagined.

Lois could see the enclosed back yard through the library windows. The grass-covered yard was equipped with a swing set off to one side and a large cement patio off the kitchen. Outdoor furniture had been arranged in several conversational groups. A picnic table with a huge red canopy dominated the patio.

Robin led Lois into the communal living room, where Lois was surprised to spot a large flat-screen TV attached to one wall. There were several mismatched couches and chairs arranged so that all who chose could view the big screen. Someone had been working on a jigsaw puzzle spread over a card table off to one side. Only the edges around the puzzle had been assembled. Individual pieces lay scattered in a jumble near the open box top, which revealed a scene of boats and water at some seaside village. The photo must have been taken in the fall. Trees among the village houses were turning vibrant colors of orange, gold, and red. It was a wonder to Lois that anyone would be able to reassemble all those tiny little pieces into the photo on the box.

Harbor House also had its own laundry room with two washing machines and two dryers, both of which were in use when Lois made her inspection. The scent of fabric softener and detergent filled the warm air. Someone had thoughtfully constructed a folding table along one wall and provided a portable metal basket on wheels with a rod above. There was no need for these residents to visit a laundromat. Lois saw several tubs of laundry detergent lined up on a shelf as well as a few extra boxes of dryer sheets.

On the second and third floors, Lois was admitted only into two vacant bedrooms. These, Robin explained, were not currently occupied. Any bedroom that had a resident was off-limits to visitors and most of the staff. The women who stayed at Harbor House needed to feel they had at least one place that was theirs and theirs alone. The larger bedroom Lois saw had two single beds and a set of bunks, probably for children, Lois thought. The smaller bedroom had just one single bed. Each room had a comfortable overstuffed chair, a dresser or two, and a small table or desk. There was also a tiny closet behind a door in each room.

"Our residents do have to share bathrooms," Robin said. "No room has its own. But for the most part, with proper scheduling, everyone has privacy. Wet towels go out in the hallway over these clothes racks. When dry, they can be reused or deposited in these nearby laundry baskets. All residents take a shift doing laundry. And everyone takes a shift helping Bonnie prepare meals. Residents are also responsible for general house cleaning. We try to schedule everything a week in advance. We work around medical appointments, school schedules, and court dates."

So far, Lois had not seen any bloody, battered women. She was relieved. She didn't know what she'd say or do when she came face to face with someone with a black eye or a cast on her arm. Lois ached whenever one of her cows limped home with a wounded leg. She and her vet were on a first-name basis. But seeing another person injured… well, that wasn't anything she could fix with a phone call. *How does the staff do it? How do they cope?*

"Shall we return to the office before it's time for lunch? You have questions to ask."

Lois nodded, shaking bloody visions from her mind.

Brigitta Johansson had just finished a telephone conversation when Robin escorted Lois back into her little office. Brigitta rose once again and directed both women to take a seat.

"What do you think of our shelter, Mrs. Caldwell?" Brigitta asked.

Lois' belly rose and fell with a chuckle as she lowered herself into a chair. "Nobody's called me 'missus' in years. I'm just Lois. This is a nice place you have. See, you need more books, though. Bookshelves looked a might lean there in the library. And I suppose you run outta laundry supplies a lot. But what I really came to ask you is, can my guild ladies make pillowcases for your rooms?

Brigitta smiled and was about to speak, but Lois, in her nervousness, kept talking.

"My Shinin' Stars don't have advanced quilt-makin' skills, so the ladies need simple projects to do. Most of the ladies are new to quilt makin', so pillowcases are somethin' they can make without too much measurin' cuttin' and sewin' up properly. I hear from Robin that you sometimes send your residents off with beddin'."

Brigitta jumped in when Lois took a breath. "That would be lovely, Lois. Yes, we try to equip residents who leave us with as much as we can offer so they don't have to start out with absolutely nothing at all. Sometimes, we give them bedding; sometimes, we even locate a few pieces of free furniture from the community. As you may have guessed, our own furnishings are secondhand."

Brigitta paused. "If you make pillowcases, might you also provide a new pillow to go inside each case?"

"Oh, yes. I think our guild can do that easy enough. I'll talk with my other guild, the Tea Baskets, 'bout maybe them makin' quilts for your beds. You could give the quilts away, too, if the Tea Baskets decide to donate."

"Oh, goodness, that would be wonderful! Thank you."

"Can I let my members know that you accept basic household supplies?" Lois asked.

"By all means," Brigitta said. "Anything you wish to donate, new or in good condition, will be graciously accepted." Brigitta turned to Robin, "Do you mind being the point person on this arrangement with Lois?"

"Happy to be," Robin said.

"That would be great," Brigitta said. "Can you prepare a list for Lois that identifies the donations we find useful?

"Absolutely," Robin said.

With that assurance, Lois Caldwell had found the long-term charity project she would present to her young guild at their next meeting. But just ahead was lunch with the staff and battered women. Lois was suddenly nervous again. She was concerned that she'd find it impossible to eat one bite in front of the wounded.

Avery needed a break for lunch. She wanted to sit down. Someplace not mobile. Somewhere, instead of eating in the cab of her truck while driving to her next job site. She drove her big bronze Ford through Arby's drive-through on her way into town, then parked it near the Tea Basket hall. The residential street seemed unusually full of parked cars along both curbs. She had to walk some distance to reach the door of the hall. Her now lukewarm sandwich would go down better with some of Nora's coffee and the old woman's consoling. Because she had not been able to attend guild meetings, she was caught unaware that this particular day had been set aside for making a quilt destined for the local Red Cross. The hall was filled with women, bustling about with activity. Women talked over the hum of a dozen portable sewing machines. Some stood at ironing boards pressing small pieces of fabric. Others sat around tables working on other small scraps of fabric. Avery saw a few seam rippers in use among them. Even Nora was bent over a table, hard at work on some task related to making the charity quilt.

Some looked up briefly from their stations to shout out a hello or to wave. Avery smiled and returned each greeting. She then placed her sandwich in front of an open chair at

Nora's table, retrieved a cup of coffee from the kitchenette, and returned.

"Avery, how nice of you to come by to help us make the Broken Dishes quilt today," Nora joked.

Avery peeled back the wrapper on her roast beef sandwich and bit into the bun. "Sure thing, Nora," she mumbled. Once she had swallowed the first mouthful of lukewarm beef and bun, she asked, "What's your job? Looks easy."

"I'm ripping out."

"Mistakes?"

"Oh yes, quite a few. Some of the gals are having a wee bit of trouble making half-square triangles today. Carolyn and Rosie gave a demonstration early this morning on how to make eight at one time. That's sure to speed up the process. Broken Dishes is made of nothing but half-square triangles, you know. But still, some of the ladies have been having trouble with their sewing machines. We always caution members to clean lint from bobbin cases once a month. But some just refuse to heed the warning. Then they get into a situation like this, and phooey, their machines act up because of all that lint in the housing. Very frustrating for us all." She held up a small triangle of mangled fabric she had been trying to save.

"Tell me about frustrations," Avery said. "We all get more than necessary, I'd say." She took a sip of Nora's coffee and watched the older woman insert a narrow seam ripper between a pair of stitched fabrics. Avery could see a great excess of wadded-up thread on one side of the triangle.

"You deal with frustrations?" Nora asked, looking over her oversized glass frames and at her tall friend. She returned to her fabric and zipped the tiny blade through the seam.

"The usual. Work. Drunks. Boss. Filing to run as an independent."

"Oh, Avery, you're not leaving our Democratic Party, are you?" Nora asked as she paused while separating her two squares of fabric to remove threads. She "erased" loose threads with the rubber-tipped end of her ripper, then added the separated triangles to a small pile on the table in front of her.

"No, not entirely. I'm filing as an independent because that's the only way I could possibly run against Hollister and keep my job a while longer. Probably stupid. I hear it'll be an uphill battle, running as an independent. But I just can't stand by and see my boss neglect the work that needs to be done. I feel I can do a better job. Besides, I also feel strongly that the people of the county deserve better."

"You go, girl," a voice rang out from nearby.

Avery twisted around to see Ximi Ling and Simone Beck approaching. They had overheard her observation.

"More blocks for you to rip, Nora," Ximi announced, placing another small stack of fabric in front of Nora and her seam ripper. Simone added a small stack of her own with a look of apology on her face as she stood by. Ximi picked up the small collection of mistakes that Nora had already separated.

Nora let out an overly dramatic sigh. "Having to undo what others have done is so disheartening."

Avery was not sure if Nora referred to sewing or to roadwork.

"When the right time arrives, Avery, you should announce to everyone in the guild your plans," Nora said. "These gals are a force to be reckoned with. Remember last year when everyone pulled together after the big storm? You were instrumental in organizing that. I wouldn't be one bit surprised if they all, no matter what political party they belong to, all of them, will help you again."

"You're really planning to run for county engineer?" asked Ximi.

Avery suddenly became aware that the word could spread quickly in small communities like Athens. She now worried that revealing her decision to Nora and others in the guild might reach Jasper's ears before she could tell him herself.

"Can we help?" Ximi asked with eagerness in her eyes and voice. "I've never worked on a campaign before. What can we do?" As usual, Ximi bounced up and down on her toes with the energy of a child. In Nora's opinion, Ximi, the youngest member of her guild, was a child. Nora estimated she was at least seven decades younger than herself.

"We'll help you, right, Simone?" Ximi said, nudging her friend's arm.

"Well, I'd love to, but really I can't. My schedule is just too tight. I've had to cut back hours at the Thimble and Chatelaine because I need to be home by three."

Unbridled sadness pulled Ximi's expression down like the curtain on a school play. Her smile drooped, replaced by a frown. Today had been the first time in weeks she had been able to spend time with Simone. She had hoped it was a sign of their return to a more normal friendship. Simone was becoming a stranger. Simone never seemed to have any time to spend with her anymore. They didn't shop or even grab a snack at their favorite coffee shop just to chat. Simone rarely telephoned. Ximi was always the one to place a call. Sometimes, Kyle even answered Simone's cell for her. Every time, he'd tell her that Simone was "too busy at the moment to talk." As time passed, since Kyle and Simone had married, Ximi was seeing less and less of her best friend. Now, this is a chance to do something new and exciting together, proving to be yet another disappointment. Ximi decided to speak up.

"We never do *anything* together anymore, Simone. What's going on with you?"

"I told you," she snapped, "I'm swamped. Really. I promise we'll have time when things settle down. Since I've cut back my hours, quilts are backing up, and Molly needs that income. So every time I can work for her, I simply must."

Ximi had no comeback. It was unlike Simone to be so defensiveness and snap at her. She didn't know what Simone's problem was unless the problem was Kyle. Why she couldn't free up a few hours every week or two just to spend a little time together was hard to figure. She turned back to Avery.

"Well, Ave, you can count on me. I'm yours. What can I do now? Can I draw anything on my drafting board for campaign signs, posters, or fliers?"

Avery had forgotten that Ximi, an architect, was also an accomplished artist. She then recalled the professional fliers Ximi made for the new Shining Star guild. Then she recalled that Ximi often designed her own modern quilt patterns. Avery smiled. Yes, indeed. She had a special job for Ximi Ling. Campaigns need a good designer for yard signs and posters.

9

Simone arrived home feeling renewed. That afternoon spent with Ximi Ling and her Tea Basket guild had been pure delight. She'd nearly forgotten how much she enjoyed being with Ximi and working on projects with her. Nora was always a source of insight. The raffle quilt for the Red Cross in the Broken Dishes pattern was coming together and looking gorgeous. Yes, she missed her guild. She had to admit that fact to herself now that she was home. Most of all, she missed spending time with Ximi. She had recognized the disappointment on her friend's face when she had backed out of working together on Avery's campaign. She knew she shouldn't have snapped at her. This reflection on the hurt she inflicted on Ximi made Simone feel sudden guilt.

The Instapot waited on the counter. In less time than it took her to shower, she had a meal ready. She heard his keys hit the dish on the table in the entry. She heard the thud of his bags hit the floor. Like Pavlov's dog, she retrieved a cold beer from the refrigerator and placed it before him just as he sat down at their table.

"You know, babe," Kyle began as he popped open the can, "I've been thinking. You work too hard. You worked in town at one of those guild things today, didn't you? You need to ease up."

He knew where she had been, and he didn't wait for her to answer.

"I think you need to quit working at the Thimble store. Shade is too far away to be driving every day for what little that woman pays. Besides, I make enough money as head coach, so you don't need to work. What will people say if they think I can't support a wife on my salary?"

Simone sat down at her own place and began to protest. "But Kyle, I love my work. It's not 'work' exactly, it's more like creative play. It's a pleasure."

"Well, there's just no need for you to work. You just tell Menear you're quitting. Give her notice next time you go out. No. Call her. Tell her you're quitting. Do it."

"I can't do that, Kyle; she needs me," Simone whined.

"You heard me. I need you, too. I need you here. I have an image to maintain. What's more important, that little job of yours or your duty to your husband? You quit that job. It's time you stayed home. You'll see. Home is where you belong. And you need to do less with those quilty women in that silly club of yours."

Soon after Nora's suggestion, Avery stood before her old guild to announce her decision to run for office as an independent. She explained that the democratic ticket had its candidate, the incumbent Jasper Hollister. And even though he was her boss, she told her audience that she strongly felt she could do more for the county than Hollister if she were to win in the fall.

"But, I have obstacles to overcome. It means I have to acquire permission from the voters of Athens County before I can have my name placed on the fall ballot. To do that, I need to circulate a petition and get signatures from voters that it's okay with them that I run. This is before I can officially campaign. Nora suggested I ask if any of you might care to help out in that regard."

To her surprise, applause filled the meeting room of the Tea Basket Hall. There were quilt ladies who were neither Democrats nor Independents with hands raised, too. Another surprise. Did this indicate that she might have bipartisan support? Nora had been correct. Avery was going to get widespread support, at least from the women of her guild. She wondered if those guild members who were Republicans felt, in this instance, that it was alright for them to do so only because the Republicans didn't have their own candidate to oppose Hollister in this election. Or maybe, just maybe they really did think she was a good candidate for the job. Whatever their reasons, there were many hands raised, willing to help her acquire those needed signatures.

Rosie would train volunteers. She would instruct them on how to collect voter signatures. Ximi Ling's hand shot into the air, waving enthusiastically with a question. Could she be the first one in line to canvas? Rosie tempered the woman's eagerness with a shake of the head, and her hands raised in surrender to Ximi's exuberance. "I need someone to help organize our members into pairs to cover the county with petitions. Can you take on that task?"

Ximi's eyes lit up, and she smiled broadly, popping a bubble in her mouth. She had never been a campaign volunteer. This was something new and exciting to her, something to look forward to, even if her pal, Simone, might not share the experience with her. Her eagerness to volunteer for any task was well known. She was the most willing member of both guilds to tackle any task. No one present that day was surprised by her enthusiasm for this project.

Unlike the unbridled joyful thinking of Ximi Ling, Avery found herself doubtful that she could acquire the signatures required, one percent of the total votes cast in the last election. She was sure the process of collecting those signatures would take weeks, maybe the entire summer. Then, she worried that if she did get them, there would be no time left to actually run a campaign.

Ximi organized helpers from both Tea Basket and Shining Star guilds to assist Avery, and they went to work. Avery had the willingness of her guild sister, and with Rosie's leadership, the Underwood for Engineer petition not only met but far exceeded acquiring the required signatures, just in case some were disqualified.

With petition sheets in hand, Avery walked into the board of elections office to make her delivery. She turned the stack over to the staff, accepted a receipt, and was told the next step was verifying that the signatures were valid. They would let her know when their work had been completed and if she was then certified to be a candidate.

With her head still swirling over the rapid accomplishment of this preliminary step, Avery walked next door to the courthouse. She nodded to the deputy and passed through the scanner. She walked a few feet down the cool corridor to the prosecutor's outer office door and entered. There, she greeted the secretary and explained that she had only stopped by to let Joe O'Feeny know about her progress.

The secretary nodded toward his office door. Seems Avery had permission this time to skip any formal announcement of her arrival.

Joe was seated behind the desk working on paperwork when she rapped on the doorframe. He looked up and smiled broadly, seeing her. His dark blue suit, crisp white shirt, and red tie make him look professional in every sense. He offered his hand and gestured for Avery to take a seat.

"Want a coffee?" he asked.

"No. Thanks. I just wanted to tell you that I delivered my petition to the board of elections."

"It won't take the board too long to validate. They're pretty efficient," he told her. "I'd guess you'll get your answer in a month, maybe five weeks. Then, the real work begins. As I recall, you aren't wise to the ways of politics, are you?"

Avery wanted to defend herself, but he was correct. Every part of this process was new to her. Joe had been helpful in the past, even when he told her that he couldn't endorse her. So maybe she should listen to what he had to say. "I don't suppose you'd care to enlighten me?"

"You don't know the rules of the game, maybe even a little lacking about where to canvass for votes."

Joe smiled and ran his hand down his red tie. This was a tell of his that defense attorneys never cared to see. It meant O'Feeny knew something they didn't. "Why don't I treat you to dinner tonight? I'll fill you in on the voters of the county and some procedural guidelines you need to know over pizza and a beer. Would that work for you?"

Avery grinned, thankful that his early remark had not been a putdown but an honest assessment of her lack of abilities and expertise. "I think I'd like that. Yes. I'd be grateful for any help you have to offer."

"Good. I'll be out of here around six. How about you?"

"We work ten-hour days. I'm on my lunch break at the moment. I won't be off until after seven."

"Meet me around seven-thirty then. There's a new pizza place that has indoor service down on State Street. Meet me there after you get off. I'll get us a table in the back."

Avery shook O'Feeny's hand and left the courthouse past the deputy who was taking an old man's pocket knife away for safekeeping. For the first time, she felt a sense of accomplishment. All the credit was due to Rosie. She could relax, knowing there was little for her to do but wait for the board staff to do their jobs. She also felt a sense of anticipation toward her upcoming campaign and pizza with O'Feeny.

The time for Avery to announce her independent candidacy to Hollister had arrived much sooner than she thought possible. She had accomplished her first campaign hurdle with the help of many. She had acquired the signatures of valid voters as the laws stipulated. Avery Underwood would be the only woman and independent candidate for county engineer. Soon, there would be Fourth of July parades, Parade of the Hills, local festivals, and other events with marching bands, and she, the candidate herself, perched on the back of a convertible tossing candy to kids throughout the county.

As Nora had predicted, members of the Tea Basket and Shining Star quilt guilds had proven to be of great help to her. Long-time democrats worked alongside lifetime republicans to canvass voters for signatures. The real estate agent, Rosie Dyer, agreed to be her campaign treasurer. With no money to speak of, Rosie handed over her own twenty-dollar bill at the bank to open up an account for the new Underwood political campaign. Between Rosie's contacts in the business community, along with her friend Carolyn Ashcroft's connections with the local medical associations, the word of a new female independent running for county engineer spread across the county like autumn leaves on the wind.

Hollister bellied up to the counter and slammed his cell phone down. "Underwood, at last, is finished here. I want you to go through her desk," he ordered Sheila. "Box up her personal belongings and drop them outside tonight when you leave. The last time I want to hear that Underwood has been on this property is when she picks up her junk tonight. Do you understand?"

"Yes, sir," Sheila said, her eyes catching Avery's.

Avery had delivered the news to her boss. Hollister did not take it well. To make some sort of point, he ignored the fact that she stood right next to him. He could have told her to collect her own things. But he was trying to make a statement. The statement was that he was a jerk.

He finally turned to face her, his face red with anger. "Well? What are you doing still standing there like a dumb ass scarecrow? Give your keys to Sheila and beat it! This time, you *are* gone," he yelled. With that, he stomped off toward his office, slamming the door closed behind him.

"Sheila! Where's my phone?"

Avery noticed his phone on the counter where he had just left it. He was always careless to leave it about. Beside it was his metal file box. She opened the box, felt for something under the upper edge of the clip, and smiled. Then she placed his phone inside the box, closed and fastened the lid.

Sheila grinned. "Don't see it anywhere, sir," she yelled back.

Avery walked toward the exit past her desk piled high with paperwork yet to be completed while Sheila reluctantly rummaged for a cardboard box under the counter. Avery began a slow boil with her hands in her pockets, preparing to leave. She recalled soon after she had been hired as his assistant, Hollister began to reduce his hours in the office. He was slacking off the job, off *his job*. That affected *her job*. Over the months, she became more and more frustrated. She had wasted her own time trying to track him down when she needed him for answers or a signature. She felt used and put upon by his constant absence. But she had found a solution.

Months earlier, Avery had slipped an Air tag inside his metal file box to pinpoint Hollister's location. The device solved that problem. One time, when she required his immediate signature, she located him on the fifth hole of a golf course during office hours. Another time, she tracked him to a diner with cronies chowing down on midafternoon fried chicken. And yet another time, on a lovely sunny and warm day this spring, she found him angling for fish at a private pond off Rainbow Lake Road. Hollister was always aghast at how she had so accurately pinpointed his location every time. But Avery never let on the source of her amazing detective skill.

That she was left to do his work had started her thinking she should be the one to get his pay and his title. She was the one who more and more was forced to shuffle through all the paperwork, conduct the research and writing of grants, deal with personnel issues, and handle day-to-day operations for the department. Even before she was hired, she had seen the need for a highway department that was more proactive than reactive to the county's crumbling infrastructure. Hollister's cavalier approach to work had finally pushed her decision to the fore. Hollister may have been content to cash his paycheck and chase problems rather than work to prevent them, but she was not. Since the day of the big derecho last fall, she had stewed over the decision to run for his office. Finding him fishing was the final blow that pushed her in the direction of the courthouse. That was the day she walked uptown from the Tea Basket hall after a cup of Nora's coffee and into the board of elections. Today, the Tea Basket's support gave her confidence and, finally, the right to oppose him, job or no job.

Avery stopped before she reached the door, spun around and returned to Sheila's counter and dropped her keys next to Hollister's file box. She nodded toward Sheila and then walked for the door. She paused for a moment with her hand on the door and turned to the clerk, "See ya, 'round, Sheila."

The bright sunlight outside the engineer's office forced her to squint. She pulled a pair of sunglasses from her tee-shirt pocket and exchanged her prescription lenses for them. Strangely, she felt a sense of relief, not sadness or uncertainty, for losing her job and only source of income. When Jasper erupted in outrage, for a change, she had the sense that she was in control, not him. However, she certainly had not counted on the existence of a regulation against civil servants running for public office. That had indeed been a nasty surprise.

When the sunglasses allowed her eyes to adjust to the sunlight, she noticed some of the crew standing around a grader. They knew what had happened inside with Hollister. Word was continuing to spread. Then, as her sight improved even more, she saw that they were giving her a thumbs up. Avery smiled, returned the hand signal, and moved off to climb into her truck.

Avery's first stop would not be with personnel at the courthouse. She planned to pay a visit to Joe O'Feeny, chair of the Democratic Party, county prosecutor, and frequent late-night pizza partner. She punched up Joe's private phone number on her cell. "Hey. Avery here. I need to talk. Got a few minutes to spare? Yeah? Great. I need to ask you more questions. Meet me for a coffee?"

10

Avery caught sight of Joe waving from their usual table in the back of Donkey Coffee. She made her way past clusters of other small tables occupied mostly by college students bent over books, laptops, or phones. She pulled out a chair for herself across from O'Feeny and sat down. A cup of her favorite brew was waiting. Two large muffins also waited, crowded together on a saucer too small to hold two of them. Joe had already eaten half of one.

She and O'Feeny had spent several hours together at this particular table in the back of Donkey Coffee. She would meet him for his midday coffee breaks. He would discuss campaign laws. She would keep O'Feeny abreast of progress, gathering signatures on her petition. By day's end, he would treat her to a pizza or a bag of Miller's Poultry for dinner, and they would continue to discuss political issues. Avery would ask questions. Joe would answer. But now that she was a viable candidate, these meetings would change focus.

"So, how's your day going?" He asked, his voice full of sarcasm. He nodded toward the whole muffin and the cup of coffee waiting for her.

Avery suspected he knew she had made her announcement to Hollister. She gave him a lopsided smile and broke the whole muffin in half.

"Just great," she snorted. "Jasper's pleased to see me go. Tell me something. Are you *sure* I do have to quit my job *now*?" She bit into the muffin top savagely. "Hollister told me I had to quit way back when I announced I wanted to run. Well, no, that's not quite right. Hollister *ordered me* to quit back then. You told me I didn't have to--yet. Was he telling the truth?"

"Ah, no, and yes."

"What?"

"No, you didn't have to quit when Jasper first told, ah, ordered you to. You weren't yet a certified candidate. Your civil service position was safe."

"But you knew then I would eventually have to quit? Even that day when you suggested I file as an independent?"

"Yes. Now that you're a certified political candidate for a county leadership position, you cannot be a civil servant and simultaneously campaign for public office."

"So you knew. Why didn't you warn me I *would definitely* lose my job? I could have been job hunting. You led me to think I had options back then. You withheld that fact. Why?" Avery took another big chunk of muffin and swallowed hard.

"Well, mostly, I didn't want to kill your dream. I thought knowing you'd lose your job might make you decide not to run against Hollister. I saw in you great potential for an office holder, for an engineer, that I didn't want the county to lose."

"So how am I supposed to run, let alone survive, now that I am about to have no income? I've depleted most of my savings after I came to Athens when I didn't have a job *the last time.*"

Joe smiled kindly, nibbling at the last of his own muffin and chasing it down with a sip of coffee. "I was planning on that question coming up."

"What? Me asking how I'm going to survive, or how I was going to afford a campaign?"

Joe shook his head. "I think you have an excellent shot at unseating Hollister. I honestly do. But if you need support other than with your actual campaign, I was thinking, hoping actually, that you'd approach me and allow me to keep you afloat. You'll get plenty of donors for your campaign. I know you will."

Avery looked at Joe. She had been angry with him when she walked in and sat down. Now, she was confused.

"You thought maybe you'd what, pay my rent or something like that?"

"Sure. That's something I could do."

Avery looked hard at Joe with his wild red hair, bushy eyebrows, his smile, his business attire, and his lawyer's armor. She wondered if their friendship, forged over the past weeks, meeting over muffins and coffee or over beer and pizza to discuss the ways of politicking in Athens County, might have meant something more to Joe than she realized or intended.

"Look, I'm not the type to become a 'kept woman' O'Feeny."

"I'm aware of what kind of person you are. Have been since that first day in my office. I've gotten to know you even better these past weeks. I know you're independent, more than just independent politically. I know you're smart. I know you care about good highways. You care not just about things that relate to your career and your political ambitions, but you care about people. I have no intentions of 'keeping' you, Underwood, if that's what you're thinking. But, if you allow me, I will support you financially while you pursue this dream of yours. Six months isn't so long. I won't make any unwanted demands in return. I'm not that kind of guy. Politically, as I explained when we first met, I cannot publicly *endorse* you. You know that. But privately, in this matter, I can provide support. And I will. I want you to win, and I want to help at this stage."

Joe raised his coffee cup. "To your political success, my friend," he said, waiting for Avery's response.

Avery thought for a long moment, then cautiously raised her own cup to his, "To success."

That evening after the courthouse closed, and for many evenings that followed, Joe O'Feeny appeared on Avery Underwood's apartment doorstep carrying a hot pizza from Avalanche or a bucket of deep-fried chicken and potato wedges from Miller's Poultry or Thai carryout from Dr. May's. If he didn't feed her, Avery would eat a peanut butter sandwich from her scant pantry. Eventually, the two worked out a permanent schedule of alternative deliveries. Avery would call ahead to order and text Joe. Joe would pick up the order after work and deliver it to her apartment. He always picked up the tab and gave the receipt to her so Rosie could log the amount in as a contribution.

Simone found herself sitting alone once again at yet another sports department event. She had dressed to the nines according to Kyle's preferences. The pair attended this particular dinner to honor outstanding seniors on the team. The soon-to-be graduating athletes were tall, muscular, and fit. Bulging biceps stretched wide the sleeves of their sports coats. The big players wearing their colorful jackets reminded Simone of those big commercial Christmas ornaments in department stores. In fact, they were ornamentation to Coach Kyle Beck, just like she was, just hanging around to make him look good. But these young men were so much more than she. They would soon have their own paths to follow, far from this college, out on their own pursuing careers beyond the reach of Coach Beck. Simon, on the other hand, would never get far from Kyle Beck.

Some part of Simone longed to mother these young men. She imagined what it might be like if she could treat them as her own. But, of course, those were foolish thoughts. Of course, she could not. She rarely had an opportunity to interact with them. She rarely had the opportunity to interact with anybody anymore. She had her place in the stands or in the house. The players had their place down on the field.

Still, before festivities began, Simone made a point of greeting each young man as if she knew him. She offered her congratulations on their academic successes and her hopes for their future careers. She asked a few of them about alternative job prospects if their dreams of landing a spot on a professional team didn't happen. Full of confidence, none offered up a Plan B. Then, they were whisked away to the front table with their coach, where they received awards, certificates, and praise from him and other college officials. Simone, like every spectator present, applauded each recognition from her place on the sidelines, seated alone at one of the tables. She had no Plan B either.

Simon's thoughts wandered. She didn't listen to any of Kyle's speech. Instead, she let her mind wander and puzzled over his behavior toward her. She felt less than the perfect wife she'd planned to be. *Where have I gone wrong to cause him such doubts? Wasn't I successful before our marriage? But now, I have no job by which to measure success. Not anymore. I loved that job at the Thimble and Chatelaine, too. Why is it so hard to be married and have a job at the same time? I know I could have done it. What more can I give up to please Kyle?*

She began to feel an emptiness inside. More than that, she felt confused by all these thoughts. Who was she now that she had become only Mrs. Kyle Beck? What had gone wrong so soon?

Someone spoke into her ear. The voice brought her back. It was old Dr. Mathias from the English department. "Alone again, I see."

"Always," she said.

"What you need is a posse of doting friends, m' lady." The old professor said as he pulled back an empty chair next to Simone and sat down. He was wearing the same bright blue bow tie he'd worn the last time they spoke.

"I used to have something of a posse," Simone admitted, thinking then of her friend Ximi. "But I seem to be more and more a party of one. No posse. No purpose, really."

"Oh, surely you have a purpose in this world," Mathias said.

"I'm not so sure anymore. At least no purpose beyond being Mrs. Kyle Beck."

"Oh, come now. As I recall, you hold an advanced degree in one of the humanities. Am I correct?"

Simone sighed. "Yes."

"Ah, I thought so. You do know that the university will hire spouses of staff members. They find adjunct teaching positions for them. You could apply. I'll give you a good reference if you want to give it a go in the English department again. Might give you that purpose for which you think you lack."

"Thank you, no. Kyle doesn't want me to work. Thinks it might be bad for his image as a good provider."

"*His image?*" The old professor scoffed. "Nonsense! Lots of spouses do it. *His image* be damned. What about your self-esteem? What about your need for ... let's say ... some intellectually stimulating conversation? The exchange of ideas, old and new? *His image?* Balderdash!" Mathias said loudly.

Kyle had concluded his speech and was making his way toward their table. He overheard the end of Mathias' exchange with his wife.

"Simone! We're finished. Time to go." He acknowledged the old professor with a cool glance.

"Mathias, do you attend all my functions? Are you trying to get a free meal at the athletic department's expense?"

Mathias pretended to be amused. "Ah, my scheme has been revealed. Though you think that's what I do, Coach Beck, I'm actually a tutor for many of your academically challenged ball players. *They* invite me to every meal. I always give them extra credit if they do. Keeps them on your eligibility roster that way."

It was Kyle's turn to pretend to be amused. "Well, don't go hitting on my beautiful wife while you dine at my expense."

"Oh, I wouldn't do that, sir. What would she have with an old harmless codger like me? But I have noticed she spends too much time alone during these soirees. Surely I can help a lady avoid boredom once in a while?"

"Just tutor my athletes, and don't bother Simone."

Mathias stood, then bowed dramatically to Kyle, as a serf might have done to one of the higher stations during the Middle Ages. "I will then depart and leave you, Mrs. Beck. But I leave you with this thought, Coach: do not isolate this remarkable woman from the world. She has much to offer."

Mathias turned away, leaving Kyle and Simone alone.

The banquet hall was nearly empty by the time Mathias passed through a doorway out into the hall. Kyle's face had gone several shades deeper than when he had first approached. His eyes darkened. He turned them onto Simone with an intensity she had never before seen.

"I don't want you talking to that old fossil again. Ever! As a matter of fact," he took her arm in his grip, squeezing her flesh and forcing her to her feet, "I don't want you talking to *anybody* unless I say it's OK. Do you understand?"

Simone fought back tears that threatened to spill from her eyes. She didn't know what to say to this sudden act of hostility toward her. *What have I done wrong this time?* She attended the event just as Kyle had told her to. She dressed the way he liked her to dress. She didn't speak in any manner to embarrass him. But now, now she wasn't to speak at all?

"Kyle, you're hurting me. I didn't do anything wrong. Mathias came to me."

"Don't argue with me. Don't *ever* argue with me. Not now, certainly not in public. You're always trying to pick a fight. So shut it. We're going home. Now. Don't ever talk back to me again. Understand?"

Avery signed the necessary paperwork to conclude her employment as the county's assistant highway engineer, with Joe O'Feeny standing by her side. While she penned in the necessary lines, he chatted casually with the county clerks who knew him well. Avery handed over the forms and turned to Joe.

"What's next?"

"I believe, candidate Underwood, you need to kick off your campaign. Do you have a committee? A treasurer?"

"Treasurer, yes. Money and committee, no."

Joe took the Xerox copies of Avery's severance forms, flipped the stack over, and began to scribble on the back of one sheet. "Here are some individuals with name recognition and solid reputations. Tell them I referred them to you. Ask them to serve on your campaign committee. Let them know you'll oppose Hollister in the fall. I'm sure they'll jump at the chance to rub his nose in a little road dust."

Avery accepted the papers and looked over the scribbled list. "Thanks, Joe. Why are you doing this?"

"Because I can." He leaned close to Avery's ear to whisper, "*I think Hollister is no good for my party.* Be sure you tell voters at every campaign event that you're a disgruntled democrat. When you become the *next* incumbent, the party can and will back you. Promise."

Lois stood in front of her Shining Star guild in a mid-calf length dress of lightweight denim. She had bought it as an experiment. Lois felt more comfortable camouflaged behind floral prints or polka dots. She feared how wide a solid color might make her look. She fumbled nervously with a piece of paper where she had written down what she wanted to cover with her members. Lois believed that her rise to the office of guild president was premature and unwarranted. But the other two presidents, first, short-tempered Evelyn, then very capable Avery, had both abruptly departed the post, leaving her to fill the void. She was nervous.

Evelyn North had gone off on a world tour following her unfortunate experience during the big storm, leaving what little survived the ruin of her house stored in Lois' guest room. Then Avery took a job with the county, which took away all her free time. Now here stood Lois, sucked into the role of president like a dust bunny into a vacuum. She had been happy to work behind the scenes as their old secretary. Now, she had to stand right up front, in god-awful blue denim, and address her members.

"Uh, yes, well," she began. "Like we talked about some weeks past, we need to have a charity. Well, I visited Robin Prescott and Brigitta Johansson at Harbor House. That's the shelter for battered women. They have a nice place there. But they could use a few household supplies on an ongoing basis. I thought maybe we could be the ones to provide a constant supply by donating a few things every meetin'."

"What do they need, Lois?" Asked Ximi Ling from her chair in the front row. Ximi's friend, Simone, "Couldn't go," her husband told her over the phone when Ximi called to ask if Simone would attend.

Lois looked down at her paper and read off the list of items. "Bathroom supplies like toilet paper, tissues, hand soap, toothpaste; that kinda stuff. Kitchen supplies like dish detergent, as well as washcloths and paper towels. Then, in the laundry, they need pods, dryer sheets, and maybe even laundry baskets that their residents can take when they leave the shelter."

"Then, um, if you agree, when the ladies leave Harbor House for a place of their own, I thought we could make pillowcases for them. Course, that means that we also have to provide the pillow that goes inside each case."

Lois looked up from her list. "How do you all feel about that?"

Ximi's hand shot up. "I love it, Lois! I've made pillowcases before. I'd be happy to help and show anyone how to make them. They're real easy. We can all be on the lookout for pillow forms when they go on sale. We all get coupons for some of the supplies you listed. I'm willing to pick up one or two extra items every time I go to the store. I also have a brand-new laundry basket that's too big for my needs. I'll bring it in tomorrow, and we can start filling it up with household donations right away."

Members of the Shining Star guild nodded approvingly.

"Um, any more discussion?" Lois asked.

There were no comments.

"K, so I guess we should have a motion and a vote."

Ximi's hand flew up once again. "I make a motion that the Shining Star Quilt Guild donate household items to Harbor House on an ongoing basis and that our members make at least two pillowcases every year for Harbor House and fill those cases with brand new pillows."

"I second," came a voice from the back of the room.

"K, then. I think we should vote for or against Ximi's motion," Lois announced.

"Those for?"

Hands shot in the air.

"Those against?"

No hands.

Lois smiled and sighed with relief. She didn't know why she always got so nervous standing in front of her friends. "Well, looks like Shinin' Stars now has a charity for the year. I'll tell Robin. She'll be the one who'll pick up our donations for Harbor House. I think I'll put a signup list near Ximi's basket. Everyone should take a turn to supply a new basket. Whoever signs up to provide that next one should bring it in soon so that when Robin takes away Ximi's, we'll have the replacement ready and waitin' immediately. Thanks, everyone."

11

The traffic light turned from yellow to red. Kyle stomped hard on the brake pedal, stopping the car abruptly. The light change wasn't the cause of his irritation. His jaw muscles flexed. He gritted his teeth. Simone sat beside him with a pained look on her face, fighting back tears. Kyle said nothing. When the light changed back to green, he put his foot down on the accelerator, squealing tires driving away from the intersection. He sped down the street but got only a block, caught again by the next traffic light. That seemed to irritate him even more.

"How many times do I have to tell you *not* to argue with me?" he yelled.

"But Kyle... I want…" Simone began pleadingly.

"Just shut it. Now that you don't have a job, there's no reason for you to have a car. I'll take you wherever you need to go."

"But I'll be home alone, all day, while you're at work."

"You heard me. We're selling your car. I've already put an ad in the paper. That's the end of it."

Simone turned her face toward the side window. A single tear trickled down her cheek, which she wiped away with her hand. She loved her car. She loved Kyle, too. She did not want him to see her cry. She had already learned that crying only made matters worse with him. He had bullied her just a few days ago to quit her job at the Thimble and Chatelaine.

When she broke down in sobs, then he'd called her a "baby." In his anger, he threw her purse across their living room. That, in turn, caused her to shed even more tears. Those tears brought him very close to striking her.

They were moving again at a more reasonable speed, but Kyle reached over and jerked his wife around. "Look at me when I'm talking to you. You heard me. The car is gone. Period. End of story. Get over it."

Avery withheld the source of the names on the list of potential committee members as she handed the list to Rosie Dyer, campaign treasurer. Rosie looked at her with some curiosity as to how she came to know these people, but she quickly and eagerly agreed to contact all of them. Since Avery's little apartment was too small to assemble a group larger than two people at the same time, Rosie suggested the committee gather at her spacious ranch house in The Plains as an alternative.

Avery soon realized that Rosie knew nearly every person Joe had suggested. She shouldn't have been surprised. Rosie, as a long-time real estate agent, had probably had some previous contact over the years with half of the country's population. Within a few days, Rosie's phone calls filled Avery's committee from Joe's list.

"I don't know how you came up with these names, but these folks are perfect. They're the kind of gatekeepers that can make a big difference in people's perceptions of you as a viable candidate. All of them are politically active. And guess what? Many of them have had disputes with Jasper at some point in the past. Every one of them was eager to come on board as soon as I told them you'll oppose him in the fall."

Avery smiled, thinking of Joe O'Feeny's comment about rubbing Hollister's nose in the dirt.

She arrived at Rosie's the morning of their first committee meeting prepared to lead and organize. She carried Ximi Ling's campaign artwork, mockups for signs, bumper stickers, and banners. She also carried a trusty project clipboard and several pads of legal-sized note pads ready to work.

Those gatekeepers, as Rosie called them, were already eagerly assembled and seated around Rosie's dining room table when Avery arrived. She shook hands with each person. There was an ex-deputy sheriff, a volunteer with the local extension office, a dentist, a couple of shop owners, and a farmer who ran a cow-calf operation south of town.

Her committee members launched into discussions at once. The energy they generated began to take over. Avery soon realized they were all very well-versed in politics and campaigning, but she was not. She happily relinquished all campaign planning to her group of experts and not at all reluctantly. She only had to sit back, answer an occasional question, and then watch them draw up her battle plan. By the end of that first afternoon, huddled around the ornate table, the Underwood for Engineer campaign came to life.

Before canvassing voters could begin in earnest, Rosie was selected as the campaign chair and still remained its treasurer. She explained they'd need an advertising budget for billboard and yard signs, radio spots, and leaflets. Ximi's artwork was approved. To Avery, the need to reproduce it sounded very expensive, perhaps too expensive. She was keenly aware she was but one paycheck from becoming a destitute and unemployed bum. Rosie told the committee the campaign had but twenty dollars in the bank, less the expense of printing checks. That abruptly translated to mean they had nothing yet.

Several committee members immediately withdrew wallets and purses to hand over cash or to write checks. Rosie smiled at Avery.

Avery expressed her thanks. "I really appreciate your generosity. I didn't expect to hit you all up for donations. I mean, look at the work you're doing. But thanks. I hope I can conduct this campaign with dignity and all the energy it deserves. I appreciate your confidence in me." She remembered what Nora said about enlisting the aid and assistance of the Tea Basket members. The Tea Basket Guild was to meet the next morning for their regular monthly business meeting.

"I would like to attend the guild meeting tomorrow. Perhaps I can make my announcement there if Nora agrees. I'll even ask for a few donations from members, and who knows, I might collect a few dollars more for advertising."

The committee agreed. They thought having their candidate surrounded by women sounded like a good visual to kick off her campaign. As their initial planning was completed, the group took a break from the morning's meeting. Rosie had a box of donuts and a pot of coffee waiting for them in her kitchen.

Rosie pulled out her blue cell phone and punched up Nora's number. Before Avery had finished getting herself a cup of coffee from the kitchen, Rosie had acquired Nora's blessings so that she could announce the Underwood campaign from the Tea Basket hall.

Rosie next called the local newspaper's telephone number. "The Underwood campaign, Avery Underwood candidate, the first and *only woman* ever to run for county engineer, would announce her bid for the office in the morning," Rosie announced to the editor on the other end of her call. "She's going to make her announcement from the Tea Basket Quilt Guild's building on the corner of Morris and Shannon Streets in Athens. That's right. She's going to run against her old boss, Jasper Hollister. Yes, you're welcome to attend. We look forward to having the press cover our event."

After a thumbs up to the candidate and committee members, Rosie called the local radio station to drop the same scoop. She finally slipped the phone back into the pocket of her blue blazer and nodded to the committee with a big smile on her face. High fives were abruptly followed by much congratulations directed at the new independent candidate for county engineer.

Avery felt stunned. She couldn't help but wonder, had she climbed aboard a moving train? She only hoped the locomotive didn't run out of steam, or in her case, money before they reached their final destination in November.

Avery was the last person to leave Rosie's home after the meeting broke up. She drove back to her apartment, not remembering any part of the trip down the four-lane. Rosie drove separately in her own blue Ford Edge, following Avery's bronze pickup.

Rosie had ordered Avery to look her best for the morning's cameras and every day after that. She was now a candidate and needed to present herself as such every moment in public. Avery unlocked the front door to her little apartment and pushed the door open. Rosie walked past Avery and vanished into the bedroom. Avery could hear the sliding door to her closet open. Her friend soon returned to hold out two hangers, each bearing one Oxford shirt. The always professionally dressed business woman's incredulous face said it all.

"*This* is all you have that's remotely *dressy*?"

Avery shrugged her shoulders and gave a lopsided, apologetic smile. "What can I say? I work on dirt roads all the time. I have a new hard hat if that helps."

"We're going shopping!"

"But Rosie, I don't have a lot of money for clothes at the moment!"

"Well, I do. I have a charge card, and this will be my early birthday present for you. Now, turn around and scoot. I'm driving."

Rosie bought Avery three pairs of Dockers and argued that Avery needed to substitute them for her customary dungarees. Avery conceded. The next morning, she "dressed up" in one of the oxfords that Rosie deemed not to be good enough for any occasion and a pair of new Dockers. She stood attired in her new official look in front of a crowd of mostly women who had assembled in the Tea Basket Hall about to give her first political speech. That realization made her nervous. She did not want to appear or sound weak. Now was the time to act the part of an office holder, responsible for a staff, responsible to the voters. She recalled the staff, the good workers, the friends like Sheila Harper, and even the bad ones like Pat, the guy she had disciplined for drinking on the job. She reminded herself that Jasper Hollister was one of the bad workers. Jasper didn't drink on the job. He fished or ate or did anything *but* his job. That was to be her starting point, an opening salvo against Hollister's work ethic. She'd go right for his weak spot.

The first floor of the wood frame building was packed. Tea Baskets made up the majority of those seated inside in rows of chairs set up for their regular monthly meeting. But this was not a normal guild meeting. Nora had obviously been on her phone the previous day encouraging her membership to be present for this event for one of their own. There were many Shining Star members seated among them, including Lois. Lined along the back wall where the old storefront windows backlit them so that Avery was unable to make out faces stood a few reporters and interested strangers.

Avery wasted no time once she walked through the front door. Nora nodded to her and motioned for her to approach the front of the room. Nora shook her hand with a big smile on her face, then walked away, giving Avery the floor without any ado.

"Hello," she said to the crowd of women assembled in front of her. "Ladies of the Tea Basket Quilt Guild and Shining Star members, too, you all know me well as one of your members who now only visit on occasion to enjoy some of Nora Radnor's excellent coffee. Some of you in the press corps, standing there in the back of the room, know very little about me. My name is Avery Underwood. Today, I'm announcing my independent candidacy for the position of county engineer on this fall's ballot."

Avery was surprised by a sudden round of applause from the crowd seated in front of her. Their enthusiasm brought a broad smile to her face. She caught herself about to make a nervous adjustment to her glasses, which needed no adjustment at all. As their applause faded, she managed to return to her speech with a bolstered calmness.

"Until very recently, I used to work in the engineer's office. I resigned from my position as your assistant county engineer in order to run for the office as chief engineer. During my time of employment, I've met many residents who are displeased, to say the least, by the deteriorating condition of our county roadways. I whole heartedly agree with them. Something must be done. I believe that something begins with new leadership."

"I hold all the civil engineering credentials the Ohio Revised Code requires for the office of county engineer. As a matter of fact, I exceed those minimums. I'm also certified and licensed to operate every single piece of equipment owned by the department. Hollister does not. I stand here before you today to say that I have already been doing Hollister's job for him for the past several months. He has chosen to be absent, in excess, leaving the administration of the office to me all too often."

Avery looked down at her cell phone in hand and fiddled with the display for a moment before going on. Anyone in the audience watching would have thought she was cueing up her speech. But Avery was speaking from memory.

"For instance, today, it's 10:30 on a Monday morning." She held up her smartphone, showing the hour on the display. "You'd expect your county engineer to be on the job, dealing with personnel, supervising the work being done on bridges and roadways, researching or writing grants. But no. If anyone wants to find their hardworking incumbent county highway engineer this particular morning, or any morning, for that matter, look no further than the back room of Donkey Coffee, where every morning Mr. Hollister works very, very hard on county time putting back two cups and a Danish while serving the citizens of this county."

The newspaper's cub reporter, accompanied by a photographer, made a hasty exit from the hall, leaving behind the veteran reporter to record Avery's speech. Avery had a good guess where they were heading and knew exactly what they'd find. Corroboration. She smiled and continued.

"I promise to be a different county official, a diligent, hard-working engineer for the people of Athens. You'll find me on time every morning, on the job. I promise to work more than eight hours, more than five days a week, and harder than Jasper Hollister could ever imagine possible. I will do this because I care. I care about the condition of our roads and bridges, and I care about all the people who must safely travel on them."

"I cannot win this race alone. I know that. I need supporters at the polls who believe in me and what I can accomplish in office. This campaign needs your financial support, too. So, in announcing that I've been certified to run on the fall ballot as an independent candidate, I ask you for your support, both financially now and with your vote at the polls this coming November."

Avery concluded her speech by reciting the address where people could send contributions, Rosie's home address. She was prepared to take questions, but there were few. Some members of the press had quickly vanished from the hall with copies of her vitae on their way to meet deadlines for the presses and for the next news break. They left behind a room full of fellow quilt enthusiasts, some of whom were already waving checkbooks in the air.

Rosie commandeered a seat at the officer's table in front of the room and spread her treasurer's record-keeping paperwork out in front of her. She motioned for the first contributor to step forward. That contributor was Nora Radnor, who placed her checkbook on the table and began scribbling down the amount of her donation, which was one hundred dollars.

There was a clamor of chairs scraping across the wooden floor and voices being raised. Several of the Tea Basket and Shining Star members queued up behind Nora. Some of the quilters, seeing the line in front of Rosie grow long, decided to take a break in the kitchenette before they offered their contribution. Others climbed the stairs to the second floor, opting to mail in a check at a later date. Working on sewing projects seemed like a better use of time than standing in a long line.

President of the Shining Stars, Lois Caldwell, decided to remain after most everyone else had finished writing checks or handing over a few dollars to Rosie. She wanted to share her own scrap of news with Nora after the excitement of Avery's announcement died down. Nora was busy, as usual, in the kitchenette. Ximi Ling had joined her and was washing cups while Nora dried. Lois killed time by helping Avery stack chairs. When the two finished hauling chairs to the garage behind the hall, they returned to the kitchenette to join Nora, Ximi, and Rosie, who had just finished recording the last donor's information.

"Been talkin' to Brigitta Johansson at the battered women's shelter where Robin Prescott got work," Lois began.

"You've been busy," Ximi said.

"Johansson said they could use beddin' as they sometimes give theirs away when women leave."

"Really?" said Nora.

"Yeah, she said some ladies have very little of their own because they left their homes in such a rush. They might have nothin' at all to start over with."

"What a shame," said Rosie, "I never thought about the struggle of starting over that those women must face."

"Anyway, my Shinin' Star gals are makin' pillow cases for the shelter to give away to the ladies. Maybe we'll make some special ones for the little kids, too. So, I was wonderin', could Tea Baskets make a few bed quilts for the shelter? All the shelter beds are singles. Figured with our quiltin' machine upstairs, we could finish a bunch in no time. I'm getin' the Shinin' Stars started on pillow cases right away. Might even do a class on different hem finishes at our next meetin'."

"Oh, Lois, that sounds perfect," Nora said. "I'll bet we can get several members to start piecing nine-patches or strip quilts from jelly rolls immediately. I'll ask ladies to contribute fabric from their stashes. I think we could get busy right away."

"Simone might have time to quilt some for the project right here," said Ximi. "I heard she quit her job at the Thimble and Chatelaine."

"Quit her job? Why'd she do that?" asked Nora. "I thought she loved quilting for Molly."

"Simone's husband put pressure on her to quit," Ximi said. "I talked to her on the phone the other day. She sounded so broken up but said she had to keep peace with Kyle."

"Really?" Lois asked. This was news to her. "So she didn't simply decide to quit on her own?"

"I suspect Kyle's not that perfect prince everyone thinks he is. I think he's abusive," Ximi said. "Remember the talk Robin gave? I noticed after her talk that he exhibits some of the warning signs from comments Simone mentioned, like demanding dinner and ordering Simone around like a servant."

"Lord, no!" Nora said, taking the only empty chair in the hall and sitting down. "That might explain what I saw the other day."

"What'd you see?" Lois asked.

"Just a few days ago, the two of them were sitting in the coach's car at a traffic light near the Convocation Center. I was driving up Richland Avenue in my car. I waved, but they didn't notice me at all. It looked to me like Kyle was reading the riot act to Simone. She had her head turned away from him, looking away like, out the window toward the river, you see. I think he jerked her arm and made her look at him. At the time, I thought surely I was mistaken. But my light was green, so I had to drive on."

The small group of friends looked at one another with both concern and some skepticism. They knew Simone to be educated, wise, and not in the least a pushover. But Nora was also not one to fabricate stories about her fellow guild members. And everyone was now beginning to wonder. Who was Coach Beck in his personal life? And how could Simone have become a victim of abuse so soon in their marriage that Nora's observation and Ximi's belief seemed to suggest?

New Shining Star guild members bent over their sewing machines hard at work in the Tea Basket Hall. The women were spaced out at six-foot tables in the big room on the first floor where Avery had made her public announcement only a week earlier. Today, black electric cords from their machines sprawled across the wooden floor into several multi-outlet extension boxes. Progress was going slow for many of them who were new to making pillowcases, and some were even new to sewing on an electric machine. The occasional "Oh, shoot" or exclamation of *"What?"* peppered the air. Lois Caldwell and Ximi Ling, her assistant, walked from outburst to outburst, quelling frustrations. Nora Radnor was present too, as she most always was, at the ready with a seam ripper in the pocket of her linen suit or a fresh cup of coffee from the kitchenette.

"You gals are doin' just fine," Lois said, encouraging them along. "Remember, this ain't brain surgery. As long as you don't get happy with your scissors, we can fix sewin' mistakes and put you back on track. You're workin' with one piece of fabric folded in half along the long side. You only need to make two seams. The hard part is already done. You've got your simple hems finished. I know it might sound goofy to sew the right sides out the first time, but trust me, and do it. Go slow, and don't work ahead. Concentrate on makin' your seams a perfect quarter inch wide. Wait for the rest of the group to catch up. When you finish the bottom seam and the side seam to your pillow case, stop and wait for the rest of us."

Lois shuffled along the work tables, inspecting each beginner's progress, offering a smile and nod of encouragement. "Who isn't finished with the first two seams yet? Raise yer hand."

No hand went up. "K. Now cut the thread and remove the fabric from your machine. Trim off a tiny triangle at the two corners of the bottom of your pillow case like I showed you in my demo. Then, turn your pillow case inside out. Work those two corners out so you have nice-looking square corners. Finger press those seams open real good."

Lois wore the blue denim dress she had worn to town the other day. She still wasn't sure if the thing looked good on her, but Lois was not one to waste money. She'd purchased the dress, so she would wear the dress. The hem fell nearly to her ankles when it was supposed to have stopped mid-calf. She'd decided one day she would rip out the hem and shorten it. But today, she had other things to do. On her feet, she wore her go-to-town comfortable lace-up old lady brown shoes. They had cushioned soles perfect for standing over a student who was taking too long to complete a simple task. The three-quarter length sleeves of the dress covered her upper arms. Bat wings, she called them. For that, she was grateful.

No one ever criticized Lois for her dress size or her appearance in spite of her self-consciousness. Her kindness and patience were the only things that her friends in both guilds ever recognized. This day was no exception. Lois was being very patient.

"This next step will seal those two seams you just made inside a second pair of seams. When your pillow case is washed, there won't be no threads to ravel out. And when you stuff a pillow into it, the pillow won't make ravelins'. Set your seam guides for a width of three-eighth inch. That's right. Use your measure if you need to. Now, with your pillow case turned wrong side out, sew the short bottom raw quarter-inch seam inside a new three-eighths seam. Go slow. Sew all the way to the end."

"Remember when you were a beginner, Lois?" Nora asked, handing her friend and fellow guild president a lemon Oreo.

"Long time ago," Lois said, popping the cookie into her mouth and remembering her own misgivings while sitting for the first time in front of a sewing machine at a guild class. Lois had been positive that all eyes were watching her struggle and make mistake after mistake.

"Yes, it was. And look at you now. Guild president and leading a class for new piecers. You've come a long way."

Lois folded arms across her chest with some satisfaction. "Do you 'member when I was scared of Evelyn North, too?" she asked.

Nora smiled. "Many people were afraid of Evelyn. But you tamed her. *You* did that. Have you heard from her lately?"

"Post card now and then. She's enjoyin' her world cruise with some of that insurance money she got. Hope when she comes home, she's become a kinder woman."

"Me too. Dealing with nasty people is frustrating."

"K ladies. Now repeat that step by sewing the side seam inside another three-eighths seam. "When you finish, clip the corners, turn your pillowcase right side out, and your first pillowcase will be finished."

12

Tea Basket and Shining Star members had donated enough money after Avery's speech that Rosie was able to order and pay for yard signs and fliers that afternoon. The front page newspaper article, which ran the day after Avery's announcement, also generated a small flood of mail-in contributions. The news article was accompanied by two side-by-side photos. One image showed Avery looking much like an engineer, smiling in front of a crowd and wearing one of her two Oxford shirts and a pair of crisp new blue Dockers. The other showed Jasper Hollister holding up a half-eaten Danish, looking every bit the slacker Avery was quoted to have accused him of being.

Without sufficient money to rent office space, the Underwood campaign headquarters remained in Rosie's dining room. Rosie was fine with the arrangement. Her house was soon crammed with cardboard boxes containing plastic sleeve yard signs and more boxes stacked high in a corner containing wireframes for the sleeves. Volunteers had spread county and township road maps all over her elegant dining table. On top of those, they'd scattered volunteer lists attached to clipboards. A regular parade of young people shuffled cars on and off Rosie's short driveway, picking up maps and getting assignments before heading back out to canvass for their candidate.

At her campaign headquarters, Avery's big Ford nosed up to a makeshift sign tacked to the trunk of Rosie's maple tree at the end of the drive. A whitewashed board with blue letters announced the space as "Reserved for the Candidate." Avery picked up her travel mug of leftover coffee, climbed out of the cab, and paused to smile at the crude lettering. Somehow, it seemed perfectly alright not to be fancy or costly. Hers was, after all, a grassroots campaign. No party backing. No big money.

She had arrived early this morning and would do so every morning, ready to begin her own round of canvassing for votes. The sign reminded her that all this work was being done for her benefit. She was both grateful and humbled. Only a few days later, a volunteer slapped magnetic signs on both front doors of the F350 advertising her bid for the office of county engineer. Rosie had obviously found enough money to have them made.

Today, as with every day, she planned to knock on as many doors as possible. Even though she wanted to be the only one to ask for votes, she was grateful to have acquiesced to her campaign manager, Rosie, that others would also be canvassing for her.

"No. You cannot do it all yourself. Not possible," Rosie argued. "The committee assigned you to canvass in the most populous neighborhoods. Volunteers will hit the outlying areas. You knock on doors in the towns. Athens, Nelsonville, The Plains, and Albany are your beat. After them, if you finish, then you go to as many of the smaller villages like Torch and Shade as time permits."

Still, Avery protested. "But Rosie, the people most impacted by county roadways live in the rural areas. That's where the engineer's office has the biggest impact."

Rosie argued back. "No. You stick to the towns. That's where the most votes are. And yes, it is the rural folks who use the county roads. But it's the townies who have more votes. If and when you finish your assigned municipalities, then you can visit the people who have to drive on the worst of Hollister's roadways. That's just how it's got to be. Stick to the plan laid out by your campaign committee. Trust them, Avery. You have to get the votes before you can help anybody."

Avery knew Rosie was right. She needed votes to unseat Hollister. If she won, then she could actually do something for the rural residents by improving and maintaining their roadways. First things first. Reluctantly, she sighed and nodded in agreement.

Avery kept track of each address where no one answered her knock on the door. She wedged a flier in the door, intending to return as Election Day neared. Perhaps, if they had enough money, she thought they might mail additional literature if she wasn't able to return. She stuck to the neighborhoods she had been assigned and hit the pavement by nine every morning. She would still be knocking on doors by seven every evening. That's when Rosie had ordered her to stop working. She felt grateful not to have her old job anymore. She needed every hour to meet potential voters. She wondered if Jasper was also out of the office, as usual. But now, was he out seeking votes, too?

When Avery was met at the door by a woman, she was sometimes greeted with a smile; a thank you for her literature, and, too often, a look of doubt when she explained her purpose. Avery tactfully countered skepticism using her flier. She'd point out her advanced level of education in civil engineering, her years of experience supervising road crews constructing state and national highways, and list her credentials and certifications. She usually concluded by asking the woman with a furrowed brow about her own level of education. She reminded these skeptics that there has been "a first woman" to take on traditionally male jobs in other professions. She'd conclude by saying with as much bravado as possible, "I hope, with your vote, I'll be Athens County's first Highway Engineer."

Saying this so often, she was beginning to believe it.

She met women who were office supervisors, small business owners, doctors, and lawyers, and she even shook the hand of the city's mayor, who was definitely not an independent. Most of the women with professional careers wished her well. She took that as a good sign. For those who somehow managed their lives on minimum wage jobs, Avery gently encouraged them to go after their own dreams. She'd hold up one of her fliers and point to it. "You, too, have the power to accomplish whatever you put your mind to," she'd say. "This is mine." She meant it.

Encounters with a few good ol' boys didn't always go well. At times, Avery was met with outright cynicism. One grizzled old-timer snorted and scoffed. He told her she was "half-baked to run for the job." There were others who said something similar but in rather crude and ungentlemanly terms. She took their negative attitudes in stride with a smile. She was wise enough to know there are some whose way of thinking would never change.

Once in a while, she could divert some man's attention to the topic of vehicles, trucks in particular, of which she was rather fond. Often, she'd notice a small pickup parked in the man's drive, obviously his. In her observation, she revealed her knowledge about her F350's engine and towing capacity compared to his truck. But she'd always compliment these men on their choice of a vehicle. "Reliable. Great gas mileage. Easy to maintain," she'd conclude. She'd recite her V8's eight-liter engine, its four hundred horsepower with four hundred forty-five lb-ft of torque and its payload capacity of three thousand pounds and towing capacity of thirty-eight thousand pounds. All the while, she'd be listing her truck's specs and looking off at the man's small truck.

Given enough room in their discussion, she'd wedge in some additional statements that proved her knowledge of roadway equipment, their cost to operate, what equipment she knew the county currently owned that would soon have to be replaced, and how much it would cost. Once in a while, she would detect just the smallest glimmer of realization in the man's eyes. Maybe it wasn't a great illumination in his consciousness, but at least a small flicker that he might consider her actually capable of having the knowledge and ability to do the job of an engineer. She'd then offer her hand to depart, but she always paused, would turn back and ask for the man's vote, even if she sensed the mind was as frozen as an engine without oil. Avery and her F350 spent hundreds of hours knocking on doors and talking to voters over the months leading up to the election and encountered more skeptics than she cared to count.

One morning, Rosie grabbed her sleeve before she was out the door. Rosie handed her a gas company credit card.

"What's this for?" Avery asked.

"You really are new to politics, aren't you? Rosie asked. "This is for you. It's to keep your truck on the road during the campaign. Just charge the fuel with this and keep a log of your mileage. Give me the receipts and your odometer readings every time you fill up with gas. This is a campaign expense, not your personal expense. Whatever you do, whenever you do it, if it's related to the campaign, you get a receipt. That includes meals, kiddo."

Avery signed the back of the card and wedged it into her wallet. "Meals?" she asked. To Avery, that sounded too much like something Jasper would do on company time. "Oh, I don't know about meals, Rosie. That sounds unethical."

"It's perfectly legit as long as it's campaign-related. It's not for pizza with Joe."

Avery's eyes widened with surprise. "You know about Joe?"

"I know lots of people, Avery. Lots of people know Joe. Lots of people know you two are on friendly terms. Should I know anything else?"

"No," Avery said hastily and with a bit of surprise in her voice. "Absolutely not. We're just friends. He's been helpful, really helpful, for the campaign."

"That list of names for the committee came from him, didn't it?" Rosie asked.

"Yes," Avery admitted. "He said giving me those names was all he could do at the time since he had to publically back Jasper as the incumbent. I was surprised when he handed me that list. Like you, I guess, he knows everybody in the county, too."

"Joe's one of the good guys, Avery. He's a carnivore of a trial attorney, though. Never get on his bad side. He has the memory of an elephant, the fangs of a viper, and the vindictive nature of a woman scorned. I've seen him work a trial. He can sneak up on a defendant on the stand, bite the guy's head off, chew it up, twist it back on, and the poor slob won't even feel pain until the jury declares him guilty. He can make witnesses say things they shouldn't say. Seen it more than once, too. I think Joe lives and breathes to put criminals behind bars. He's very good at his job because he's tenacious. So, how is he with you?"

"Obviously, I'm no criminal to be prosecuted. Joe's a friend, always professional when we're together. I've never seen him work a trial, of course. We sometimes have coffee, sometimes a beer, and a pizza once in a while. Joe delivers carryout to my door most evenings since I'm, well, broke and destitute. We talk a lot. That's all. Campaign stuff. You know."

"Well, you win this election, and I venture you'll see a lot more of Joe O'Feeny."

Good to his word, O'Feeny paid Avery's rent through the end of the year. When he dropped the receipt off at her real estate office, Rosie took the opportunity to confirm the Underwood-O'Feeny relationship or lack thereof. She was disappointed. Not a hint of romance from either of them.

"Yeah, but I heard from a little bird that you deliver dinners to her."

"That's true. On occasion," he said without hesitation.

Rosie gave him a questioning look.

"Ms. Dyer, not every male in this town is out to hook up. Students maybe. But Underwood and I have a working relationship, that's all. I assure you. My intentions, if you're checking up on me, are purely professional in nature. It's refreshing to find a woman in the area who's vested in learning the ropes of local politics and, I hope, on the verge of unseating Hollister."

"If you say so," Rosie said with some disappointment in her voice.

"I do say so, Ms. Dyer. Have a nice day."

And with that, Rosie's hopes of romance died a sudden and painful death.

Simone stumbled. Her bare feet brushed through damp leaves scattered on the dark forest floor. Sounds seemed muffled by a thick blanket of fog that night. Drifting clouds overhead obstructed a meager light cast by a pale moon. She had made a grave mistake. She should not have entered this forest hollow. Now, in this darkness, she was truly lost. In her panic, she even forgot where she'd intended to go. Her toes were freezing. To her recollection, there was no forest as thick as this one near her home. Was she even near home? She shook her head, struggling to remember the fog in her mind as thick as the one through which she stumbled. No, she did not live near this or any forest. No one she knew, except maybe her friend, Ximi Ling, lived near a wood lot.

But Ximi's house was too many miles away for that to be her destination. She had lost her mind, not her way. That was it. She had finally become unstable, gone completely insane. She had no business whatsoever traipsing around in the middle of the night, barefoot, in such a location. What would people think?

Something stirred behind her. She spun around but saw nothing in the murky darkness, only mist that swirled around the gnarly roots of a moss-covered tree.

Which way was she to go? Should she turn back and try to follow the path by which she had come? In her muddled mind, Simone couldn't even remember how she had arrived at this isolated spot. Her heart rate increased. Her hands, which had been cold and stiff, began to grow damp with increasing anxiety.

She heard another faint sound. Breathing. The sound of air flowing in and out of the nostrils of some monster, she was sure. Now, she was gripped by primal fear.

Terror finally overtook her completely. Simone tried to bolt for safety, tried to force her feet to move, to run. But her feet refused to respond. Her legs were bound, half buried in thick mud. The sludge prevented either foot from rising. The harder she tried to pull a foot up, the tighter the sludge gripped.

The disembodied breathing grew near. Still, she saw nothing staring into the darkness.

Suddenly, maybe because she had stopped trying to struggle, her feet were free. She jerked them up, ready to run, but it was too late. She watched in vain as a mighty swing from a broadax of glistening steel severed both feet and her hands in one giant arching swoop of the handle.

Simone sat upright with a scream. Upright. In her own bed.

She trembled, her nightgown damp with sweat. She looked out the bedroom window. There, leaves—more gray in the evening light than green—clung to the only maple tree in her front yard. It had been a nightmare. A bad dream. She struggled to slow her breathing. She brought her hands up in front of her face. Both hands. Still attached to her arms.

Kyle rolled over just enough to see his wife sitting up beside him.

"What the …? What is it with you? You insane?" he grumbled.

Simone tried to calm her voice so that she could speak without trembling. "Maybe. Just a nightmare. I had a nightmare. That's all."

"You're lame. You woke me up. You're worse than a little kid. Forget about it. Go back to sleep. I have to get up early," he muttered, rolling away and pulling the sheet tightly over his body.

Simone remained upright, allowing the dampness of her nightgown to evaporate and cool her body. She listened to the real sounds of the night, crickets somewhere outside, to Kyle's slow and rhythmic breathing beside her.

The next morning, as she watched Kyle drive off to the university, Simone thought she would call Ximi. She had been neglecting their friendship for weeks... months, actually. Theirs had been a friendship as tight as two could possibly be. Too many excuses had kept them apart. She found it easier as time went on to avoid Ximi altogether rather than admit to her neglect. Then there was the other problem. Phone conversations with Ximi, if Kyle was around, almost always resulted in some form of rebuke from her husband as soon as she disconnected.

"You spend too much time with that Chinese woman," he'd say.

So she reduced her phone calls. Sometimes, she never answered incoming calls from Ximi, just let them go to voice mail. Sometimes, she never even replied to the voicemails.

She worked up the courage to admit her neglect. She decided she'd admit she was a failure as a good friend. Take the blame. Ask for Ximi's forgiveness. It was past time to reconnect, especially after that nightmare. Ximi was a good listener. And Simone felt the need for a friendly ear to share the story. She was also proving to be a failure as a good wife.

Maybe she could fix the friendship. She was unsure what to do about her faults as Mrs. Kyle Beck.

She picked up her cell phone and made the call.

"Hi."

"Simone? Oh, my God! Hey, you're calling *me*. That's great. What's up, girlfriend?"

Instantly, Simone felt more joy than she had in weeks. Ximi's upbeat voice and the constant bubbly attitude possessed magical healing qualities. There was no blame in her friend's tone of voice. No sarcasm. She sounded just like the old Ximi she knew. Her friend. No one could speak with Ximi Ling and not feel good about themselves. Her effervescent nature transferred to everyone around her. Simone heard Ximi pop a bubble. Still chewing gum.

"I need to tell you about a dream I had last night. You were in it, sorta."

"I was in your dream?"

"Well, it was more a nightmare."

"What did I do? Why were you scared? What happened?"

Ximi's questions came rapid fire, the same way she drew, quick sweeps of the brush, broad strokes that created beautiful scenes in only seconds. Simone realized how much she missed spending hours in her company.

"*You* didn't do anything, exactly. But in my dream, I became aware of you, or your place, maybe. Anyway, I thought about you in my dream."

"Nightmare? You said you had a nightmare. What happened?"

"Well," Simone began slowly, recalling the forest, darkness, and fear. "I was alone. Lost somewhere. I don't know where I was exactly. Maybe that's what was the most frightening. I thought maybe, maybe, I was looking for you. I dunno."

"OK. So you found me now. What happened then?"

"Something... I was afraid. Really afraid. I thought I was going to die. I tried to run…"

"And just like all nightmares, I'll bet your feet wouldn't move. Am I right? Isn't that always the case? Terrible feeling, isn't it? Weird."

"Exactly! But I did move… eventually… I did break free. But I was too late. A monster, maybe the devil himself, or maybe the Grim Reaper… I lost my hands and my feet. Swoosh! Gone. He cut them off with an ax. "

"Eew. Was it a really gross bloody dream?"

"Funny about that. No. Not at all, now that I recall. Where my hands had been cut off, well, the stubs of my arms looked like the growth rings inside trees. You know, the sawed-off stumps. That's what they looked like. Like my arms were two stumps of little trees. Too weird."

"Well, I'm glad you didn't bleed to death in your dream. I don't think I could handle you bleeding to death 'cause your hands got whacked by the Grim Reaper."

Both women laughed at the absurdity.

"I feel so much better just telling you about it. I've been on edge since, not knowing what caused me to have such a nightmare."

Ximi listened silently, biting her lower lip. She was debating with herself to openly bring up her feelings about Simone's isolation and the signs she was seeing in Kyle as an abuser.

"You still there? Hello?"

"Sorry, Simone, I was thinking. You haven't been around much, and that's what I would like to talk about now you've called. Have I… did I do something… wrong? We never talk anymore."

"It's my fault, Ximi. Not yours. I don't know. After Kyle and I married, I just sort of stopped seeing you. I stopped going to the guild, too. I quit my job. I sold my car. Now I'm stuck in the house all the time."

"You what?" Ximi said. Simone was one of the most independent people Ximi knew. Simone would never just up and sell her car. Simone was the one who always suggested that they drive off to places for fun at every opportunity. And Simone loved to do the driving.

"I can't believe you. You… *sold*… your… car?"

"Well, Kyle thought it would make sense since I no longer work."

"'Kyle.' Do you hear what you're saying? It's Kyle. You cave into everything Kyle wants. Kyle wants you to sell your car. So you do. Was it Kyle who told you to quit your job, too?

Simone answered with a meek "Yes."

"Was it Kyle who suggested you spend less time with the guild?"

"Yes."

"Was it Kyle who pressured you to stop spending time with *me*?"

"Yes, but you don't understand … "

"Oh, I understand perfectly," Ximi said. "I can see what's going on even if you can't.

Do you remember that presentation about spousal abuse at the guild?"

"Well, yes. But Kyle doesn't *abuse me*. I'm not a battered wife. He's never put a hand on me. He loves me. He bought me that beautiful ring. Remember? We're always going places together… "

"Are these places where *he* wants to go or places where *you* want to go?"

"Well…"

"Simone, he's isolating you from me and from everything that's important to you. You have to be careful. Think. Remember what Robin told us? Abuse begins with disrespect. If Kyle respected you at all, he would not have coerced you to stop doing those things that make you happy. I'll bet you haven't even done one lick of sewing since you married. Have you?"

"Well, I've been busy."

"I swear, that man is sucking the life right out of you, and you're letting him do it."

"No. *You* don't understand. I called because I needed to hear your voice. I wanted a little sympathy, not a lecture. You're saying my Kyle is some kind of monster. Well, he isn't. He loves me. I know it. I married him, didn't I? I'm sorry I bothered you. I should never have called."

"C'mon Simone. Listen, I didn't mean to upset you. Simone?"

Ximi was too late. Simone had disconnected.

13

Robin Prescott stopped at the Tea Basket hall, where she was met by the ever-present Nora. In spite of Nora's insistence, Robin declined a cup of her coffee. Robin had only stopped to view what Lois Caldwell's guild had so far collected for Harbor House. To her pleasant surprise, a laundry basket overflowed with donations atop a six-foot table near the front windows. Someone had also made the first pillowcase. It, too, was waiting beside the laundry basket. She saw a small tabletop sign next to the basket that listed what donations the Shining Star members should deposit into the basket. Beside that lay a clipboard with signatures running down one column. The header was penned with the words "Next Basket Donors."

"This is *very generous*. Am I to understand that I should take the laundry basket, too?"

"Absolutely," Nora said. "If you look below the table, you'll see the next basket ready to be moved up and filled. Not only have the Shining Stars been dropping off supplies, but so too have we Tea Baskets. We've started making nine-patch quilts for Harbor House beds. One is already upstairs, just off the quilting frame, and I believe it'll be finished soon. All that remains is squaring up and binding. Two of the gals practiced their machine quilting skills on it. And they did a great job. After this quilt and others are bound, we'll leave them here on this table for you to take away, along with Shining Star pillows. We hope they'll be suitable."

Robin looked over the offerings and then at Nora. "That's wonderful of you. Thank you so much. Brigitta will be impressed. I am. I'm sure she'll want to thank you personally."

"No rush, dear. Lois plans to keep the Shining Stars producing pillowcases for months. And our guild members have an endless supply of scraps for many more bed quilts. We're very happy to contribute."

Robin picked up the basket and was about to leave when Nora reached out and touched her arm, halting her exit. Nora had turned serious. "Before you go, may I ask you a question?"

"Of course."

"We've a member, well, maybe she's a former member… but we think she's living in an abusive situation. What I'm telling you is all very sensitive, you know."

"You can count on my discretion, Nora."

"You know Simone Beck, Coach Beck's wife?"

Robin nodded.

"We think she's being abused by him. She's only been married a short time. Can that happen? Can a woman find herself trapped in such a condition so soon following the honeymoon?"

"Abuse goes by no timetable, I'm afraid. There are many unmarried women who are abused. Have you talked to her and gotten a sense of what's going on between her and her husband?"

"No. We're just going on conjecture due to her absence and by what we think we've seen. I guess it could be nothing at all, just our imaginations. But your talk left quite an impression. Perhaps we're overreacting. Perhaps I'm overreacting."

"Talk to this Simone alone, if you can, before you do anything. But be sensitive. If she is in an abusive situation, you don't want your inquiries to make things worse for her."

Nora nodded with understanding, then changed the subject. "Sometime soon, you must come back. Bring your knitting. Spend a bit of time upstairs with us in the hand-sewing room. I think you'll enjoy our company."

Robin shifted the heavy laundry basket laden with supplies. She had carefully balanced the new pillow with the yellow case on top, and it wobbled precariously. "I will, but not today. I should deliver all these donations to Harbor House and show Brigitta. As I said, she'll be just as pleased and surprised by your guild's generosity as I am."

Robin departed carrying the first basket of donations from the guild. Nora closed the door quietly behind her.

Not long after, Ximi Ling arrived at the Tea Basket hall. She climbed the stairs going straight to the big room where the long arm quilting machine, the Gammil, was already humming along, Nora at the controls.

"Yay, Nora! I didn't think you wanted to learn how to machine quilt?"

Nora looked up with a grim expression. "I'm not learning. I'm failing. Failing miserably."

"Oh, what do you mean?" Ximi walked over to inspect the whole cloth that members were using to practice their stitches. "I see some great feathers there, and over here, I see a nice all-over pattern."

"I didn't make those. All I'm trying to do is a simple straight line. Look at it! It looks like the tracks of a drunken snake."

"Oh. Oh, I see. Hm, yes. Not looking too good there, Nora. Maybe you should use a ruler or a guide to help."

"A ruler? Use a ruler for a straight line?"

Ximi leaned in close to the old woman's ear. "I have to," she whispered.

"You do?"

Ximi nodded. "Yes, I do. There are many tools out there to aid in quilting. I use as many as I need."

Nora could not imagine anyone with the artistic talents of her architect guild sister having to use a straight edge.

Nora turned off the Gammil and walked out of the room with her young friend. The two entered another room down the hall, one favored by machine piecers. Both Nora and Ximi had a sewing machine set up, and the work was in progress. "You plan to spend some time on your Peony quilt?"

"I guess. Thought the work might cheer me up," Ximi said. She lifted a protective plastic cover over her sewing machine and slumped down into the chair.

"What's got you so down?" Nora asked. "I didn't think anything ever bothered you."

Ximi sighed heavily as she flipped the switch to turn on her sewing machine. The Janome beeped and clunked as it prepared for her orders. "It's Simone. She called me today, and then she hung up on me. I thought everything was going great. She told me about a nightmare she had. Then I ruined it. I started to tell her how I think Kyle is disrespectful. Did you know he made her sell her car? Can you believe it? Simone without a car?"

"Sell her car? Nonsense. How's she going to get around?"

"Exactly. And when I pushed my opinion that Kyle was systematically isolating her, she got mad and hung up. I'm worried that our friendship is over and done for. I've killed it with my big mouth and stupid opinions butting into her private life."

Nora patted her young friend on the shoulder sympathetically. "Nonsense, child. You're a good friend. You need to say what you believe. If she doesn't believe you now, maybe she will should things get worse for her."

"Do you think I was wrong?"

"I do not. The other day, I ran into her and Kyle while shopping at the grocery store. I agree with you now that I hear she has no car. Maybe he is abusing her. I noticed her hair."

"Her hair?" Ximi asked.

"Yes. On the left side of her head, it looked to me like a chunk of her hair was missing."

"No. You don't think Kyle pulled her hair out, do you?" Ximi said.

"Well, it looked like she'd gotten some caught and ripped out somehow. I can't think of anything she does that would do that. Do you? Anyway, I dismissed it all. You know she's always well-coiffed in that French twist of hers. But I could see a gap. And at first, I was puzzled. She saw me staring and tried to hide the area with her hand. When she realized I was still staring, she made an excuse. Said she'd caught her hair rolling up the car window. Now that I think about it, I'm not so sure.

Kyle was standing right there beside her sort of scowling at me. He said something like, 'She's always doing some *stupid thing* like that.' Yeah, 'stupid' is the word he used. But that bald spot was on the left side of her head. If she doesn't drive anymore, if she's sitting in his car's passenger seat, how come her missing hair was from the left side of her head?"

Ximi was worried by Nora's observation. She'd noticed Kyle was right-handed. She was now convinced this was all the proof she needed that Kyle was indeed abusive to her friend. Any visible damage was beyond isolating his wife. Ximi decided she needed to take action to save her friend. But what kind of action? She decided to call up reinforcements.

Nora, Lois and Avery assembled in the Tea Basket hall as requested by Ximi. It was Sunday afternoon following church services. Lois arrived wearing a dress of dark blue with white polka dots, her favorite "Sunday-go-to-meetin'" dress, and a pair of unusually light-colored slip-on flats. She complained to Ximi as the two walked up to the front door of the hall together.

"These shoes pinch my toes somethin' fierce. I like somethin' wider, sensible shoes that tie. I cannot for the life of me see how you can even stand upright in those stilettos you're always wearin'."

Ximi, who was much shorter than Lois, wore a solid turquoise sleeveless jumper and impossibly high black stilettos. Lois was aghast at the sight of them.

Even with the additional inches adding to her short stature, Ximi's head barely came up to Lois' broad shoulders. Ximi giggled, popped a bubble of gum in her mouth, and smiled up at her friend. She mimed someone walking a tightrope.

Nora, already at the hall, greeted them at the door wearing one of her expensive linen pant suits. Nora's lipstick, earrings, and shoes matched the peach color of her blouse under her jacket.

Avery arrived last, carrying a cup of hot coffee. Her Sundays always started slowly. Sundays were her only days off. But even then, she would be out canvassing for votes in the afternoon. Since that day of strict orders from Rosie on how a candidate should dress, Avery wore a pair of penny loafers instead of work boots. Her oxford shirt this day was crisp, white, and wrinkle-free. She had replaced her usual jeans with a pair of tan Dockers, something strongly suggested, and also a gift from her treasurer.

"Well, don't we all look fine this day?" Nora said. "Now, tell everyone why we're here, Ximi."

Ximi ushered her little committee to chairs arranged around a table while she remained standing. "I'm very worried about Simone's safety." she began. "I thought maybe between us, we could come up with a plan to save her."

"Save her?" Avery asked. "Save Simone? Save her from what? What *are* you talking about?"

Ximi started to speak but was cut short by Nora, who raised her hand. "We must tread carefully here, child. I know how much Simone means to you. But Robin has warned me that we cannot barge into her life accusing her spouse of being an abuser. We could make things worse for her if that turns out to be true."

"Coach Beck is abusing Simone?" Avery asked.

"You've been busy with your campaign, Avery," Ximi began, "You haven't noticed that Simone's been AWOL from guild. She's been absent here, and she's been totally missing in my life since she married that guy. We used to do so many things together. She's quit her job at the Thimble and Chatelaine. Now I find out she's even sold off her car. And she's done all that because Kyle *forced her to*. She should never have married him. One day after her honeymoon, she confided in me. Told me a sob story he fed her about a former lover. I'm sure he used that tale to weasel his way into her heart. You know how caring she can be for others. Anyway, because of that scenario, he fed her, she has some false sense of duty to be different or *better* than that *other woman* from his supposed past."

"We don't know for sure he's abusing Simone," Nora said. "But the other day, I did think I might have seen him jerk her around inside their car. Now, mind you, I might be misinterpreting what I saw. Again, we must tread very carefully before we take any action."

Lois had a stern look on her face, while Avery's expression was one of bewilderment. She was hearing this news for the first time.

"I'm all for takin' such a foul person out behind my woodshed and givin' him a piece of my mind," Lois said, crossing her arms over her chest.

"Whoa. Nora is right," Avery said. "We can't go about making unfounded accusations or taking drastic actions without knowing the truth. We need to hear directly from Simone what she wants us to do. We have to approach her in a way that protects her. Her husband can't know what we're doing. Can we catch her alone so she can talk freely? How do we accomplish that? Anyone have suggestions?"

A long period of silence ensued. Then Lois asked, "Why can't you knock on her door and see if you can get her to talk, Avery? You're knocking on doors all over the place for your campaign. You could make the Beck's one of your campaign stops."

"I like it!" Ximi said. "Let me come with you. Together, I'll get to the bottom of this."

"I'll drive," Lois said.

"No," Avery abruptly said. "No. You're right, Nora. We must be discrete about our purpose. I'll go in my truck with campaign literature."

"Well, don't leave me out. I want to help, too," Lois said.

"And me! This is my mission." Ximi said.

"Ok, we'll all go," Avery said in resignation.

"Does tomorrow work?" Ximi asked with eagerness.

"Go today," Lois said. "The better the day, the better the deed. If Kyle's there, you tell him you're trainin' us, Ximi and me, on how to make campaign pitches. Say we felt better bein' trained in front of somebody we know."

It was agreed. Their reconnaissance mission was planned, and about to take off. Nora declined the invitation to go along. Nora was confident her younger guild sisters could accomplish their fact-finding mission without her in tow. She'd stay behind to see if anyone needed the hall. If not, she'd lock up in a few hours if no guild members came in. She planned to return to the Gammil, holding hope that she might make at least one straight line of stitches before giving up completely.

"You gals, call me and tell me what you find out."

Nora closed the door to the hall, watching her friends walk toward Avery's truck, Ximi in the lead, outpacing even Avery's long stride... *and in those heels!* Nora was as astounded at Ximi's ability to walk in stilettos as Lois had been.

Candidate Underwood knocked on the front door of Simone and Kyle Beck's house a few minutes later. Behind her stood little turquoise Ximi in her stilettos and the polka dots that covered Lois.

Kyle opened the door. Seeing Ximi, his face took on a dark look. "May I help you?" he growled.

"If you don't mind, Coach Beck," Avery said, "You know who I am, I suppose?"

Beck nodded.

"With me are two new campaign volunteers who would like to practice their presentation on a familiar couple. Ximi, as you know, is Simone's friend, and Lois Caldwell is one of your fans and president of the Shining Stars quilt guild. When they found out that I had not yet approached you for support, they asked if they could practice their presentations on you and Simone. Would that be possible, since they feel that we're all friends? We wouldn't normally bother anyone on a Sunday, but we were all available and hoped we could catch the two of you at home today."

Beck seemed to accept Avery's story. Although he didn't want Simone in contact with Ximi, he felt awkward denying her admittance while allowing the other two inside. He capitulated and stepped aside, holding the door wide so the group could enter. Beck ushered the three into a spotless living room and then called out for his wife.

When Simone entered, she stopped short, seeing her three guild sisters standing in her living room. She smiled broadly, happy to see them. Then she looked to Kyle, who stood by, not showing any indication he was about to leave her alone with them. Simone's face took on a look of caution. Awkwardly, she broke the silence. "Uh, please,

please have a seat, all of you. What brings you here? Is something going on at guild? I'm so sorry I haven't been attending. I've been so busy lately…"

Avery took the lead. "No, not the guild. Not at all. It's my campaign. Do you mind if Lois and Ximi explain? They hoped they could break in their campaign spiel on friends that wouldn't slam a door in their faces."

"Oh, of course. We'd be happy to serve as your first contact. Wouldn't we, Kyle?"

"Yeah, not a problem," Beck said coldly, hovering over his wife's shoulder.

Lois stood up, pretending to be nervous. Pretending was unnecessary. She *was* nervous. This scheme seemed hopeless, with Kyle standing beside Simone, obviously not planning to leave the women alone. She looked to Simone, "Could we count on your vote for Avery Underwood for county highway engineer this fall?" She then tried out a questioning smile of strained sincerity.

Simone giggled.

Beck remained stone-faced.

"You forgot to ask them if they were registered voters, Lois," Avery said. "They can't support anybody if they aren't allowed to vote. That should be your first question."

"Oh, sorry. I forgot," Lois said.

"My turn," Ximi said with too much enthusiasm, bouncing off Simone's sofa to replace Lois, who took Ximi's place back on the couch. "So, are you folks registered to vote this fall?"

"Why, yes, we are," Simone offered.

Beck continued to remain silent.

"Great. I'd like to ask you to support Avery Underwood at the polls as our next county engineer."

Simone giggled again. She enjoyed having contact and doing this little role-play

with her friend.

Ximi was relieved inwardly. By all outward appearances, any anger Simone had expressed toward her over the phone had vanished.

"Aren't you forgetting something, too?" Avery asked Ximi.

"I don't think so. What did *I* forget?"

"Don't you want to hand her a flier or brochure with information about your amazing candidate?"

"Oh shoot. Yes. Ah, here." Ximi removed a flier from the top of a box Avery held out. Turning back to Simone, she placed the document directly into her hand. "You have to check these out. I did the artwork. I used *your* favorite color, too. This tells you all about Avery's qualifications for the job and a bit of her background. Do read it, Simone. Please."

"Is that it? You ladies done?" Beck interjected coldly.

"We are, sir," Avery said. "Again, thank you for your patience. I do look forward to your vote this fall. I appreciate your willingness to let my volunteers practice on you, too. As you know, Simone, they're much more at home making pillowcases and quilts for Harbor House than they are for canvassing for votes."

Kyle turned away from the three women and strode for the door to usher them out. Once his back was turned on the group, Ximi, in spite of her heels, rushed to Simone. She flipped the brochure in Simone's hand over to reveal the words "call me" scribbled on a post-it note stuck inside the fold. She looked her friend squarely in the eye and just as quickly flipped the brochure closed so the note was once again concealed inside the brochure in her friend's hand.

As the three walked out of the Beck's front door, Kyle did not see his wife peel the post-it note off the brochure and slip it into her pocket.

Avery congratulated Lois and Ximi just loud enough so that Kyle would overhear. She said, "Don't be so nervous. Most people will politely accept your inquiry even if they don't intend to vote for me." As soon as she heard the Beck front door close behind her, she glanced back over her shoulder to be sure Kyle was inside and out of earshot. She said nothing more until Ximi and Lois buckled in, and she was behind the wheel of the big truck with all the doors shut.

"He's abusive, alright. He was too guarded. He wouldn't leave her alone with us for one second," Avery said.

"I'm so glad I thought last minute to write that note telling her to call. We never would have been able to get her alone. God, he hovered around her like a, like a…" Ximi said.

Lois chimed in, "Like a fox around a hen house. And did you see how hateful his eyes were? He gave me the creeps."

"Well, good job, ladies. Now let's wait and see if she does reach out to Ximi."

Kyle Beck closed the door and then turned to his wife. "That Asian friend of yours is a slut. Did you see those shoes? Those are shoes worn by whores if I ever saw any. I don't want you anywhere near her. And I swear I'll never vote for a lesbian. Underwood's a lesbian, isn't she? Politics is beyond your ability. You don't know who to vote for. Do not vote for her. You hear me? And what in the name of God was that Lois person? I could use her on the line. She must weigh in well over three hundred. She's a monster."

"Kyle, Lois is the most kind-hearted and generous person I know. She personally and at her own expense fed many, many people in need after the big storm last year."

Kyle interrupted her. "Fed *them?* She looks to me like the only one she feeds is *herself.*"

"Please, Kyle, those women are my friends."

"No, they are not. I'll tell you who your friends are."

"No, Kyle, they *are* my friends."

That was the wrong thing to say. As soon as the words left her mouth, Simone realized she had violated one of Kyle's rules. She had disagreed with him. She had openly disagreed. No sooner had the thought occurred to Simone than she felt the back of his hand collide with her cheek. Simone suddenly found herself face down on the carpet in their living room. She could taste blood in her mouth and felt the sting of his hand across her cheek.

"Can't you do *anything right?* I told you *never* to argue with me. *Ever.* When you do, *you* make me so angry."

14

Once again, the Underwood for Engineer campaign needed more money. Campaign financing had become a constant worry for businesswoman Rosie Dyer. The funds they had wouldn't last long. She'd given Avery a gas company credit card to keep her big Ford on the road. That bill would soon arrive in the mail, and Rosie would need to cover the expense.

While Avery knocked on doors, her treasurer met with members of the campaign committee about the cash flow problem. They all agreed that what Avery needed was a fund raising event. However, this event had to be expense-free if possible, yet income-producing.

They tossed around ideas, rejecting most of them. Finally, they hit on the idea of an ox roast. Some of the gatekeepers were to find and beg fledgling musicians to play. The musicians had to agree to perform only for tips. Once bands were lined up, they'd need a farm where they could hold the event and, of course, the ox to roast. Rosie had an idea for both. First, she would run the plan past the candidate before the committee was to move forward.

Avery was canvassing in the village of Albany, some seven or eight miles west of Athens. She decided to stop at the old elementary school, where she'd been informed a small restaurant had been established in the former school cafeteria. She hoped to find potential voters there having lunch. The ancient building was no longer part of the rural school district. All the old buildings scattered around the district had been consolidated into one new campus just on the other side of the highway. Inside the old school, Avery entered and found several locals chowing down on homemade cornbread and bean soup. She had just about finished handing out fliers and shaking hands when the phone in her Dockers rang.

"Rosie?" "Yes, things are going well. I'm planning to join folks here in Albany at the old school for a bowl of soup. Why?"

"Your committee wants your permission to hold an ox roast to raise funds. We'll secure a band for entertainment, charge a fee for the meal, take donations, and you'll give a short speech asking for support. Sound like something you can do?"

"Hold an ox roast? Well, I guess, if we need to. When and where have they decided this should take place? How do you even roast an ox?"

"Need your permission first. But I thought I'd ask Lois Caldwell if she'll donate the ox. One thing at a time. Once we have the meat, then we'll find the place, then set a date."

"I thought Lois only raised a flock of hens for eggs and a few beef cattle."

"Ox is a misnomer. The ox is really beef."

"So you haven't asked her yet?"

"No. Is that something you want to do?"

"Sure. After lunch here, I'll drive out to her place and ask her if she can afford to donate a steer. I get the feeling she isn't the wealthiest of folks, but she's generous to a fault. I have a good feeling she'll be agreeable. You know Lois. She's always eager to feed people."

"Good. Call me back as soon as she tells you yea or nay."

A few of the locals overheard Avery's side of the conversation. One of them spoke up as soon as she slipped her phone back into her pocket. "So, you're going to have an ox roast, eh? Who's going to roast it?" a man asked who was seated nearby at one of the tables.

Avery looked down at the guy seated with a few friends. He was a middle-aged fellow whose middle filled out his bib overalls. He looked to be a farmer.

"Have no idea. Have to get an ox first."

"Well, young lady, I'd be pleased if you'd let me be your cook," he said.

The men seated with the farmer looked at Avery and waited for her reply.

"I've got the equipment," he went on, "and I've been working ox roasts for years. Ask around. Everybody knows me. Besides, me and my buddies here would like to help you beat ol' Hollister come this fall. Tell you what," the farmer pushed himself away from the table and stood, "I'll go out to my truck for my business card. You come with me."

Avery followed the farmer, now accompanied by his pals, out to the parking lot where their trucks were parked. The side panel of a shiny red dodge read, "Woodward's Bar B Q & Smoked Meats. Catering Our Specialty since 1984." Avery was surprised that she hadn't noticed the sign when she drove her own truck into the gravel lot.

"Here's my card," he said, opening the driver's door and rummaging inside. "You give me a call when you find your ox, and I'll do the roasting. No charge for labor or equipment. But you have to tell everybody in your ads that I'm your cook. My wife, Emma, she makes the trimmings. She does potato salad, baked beans and slaw and serves rolls and butter. I'll give you a price for her sides. You tell me your ox weight on the hoof so I can estimate the time needed to cook it. You can pay my wife from your collections at the end of that day. I guarantee you'll get a good crowd if locals know that Woodward's are catering."

Avery accepted Woodward's card. He handed her five more as an afterthought. She thanked him and promised to call if she had secured a steer. Woodward shook her hand, and then he and his pals climbed into their vehicles, leaving Avery to return to the schoolhouse. While she enjoyed a bowl of soup, she listened politely to several locals complain to her about the current condition of their roadways.

After her lunch, Avery drove to Lois Caldwell's farm. She couldn't help but think how strange it felt to have little things like the encounter with Woodward fall into place on her behalf. That locomotive pulling her train was still, it seemed, hurling down the track. If it needed a name, it would be Serendipity.

Avery parked in front of Lois Caldwell's tidy farmhouse. It looked just as it had the first time she'd seen the place, right after that big storm had thrown much of the county into chaos with uprooted trees and no electricity for much of the area. The old faded corn crib stood nearby with a tractor parked in the aisle. The shiny white siding of the house gleamed in the sun. Potted pink, red, and white geraniums lined both sides of the steps leading up to Lois' front door. A colorful old quilt was draped over the back of a rocker perched beside the screen door.

Avery knocked on the doorframe, and soon thereafter, Lois opened it wide to let her in. Lois was barefooted and clad only in a slip. She appeared to be getting ready to leave her house for town; otherwise, she would have been attired in bib overalls.

"I caught you at a bad time. Didn't I? Planning to go to town? I can come back later."

"Heavens, you're no bother. I'm just goin' to the guild hall. Mornin' chores are done. Had my lunch and a shower. Saw your truck pull up from my bedroom window. What's up?"

Avery explained what her campaign committee needed. She handed Lois one of Woodward's cards and then asked the question she had driven out to ask.

Lois was quick with a response. "I have just the steer I can butcher and have roasted. He's been a real nuisance of late. Busts outta the field every single week. I'll be glad not to be fixin' fence all the time 'cause of that devil. You let me take care of everythin' related to that ol' troublemaker. I'll get the animal to the meat processor, let Woodward know his weight, and you can hold yer event right here at my place. Got plenty of room for folks to mill about. Got electric in the big barn so bands can set up and perform right there inside. We'll throw the big doors wide open, and it'll make a great stage. You tell people to bring lawn chairs. Might need some porta-potties, though, but that's all. So when do you want to hold this shindig?"

Avery was astounded at how Lois had just managed to solve so many problems with her immediate and overwhelming willingness to help.

"Yes, Joe, she donated the steer and the land just like that," Avery said as she gobbled down a bite of fried chicken the prosecutor brought to her apartment that evening. The two friends devoured thighs, potato wedges, and slaw rather quickly.

Joe reached into the bag to withdraw another thigh for himself. Miller's Poultry was one of Joe's personal favorite take-outs. He particularly liked their slaw and loved the fat potato wedges. He always ordered a large order of wedges for himself. If Avery didn't eat all of her small order, he would finish those wedges off, too. In spite of that, Joe O'Feeny never seemed to gain an ounce of fat.

Avery didn't mind that Joe took part of her meal. He'd paid for it. He stopped at Millers at least once a week to pick up an order for the two to share.

Joe looked at Avery with a question on his mind. "So, Lois lives out of town on a farm?"

"Yes, about eight miles south," Avery said between bites. She wiped her chin with a paper napkin supplied by Millers.

"I assume her place is on one of the state routes, a township road, or a county road." It was more of a question than an observation.

"Ah, yes. She has a farmstead on Caldwell Road, named after her place, I think. It's out there a bit, but easy enough for people to reach. And she said she can provide plenty of parking in her hay fields."

"Any plans for a rain date?"

"No. Once Woodward starts cooking the steer, we're locked into the date. If it rains, you and I will eat ox instead of chicken for the rest of this year and part of next."

"So, when is this event to take place?" he asked.

"Don't know. I guess Woodward needs several days to cook an entire steer. We won't be able to set a date until the steer's weight is determined. But we also have to put out a bit of advertising for it to allow folks time to plan."

Avery watched Joe jot down a note on one of the clean napkins and then slip the napkin into his pocket. She assumed he would probably attend and just needed a note to remind himself to keep the day free.

"You think you'll be able to attend?" she asked eagerly.

"We'll see. For sure, you let me know the date just as soon as it's set."

"Will do. You want the last of my wedges?"

"Don't mind if I do."

Sheila struggled most days to convince herself to go to work at the county garage now that Avery was no longer there. She missed having Avery to talk to. She missed Avery's smile and the woman's good nature, as well as her smarts and how she took the job seriously. With the assistant engineer gone, Sheila was surrounded once again by an all-male staff. Most of all, she found it nearly intolerable to interact kindly with Hollister. The campaign against Avery kept the man in a perpetually foul mood, a mood she had to deal with every minute he was in the office. He was surly. And unlike Avery, Hollister always took the path of least resistance to avoid work at all costs. Today would be no exception. Today, Sheila was counting on his carelessness.

"What is it now?" Jasper growled as she entered his office, carrying a stack of papers, before leaving for the day.

"Need your signature on these requisitions and forms, sir," Sheila said as she placed the stack in front of him on his desk.

"Will this never end?" he complained.

Sheila had carefully marked every page where his signature was needed using a Post-it marker that was easy to peel off. But the stack of forms was at least two inches thick. There must have been a hundred colorful little post-its sticking out along the edge of the stack. Thirty-six exactly in Sheila's last count. She made sure he would find the task quite distasteful. That pleased her. She knew he'd rush through without reading anything before signing.

"Good God," he muttered. "Why do you do this to me at the end of the day? Give me these things one at a time, woman. This mass of paperwork is ghastly."

Sheila handed him a pen. "Just sign where the little colored tabs stick out. Shouldn't take you but a few minutes."

She relished watching him put forth any kind of labor. But this day, she was especially happy to watch him sign his name again and again. She hovered over him to be sure he signed every single document and took each document away with a smile just after he penned his name.

"Is that it?" He growled.

"Perfect, sir," she smiled. "Everything is perfect. Have a good evening, sir."

Avery's shindig on the Caldwell farm occurred two weeks after her fortuitous meeting with Woodward. Her committee members found three local bands willing to provide musical entertainment. Their styles ranged from loud 70's rock 'n' roll to acoustic folk guitar to foot-stomping bluegrass. Lois' barn rocked with the rhythms of drums, the occasional squelch of microphones, and the pulse of banjo and fiddle all that sunny afternoon.

The day had dawned clear and warm with no rain in the forecast. Cars parked in orderly rows in the hay field. Lois had seen to it that the hay was cut and baled early to make way for them. So many cars and trucks arrived at Avery's fundraiser that many had to park along the edge of the county roadway. Lois' field was full. Woodward's bar-B-Q pulled down ten dollars a plate. The committee charged twenty, half set aside for the campaign. Styrofoam plates piled high with beef, slaw, beans, potato salad, and rolls disappeared quickly from Mrs. Woodward's mobile serving kitchen. Her trailer was parked next to her husband's big iron smoker near the barn where her husband and his pals had labored for days roasting that no good fence crashing steer of Lois'.

The band tip jars overflowed. Avery's campaign committee mingled among the crowd, hitting supporters up for larger donations. Their efforts kept Rosie busy at her table, keeping careful donor records for each cash donation and check. Avery mingled about the crowd, accepting words of support and thanking strangers who acted like friends while struggling to remember the words in the speech she was soon to give. Rosie told her to put her speech down on paper. Avery didn't like to read her speech because she didn't like to listen to written speeches. She compromised with her treasurer and wrote out a few sentences on index cards. One card contained names to thank for this event, most importantly, Lois Caldwell. The cards were jammed in the back pocket of today's blue Dockers.

Lois kept a satisfied eye on the crowd from a distance. Pleased to see the end result of her errant steer, she ceremoniously parted with her own twenty to savor victory over his demise. She went about carrying her plate and eating as she walked. She paused momentarily only to chase a cluster of unsupervised little imps away from a barbed wire fence. She helped an elderly woman negotiate the way across the lawn toward the porta-john, offering her elbow to help steady the older woman. She was keeping her eye out for any kind of trouble. It wasn't long until she was the first to spot some. Rumbling down the road, coming toward her farm, she saw a grader being followed by a county engineer's truck.

"Jasper," she spat.

The grader slowed at the corner of Lois Caldwell's property line and there dropped the blade. With an unnecessarily loud roar of the engine and belching smoke from the tailpipe, the blade began to scrape gravel and dirt from the berm, threatening to shove aside any and all of the parked cars in its path ahead.

"What a piece of work!" Lois muttered under her breath, tossing her Styrofoam plate and remaining food into a nearby receptacle. She hurried to her truck parked in front of the house. She climbed in and drove quickly up the road coming to a dusty stop between the moving grader and the line of parked cars along the edge of the road.

"What do you think you're doin', young man?" she yelled at the driver through her open window. She had wedged her truck in his path, blocking his advance. She repositioned her pickup with the cab extremely close to the grader's blade.

"Look, lady, I have my orders," Pat, the operator, shouted down at her, tossing his head to the side to indicate the county engineer's truck idling behind him.

"*Orders* my big fat be-hind," Lois shouted back. "You tell that genius you work for to take this hunk o' metal and go play someplace else."

"Can't do that, I'm afraid." Shouted the voice of Jasper Hollister. He had left the safety of his pickup and was approaching the grader. "You all want your roads kept up. Well, this is the day we scheduled to plow the thing for ya. You have to move all these vehicles out of our way, or else."

"Or else *what*, you good fer nothin' worthless piece of…"

"Watch it, old girl. You keep that up, and I'll have to include the sheriff in this little altercation," Hollister threatened, snarling up at Lois.

Avery caught sight of the truck and the grader on the roadway some distance away. She recognized the equipment immediately. Jasper was obviously up to no good. She was just about to take off at a run toward the grader when Joe O'Feeny grabbed her arm from behind, holding her back.

"Let me go, Joe. Something's wrong. Lois needs me." Then, it occurred to Avery that perhaps Joe was meant to prevent her from stopping Jasper. "What are you doing here? Helping Jasper?"

Joe smiled. "Not on your life. Don't go up there all gangbusters just yet. You need this." The prosecutor withdrew a paper from his jacket and shoved it into Avery's hand.

"What's this?" she asked.

"It's something to wave under Jasper's nose to guarantee he backs off. Looks like Jasper saw the ad in the paper about this fundraiser of yours. You don't think like Jasper. He thinks this is *his* county road. I just gave you a permit to use the road all day long. It authorizes you to close the road to all traffic for 24 hours if you desire. It went into effect at eight a.m. this morning and lasts until tomorrow morning at seven fifty-nine. Your pal, Sheila Harper, even got Jasper's signature approving the closure. She slipped the document right under his nose inside a stack of papers she made him sign. You know how he hates paperwork, especially reading anything before he signs it. Now, you can go. Go help your friend turn that machine around and send Jasper Hollister packing."

Avery glanced at the paper in her hand and then up to Joe. She smiled and whispered, "Sorry. I shouldn't have jumped to the wrong conclusion. You did this, didn't you?"

Joe smiled back.

"Thank you," she said, then took off at a run down the gravel roadway toward Lois, the grader, and her old boss, Jasper Hollister.

Jasper caught sight of Avery running toward them. His hatred for her was palpable.

She was breathing hard by the time she reached him.

Her struggle gave Jasper great satisfaction.

Lois was holding her ground half out of her truck, standing with the door ajar, one foot on the running board of her pickup and the other foot resting on the grader's blade.

Avery stopped between the two foes. She noticed that the grader operator was the same guy she had written up for drinking on the job. "Enough of this crap, Jasper. You and

Pat, get out of here. You can't intimidate me or any of these people. Don't try to push people around with your machine."

"I beg your pardon, missy, but I'm just trying to do my job as county engineer. *Your people* are in *my way*. Least their cars are. So you go back and tell all your little supporters to move 'em, or I'll have to have 'em towed at their expense. Or maybe I'll just shove 'em into the ditch."

Avery stepped forward deep into Jasper's personal space. She stood just as tall as her former boss. Her eyes remained cool and fixed on his. She'd recovered quickly from her run. Her breathing was now even and measured. She lifted the paper that Joe had given her and let it fall open in front of Jasper's face.

"No, Hollister. *You* have no right to be here working this road today. *You* gave us a permit, co-signed by the county sheriff. This road is officially closed for our use. All of this road from one end of this farm all the way to the other. *You* closed this road, as a matter of fact. Maybe you didn't read the document before you signed it. That's just like you, to never do any paperwork properly. How was this morning's Danish, by the way?"

"If Avery's paper ain't enough for ya, Hollister, I got a conceal carry permit with a .22 in the back of this here truck of mine." Lois held up a small piece of paper, her permit, and waved it back and forth for Hollister and the grader operator to see.

Avery wondered if Hollister was about to suffer a stroke. His face turned white, then suddenly turned a ruddy red. It seemed like he wasn't breathing. Though he didn't move, neither did Avery. Finally, and reluctantly, Hollister stepped back with obvious irritation, turned, and barked an order at the driver in the grader to turn it around.

Lois removed her foot from the blade but continued to stand her ground on the running board of her truck. Avery hadn't moved at all, standing there in the middle of the road beside Lois' truck. Neither woman was about to give ground until both the grader and Jasper's county truck had completely retreated. When the backup signal began to beep loudly on the grader, Avery glanced up at Lois with a brief look of relief.

"Best you ride back with me. 'S'pect' it's almost time for your speech."

Avery climbed in beside Lois. "Thanks for stopping him."

"I didn't stop him. You did. With that paper of yours. I just slowed him down a bit."

"O'Feeny did the leg work. He got the road closed with the help of Sheila."

"So that really *was* an order to close the road?"

"You really have a concealed carry permit?"

Lois held up her little paper, and both laughed.

Few, if any, saw the drama on the road at the edge of the Caldwell farm. Joe O'Feeny had finished off his bar-b-q beef and slipped away unnoticed. Supporters were enjoying bluegrass music. And then, those who lingered received Avery's speech with enthusiasm. Best of all, they had donated enough money so that Rosie Dyer could pay Mrs. Woodward's fee, have more than enough left over to order boxes and boxes of yard signs, and pay Avery's gas credit card bill when it arrived.

Little miracles, thought Avery. They were simply the by-product of a wide support for the Underwood campaign. She *had t*o beat Jasper. People were counting on her.

Simone Beck tried to present the evening meal with style and elegance. She had prepared her husband's favorite dish. She set the table using coordinating linens, including a table runner for accent under a bowl of fresh-cut flowers and candles. And, of course, set places with the beautiful Noritake Rothschild china her guild friends had given her. Simone ached to see them all, her friends, and had wanted badly to attend Avery's ox roast on Lois Caldwell's farm. She missed them all. As she arranged silverware around the plates, she recognized just how much she really did ache to spend time with her friends. Her absence had been too long.

She then heard the familiar sound of the front door opening, keys hitting the tabletop, and a case falling to the floor. She automatically turned toward her refrigerator for his drink but caught herself and stopped. She turned around as Kyle slumped into his chair at the table without a word of hello or 'how was your day.' When the cool can of beer didn't instantly appear in front of him, he finally looked up to see instead the sad look on his wife's face.

"What's with you today?"

"Kyle, dear," Simone began, "I don't want to upset you, but I've been thinking…"

"That's a miracle, you thinking."

"Honey, please, just listen to me. I've been cooped up in this house for weeks. I never go anywhere by myself anymore. I really miss my friends. Today there was a big ox roast on Lois Caldwell's farm to raise money for Avery's campaign. All my friends would have been there. I'm sure of it, and I… "

"You mean that Lesbian, the whore, and the potential linebacker would be there? Not on your life. You keep away from those women."

"But Kyle, those are my friends."

Kyle had heard enough of Simone's whining. He stood abruptly. Picked up a plate and threw it at Simone. The dinner plate shattered into a million pieces as it hit the floor by her feet. The steak she had grilled, the potatoes she had mashed and buttered, the gravy she had stirred, and the beans she had sautéed for him flew everywhere around her. Most of the mess splattered against her legs.

"Now, just look what you've made me do!" he screamed. "This is all your fault. You always know how to piss me off with your whining and talk of those stupid-ass friends of yours. Clean this up! I'm going somewhere decent to eat. You ruin everything!"

Moving slowly, Simone bent down, gravy and clumps of potatoes dripped off her skirt, falling to the floor. She saw what had been a decent meal spread among shattered pieces of china. At last, Simone could no longer control her confusion, which was now mixed with outrage. She finally lashed out in frustration. From her perch kneeling on the floor, she snapped and yelled back at Kyle.

"Me? What *I've done*? You're the one who threw my beautiful plate! You're the one who broke my china!"

Kyle spun around in anger at this outburst. "You mean like this?" He returned to the table, picked up Simone's plate of food, and slammed it to the floor. He picked up her water glass and did the same. Then his glass crashed into the growing heap of china and mess on the floor. Finally, he yanked the tablecloth off the table, sending flowers, candles, and silverware sailing in a wide arc all over their kitchen.

"You're a whining bitch. What's wrong with you?"

He stomped out of the kitchen. Simone heard the keys rattle as they left the surface of the bureau by the door. She heard the door slam shut. Then she heard the unmistakable sound of his car engine rumble to life, the sound of tires churning up gravel as Kyle pulled out of their driveway in anger.

15

Shaking with fear, Simone blindly rummaged through her purse for her cell phone. An outlet nearby let her charge the phone. She had become scatterbrained for some reason. She would plug it in and toss it back inside her purse while the battery charged. That was one way not to forget it. She followed the cord and pulled it out. One punch and she confirmed her phone was fully charged. She punched up Ximi's number and waited for her friend to answer.

"You've reached Ximi Ling, architect and water colorist. Leave a message. I'll return your call as soon as possible. Thank you."

"Ximi? Simone here," she said shakily. "I really need to talk to you. Call me when you get this. OK?"

She tried reaching Lois Caldwell next. Same result, just a familiar voice on a recorded message. Simone then remembered the ox roast. She sighed and assumed everyone was at the Caldwell farm, probably nowhere near phones. Perhaps there was no cell reception. She'd never been to Lois' farm and had no idea where it was.

She slumped to the floor. She stared at the mess that had once been fine china and a lovely meal. Now, she was tasked with cleaning up all those shards of broken dishes and ruined food. Garbage. Her life had turned to garbage. *How could I have been so dumbto tick off Kyle? Stupid. I knew better. Stupid. Stupid. Stupid.*

Sitting in misery and self-blame amid the mess, Simone didn't hear her front door open. She didn't hear Kyle enter the kitchen. She didn't even notice him standing next to her, staring down at her with pure rage on his face. It took her some seconds to finally recognize his shoe. Only then did she shriek in sudden fear and push herself away, sliding across the messy floor.

Kyle reached down, snatching the phone from her grip. "You were calling your bitchy friends on me, weren't you?"

He punched *recent*. His suspicion was confirmed. "Ximi, and "Lois."

Kyle began to jab her phone in anger. He was deleting their numbers while she remained frozen, cowering at his feet. After every number in her address book had been erased, he threw the phone at her, where she cowered like a whipped pup amid broken dishes and food. He threw the phone so hard that the case broke open. Then he ground his heel on what was left of it.

"I told you to clean up this mess!"

Avery made a phone call that evening to Joe's private number. He picked up almost immediately.

"I did not properly thank you today for sliding that permit past Hollister. Thank you."

"All in a day's work as a political shark."

"Will you be OK with the party? You did perform a good deed for the competition, after all."

"No problem. All the credit will go to your friend, Sheila. In a day or two, she'll have a receipt to submit to your treasurer for the permit she acquired. A mere thirty-five bucks… I think, paid for in cash, of course."

"I wonder where she came up with that money," Avery said.

"Wonders never cease."

"I am so grateful you and Sheila arranged that. I don't know what might have happened if you hadn't been there with that permit. I'm afraid Lois might have ended up being one of your perps. You might have had to put her on the stand for aggravated assault or, worse, murder. I've never seen her so angry."

"Hollister has that effect on many."

Joe agreed to meet Avery at their favorite pizza joint that evening.

Avery pulled her wallet out of her Dockers, but Joe stopped her. He insisted on paying the bill. They had each devoured their share of a medium pepperoni and a pitcher of beer.

"Aren't you completely destitute yet? How long has it been since you've had a paycheck?"

"Yes, almost totally broke, but I think I can sell a quilt for a few hundred and keep meeting my obligations a little while longer. The cost of a pizza and beer is the least I can do to express my thanks. Now you've stopped me from paying you back."

"You won't be poor too much longer. Election's just a few weeks away. By January, you'll have a paycheck, a new title, and the respect of many. When that time comes, then you can buy dinner. You can pay for every meal we share next year if you want."

"By January, I *will* be destitute and *very* hungry."

"Well, don't starve yourself. I have a kitchen. I've got a cupboard full of pristine cookware that I've never used. Probably wouldn't know how to use it if I tried to cook something. If you don't know how to cook, either. I've got a cookie jar full of loose change for more pizza, subs, Miller's, or other forms of take-out."

"So *that's* been your plan all along."

"Plan? I've had no plan."

"Oh yes, I see it all very clearly now. First, you get me to run as an independent."

"I couldn't let you fail as a challenger during the primary."

"You knew when I filed, I'd be fired or at least forced to quit."

"You quit that job quite honorably to comply with government regulations."

"Then you paid my rent, keeping me under a roof and on the campaign trail all this while. For what?"

"How would it look? It's likely nobody would vote for a homeless person."

"Then, when I'm totally broke and starving, you entice me with the promise of more free take-out."

"I'm aware of what locals say about me. Although rumored to be a cruel man and a vindictive prosecutor, I am, in fact, not cruel. I often support the poor in spite of my professional reputation. But I do so hate criminals."

"And I'm a capable engineer with no reputation. But I'm able to see through your ploy. So, out with it. What are you really up to?"

Joe straightened his tie and then reached into the breast pocket of his suit coat. He withdrew a small box, put it on the table beside their empty pizza pan, and pushed it toward Avery.

Avery furrowed her brow with uncertainty. She opened the box slowly. She looked up at Joe with a questioning look.

"What's this?"

"I thought you might like a little gift. It's more *you* than me."

Avery withdrew a small metal key fob from the box. She turned it over, examining it carefully. The fob was a stamped rendition of a grader, similar to the one Jasper poised to disrupt her ox roast. "I don't get it. You want me to have this as what? A memento of our little victory over Jasper's shenanigans?"

"If you want it to be," Joe said, taking a sip of beer. "Before I was a county prosecutor," he explained, "I was a fairly decent trial lawyer for hire. I won a case for a wealthy dealer of heavy equipment against a fictitious claim that his equipment had been faulty, which led to an injury accident. He gave me that fob after the trial."

She turned the fob over again, continuing to examine the accuracy of the stamped metal. "I hope he gave you more than this little token for your legal services," Avery said.

"Oh yes. I didn't come cheap. He paid me quite well. My work as his attorney saved him many thousands of dollars in that suit. As a matter of fact, it was his generous fee deposited into my bank account that made it possible for me to run as a small-time prosecutor. That money still makes it possible for me to afford to pay your rent and buy a few meals here and there. You hang onto that fob. I think you'll be able to slip some county keys on it in a few months."

Avery wondered what had ever made her doubt Joe's loyalty toward her political ambitions.

Then Joe asked, "Could you... one day... accept something more than beer, pizza, and road closure permits from me, do you think?"

Avery looked up. She had never considered this possibility. Ever. While other girls grew up playing with Barbie and doll houses, Avery preferred Tonka trucks and sand piles. In high school, she was fascinated by math, especially algebra and geometry. She hung out with all the nerdy boys from physics class because they talked about science. None of them seemed to know how to pursue a girl, which suited her just fine. She felt safe among them, not awkward like she did at this very moment. All during her college days, she focused, obsessed really, over doing well in every subject she studied. She missed every collegiate sporting event because she was either in a lab or a library. She couldn't even to this day recite the name of her college mascot. Dating had never been a subject covered in her curriculum. *Boyfriend* wasn't even a word in her lexicon.

"Joe, I'm not," she tried to think of a kind word, but none came to mind. So she stammered, "I'm not... I'm... ignorant... I guess I should say. I've never thought about boys... men... dating, I mean."

"No surprise there. Your attire told me that," he said, taking another sip of beer and leaning back in his seat with a grin on his face.

Avery had not changed clothes. She still wore the Dockers and Oxford shirt she'd worn for the ox roast. She thought about Rosie's admonition to always dress the part of a candidate. So, she had not changed into her favorite jeans before heading out for the pizza. "I dress for work," she said somewhat defensively.

"Me too," Joe said, running a hand down his blue tie.

"You always look great. Very legal-eagle-like."

"Thank you. And I think you look great, too, as an engineer and as a candidate for office, not as some hot dish out prowling for a date. It's something I strangely like about you. You have a focus on your career that I find rare in most women. Making roads or gathering votes, that's what will win you this election, you know. Your focus. Your dedication. I also like that you're smart, though not in the ways of politics, but you seem to learn quickly."

"Are you fishing for a date?"

"No. Not today. But I am asking if you'd consider it sometime in the future."

Avery remained silent, trying desperately to think straight. Her mind was frozen in awkwardness. This was a situation she had never anticipated.

"I can see the cogs of your brain churning," he said, taking another sip of beer. "Are you estimating how much it might cost to construct a personal relationship? Where that road might lead?"

She blushed slightly. "Something like that."

"Then just think about it, OK? Take a short detour over to my place once in a while. Like I said, I don't cook, but you're welcome to use my kitchen."

"I don't cook either."

"Then we're perfect for each other. Educated professionals without any homemaking skills whatsoever. Take-out twins."

Avery slid the empty box back toward Joe and put the metal fob into her pocket. "Time spent together. Friendship. No dates. Take-out. No cooking. No speculations about any romantic relationship between us."

"Your friend, Rosie, will be disappointed. But for now, that works for me. I'm a very patient man. And if you should decide to try boyfriend and girlfriend…"

"Not boy/girl. Just friends."

"Acceptable for now." Joe raised his beer glass for a toast. "To our enduring friendship."

Avery touched her glass to his. "To the road ahead."

Just then, Avery's phone vibrated. She pulled it out of her pocket. The call was from Ximi Ling.

"I should take this," she said to Joe.

Avery's ears were assaulted by a string of rapid-fire words as Ximi stumbled over each one, trying to get the next one out. Her call was about Simone.

To Joe, Avery said, "Simone's in trouble. Ximi sounds desperate!"

Avery tried to slow Ximi down with questions. "What happened? Where was she calling from?"

"I don't know," Ximi said. "She just said, 'Help me. I need to talk to you.' She left the message in my voicemail today while we were all out at the ox roast. I just now saw the message and tried to call her back. No luck. She's not answering."

"Anything wrong?" Joe asked, hearing only Avery's side of the call.

"It's our friend, Simone Beck. Ximi received a message from her and thinks she might be in trouble."

"Beck?" Joe asked, his body tensing. He put down his beer glass. "Is that the same Beck as Coach Beck?"

"His wife, actually. Simone." Avery turned her attention back to Ximi. "Where are you?"

"I'm in town," Ximi said.

"Me too. Meet me at the Tea Basket Hall. Lois was heading over after the ox roast, so we can touch base there and decide what to do."

"I'm coming with you," Joe said, rising to his feet.

"As a friend?" Avery asked.

"As a prosecutor," he replied.

Nora was descending the steps with Lois beside her just as Ximi burst through the front door of the hall, panting from having run from her car parked some distance down the block. She noticed that Ximi was wearing running shoes this time. She could see her little friend also wore a worried expression on her face.

"What's wrong, dear? What's the rush?" Nora asked.

Nora, trying to calm Ximi down, placed both hands on the Asian woman's arms and had her sit down in a chair. "Breathe. That's it. Slow down and tell us what's wrong."

"I'm worried about Simone. She called, sounding really upset... Left a message on my cell... But now she isn't answering... My calls go right to voice mail. Avery's coming here to meet up. We need to *do something*. I just know it!"

Avery came through the door just then with a man at her heels who Nora did not at first recognize. But then she remembered where she had seen the red head of hair. He was the county prosecutor, Joe O'Feeny. A Democrat. Chair of the local party. She wondered about his presence with Avery.

"Avery," Nora said, "You've brought us a distinguished guest."

"A friend," Avery corrected.

Ximi turned around to see the pair. "We have to do something, Avery. I think Kyle's hurt her. I can't prove it. But I'm worried. Her voice... she sounded so scared."

"Did she say she'd notified authorities?" Joe asked. "What's her address?"

Ximi's eyes widened at the sound of his voice. She had failed to notice him coming through the door behind Avery. She had not thought about getting the law involved. She knew Simone's address by heart and repeated it to Joe. "I don't know if she's called anybody but me," she stammered. "I don't really know anything at all. It's just that I have a sense that she's hurt. The sound of her voice quivering like… that frightens me."

Joe pulled out his own cell phone and punched up a number, turning his back on the women huddled around Ximi. He walked a few steps back toward the door, keeping his voice low so they couldn't hear his conversation. He soon disconnected, pocketed the phone, and turned back to them. "The sheriff's office hasn't received any domestic abuse call from anyone named Beck or from anyone at that address."

"What can we do?" Ximi asked.

Avery looked at Joe.

"Be careful," he advised. "Your friend made a call for assistance only to you. Could be nothing. But if you could pay her a visit. Seeing her in person might determine what's going on. Personally, I think you *should* be worried."

"What do you mean, Joe?" Avery asked.

Joe shrugged nonchalantly. "Sometimes a call for help to a friend can mean more than it seems. That's all."

"Let's all three go," said Lois, who stood nearby but remained silent to this point. She was still in full offense mode from the incident with Jasper and his grader. She was ready to battle anyone trying to take advantage of one of her guild sisters.

"Any chance you could use your campaign as a pretext for a visit?" Joe asked.

"No," Avery replied. "We already did that. Kyle was at the house. He never left her side the whole time we were with her."

"Sounds like a familiar tactic," Joe said.

"Tactic?" Nora asked.

"An abuser will hover around his victim. Never leave the woman alone with anyone."

"Then let's use Tea Baskets as an excuse," suggested Lois. "Don't we have a stack of tops for bed quilts needin' quiltin' and a bunch of pillows that need deliverin' to Harbor House?"

They looked at each other. It was a weak excuse just to make a house call, but it was the only one they had.

16

"Call 911 immediately if you find harm done to your friend," Joe instructed Avery. "Then call me."

Joe decided not to accompany the women to the Beck home. He backtracked on his earlier prediction, too. As nonchalantly as possible, he tried to reassure them.

"I'm thinking you'll probably discover everything alright with your friend."

His plan was to retreat to his office until he heard otherwise from Avery. In reality, what Joe did not say was prosecuting a case would be complicated if the prosecutor was also a witness to a crime. In this case, Joe wanted to be the prosecutor, not a witness, to bring this particular man down.

Avery nodded goodbye to Joe as he departed for his office. The three friends left Nora in the hall. Avery's long strides brought her to her truck first. She opened both passenger doors for Lois and Ximi. Ximi hopped easily into the back seat, pulling her door closed immediately, eager to get to Simone's. Lois struggled slightly to climb up into the front. Avery jogged around to the driver's side and stepped up into the F350, taking her place behind the wheel while Lois pulled her door shut, and her two friends fumbled with rarely used seat belts.

Ximi leaned forward from the back seat of the extended cab to better engage her friends. "What's the plan? How are we going to do this?"

"Let's see," Lois turned around and said, "If Simone can get quilts to Harbor House."

Avery turned the key in the ignition and put the truck in gear. As she pulled into the street, Lois asked, "Was that Joe O'Feeny, the prosecutor, with *you*?"

Avery smiled. It had never occurred that Lois or any Tea Basket member might be interested in her affairs. *Affair.* The word, wrong choice of word, both amused her while at the same time making her feel slightly uneasy. Was that because of the idea of an affair? Or was it because now her friends knew something about her just being in Joe's company? She brushed off feelings.

"Yeah. I tried to buy him a pizza dinner to thank him for that road closure permit."

"Smart guy," Lois said, satisfied with her answer.

Avery drove the distance to the Beck house with no further conversation between the three. Ximi was unusually subdued, staring intently out the side window. Lois stared straight ahead, watching the truck pass under the glow of street lights. When they arrived at Simone's, they all piled out at once. Avery, once again in the lead, knocked on the front door, flanked by her companions.

To their surprise, Simone opened the door.

Simone looked surprised but seemingly unharmed and dressed as neatly as ever. Her long hair was tied up in her usual French knot. Her makeup looked professional, though somewhat heavy. She invited her friends in at once and ushered them into the living room. The house appeared as spotless as Lois recalled it being the last time they had been inside.

Avery noticed that nothing seemed out of place.

Before they were seated, Ximi could contain herself no longer and launched into a string of words.

"I'm so sorry. I couldn't call you back sooner, Simone. My phone was on the fritz. Just got it fixed today. Then I did call. But you didn't answer. I was worried about you. You told me to call at once. And…"

Simone held up her hands in surrender. "Whoa. It's OK. It's OK. I called you only because I wanted to apologize to you for my behavior a few days ago," she lied. "I was out of line. I know you were only trying to be a good friend. I was being overly sensitive. But really, everything is fine. My phone is… out of commission, too, at the moment." Simone took a seat on her couch, and the rest followed her cue, with Ximi sitting next to her friend.

"You don't need to worry about me. Not at all. Not one little bit. Kyle is not the man you think he is, Ximi. He's not a bad person. I should apologize again because I've been cleaning. I can't hear it ring when I'm running the vacuum, so I just turn it off. But I'm perfectly OK. See?" Simone spread her arms wide as if to allow her guild friends to examine every inch of her body.

Ximi hugged Simone. Simone hugged back. "You said your phone was on the fritz."

Simone tried to explain as quickly as she could. "Ah, yeah, having problems with reception, that's all."

Avery looked at the embrace of the two friends. She had a difficult time understanding how some people found it so easy to demonstrate care for others with just a simple embrace. Looking on made her feel like she was intruding. She averted her eyes to the wall to give them privacy. Her wandering observation followed the wall down to the floor, along the baseboard, and stopped at a spot under the edge of a credenza in the hallway leading to the kitchen. Something caught her attention. A small white piece of something was wedged under the edge of the cabinet. She got up without thinking and pried the edge with her fingernail until it came loose. She stood there holding a piece of broken china. "I think your vacuum missed this," she said, turning the shard over to Simone.

Simone's cheeks turned visibly pink, even through her heavy makeup. She accepted the broken piece of pottery into the palm of her hand.

"Oh." She said, laughing nervously. "I dropped a cup the other day, and it broke into a million pieces. This apparently escaped my cleanup attempt."

"Looks like a chunk of that Rothschild pattern," Lois said, eyeballing the bit of pattern on the small wedge in Simone's open hand."

"Oh dear, yes. I'm so sorry, too. I love that set, which came from all of you. I'll have to order replacements."

"*Replacements?*" Ximi asked. "You broke more than just a cup?"

"Oh… ah… yes. I broke the saucer, too. I was very clumsy. Slipped, carrying them to the sink. Both crashed to the floor."

An uncomfortable silence fell on the group.

Avery decided to move the conversation toward their fabricated reason for stopping. "We came here to ask if you could help us deliver quilts and pillows to Harbor House."

Simone was grateful the topic of broken dishes had been dismissed. "Oh, thank you, but I thought someone from Harbor House was going to pick them up from the hall. I read that in the minutes. Anyway, I don't have a car anymore, so I can't be of much help."

Lois chimed in. "They were, and they do. But we all wanted to make a special trip soon. We want to meet some of the women who might be recipients of our handiwork. Let them know we support them since they're forced to seek shelter. Thought you'd maybe like to join us," she lied.

Simone's emotions were raw. She struggled to maintain an even expression on her face. She was relieved the topic of broken dishes had been forgotten so quickly. But now, she needed to avoid the wrath of her husband. She couldn't leave the house without his approval. She was desperate to keep that secret from these women and satisfy the man who seemed forever to be at odds with her behavior. Not knowing when he might return, she needed to get them out of the house as quickly as possible.

"Well, thank you, Lois, but I must decline. I need to stay here. I've much to do before Kyle returns."

"Are you sure you won't go with us?" begged Ximi.

"Yes. Quite sure. Is there anything else?"

With little more to achieve, Ximi looked at the others with sadness. She hugged Simone again, then Lois and Avery said their goodbyes and retreated to Avery's truck. As Avery backed out of the Beck drive, she saw Simone in her rear view mirror. Simone was standing at her front door waving. Avery could have sworn the woman was crying.

They had traveled only a hundred yards down the road when Lois could no longer hold her thoughts. "Was it a broken cup, or a broken saucer, or more? That's what I want to know. She didn't have 'much to do.' That was an excuse. My gut says lots of her dishes got broke, and she's not bein' honest 'bout who's done the breakin'."

"I feel the same," Ximi said. "She didn't look all that beat up like I imagined. So, I guess I was panicky for nothing. Still, I can't shake this feeling that something is wrong."

"What could she possibly have to do anyway? Did you see that house of hers? Not a single item outta place, 'cept that little speck o' broken china you spied, Avery. A body could eat a meal off her floors; they're so clean," Lois said.

"We tried," Avery said. "Kyle wasn't there to stop her. If she was in a bad situation, we offered her the way out. She chose not to take it. So everything probably is okay between them, and we're mistaken."

"Well, I, for one, am *not* convinced," Lois said, folding her arms across her bosom in defiance.

Ximi found herself feeling alone in the back seat of Avery's truck. No further conversations were exchanged among the friends on the drive back to the hall. Lois stared out the window again. Ximi sat sullenly behind them, looking straight ahead at nothing. Avery concentrated on driving and frequently checked her rearview mirror, thinking about the image of Simone standing alone in a doorway.

When they returned, Nora peppered them with questions, but no one had anything to report other than Simone's insistence that all was well. Avery soon excused herself to go home. It had been a long day, and she needed sleep. Her campaign staff of volunteers had undoubtedly identified a neighborhood for her to canvas tomorrow. She'd need to get an early start. Lois left for her farm. Only Ximi lingered to stew a little while longer, resigned to hearing words of wisdom from Nora about the virtues of patience and the difficulties one must sometimes endure to remain a good friend.

Avery called Joe from her truck. He was still in his office. She thought he sounded somewhat disappointed that they had found nothing out of place at the Beck house other than one piece of broken china. She mocked Joe for sounding like a zealous prosecutor looking for a crime to prosecute. She suggested he consider corporate law. It might cure his case of cynicism and suspicion about everyone.

Joe roared with laughter at the thought of him tied to a law firm, swimming with a school of corporate lawyers. "No, thank you."

He had tasted private corporate law. But Joe O'Feeny lived for criminal law. He was the one barracuda in this small pond of unlimited jack and mullets. That's what gave him reason to rise every morning. He liked sitting in the prosecutor's office at any hour, and he enjoyed putting bad people behind bars. Joe ate criminals for lunch. This evening, he was sure he'd caught the scent of a nearby culprit and found he needed to be content to lurk in the shallows, waiting for the guy to reveal himself for what he was. His prey eluded him this day. Who knew what tomorrow would bring?

He asked Avery if she might come over tomorrow so they could dip into the takeout jar at his place for more Miller's chicken. Avery thought maybe she'd be able to meet him around seven. Joe agreed. Then Joe changed his mind and asked her to think about going to a restaurant for a sit-down meal instead of takeout.

Avery agreed, but she didn't know why she'd done so and agreed to do it so quickly. She usually knew why she did things.

Avery arrived at Rosie's house the next morning, rested and ready for work. Just as she stepped out of her truck, she passed a supporter who was leaving with a campaign yard sign. She was pleased to see the sign going out. She nodded to the man and thanked him for his support.

The man smiled back. He lifted the sign and said, "This one better stay put, eh?"

The comment seemed odd. She brushed it off as she bounded up Rosie's front steps two at a time, then walked into the dining room. As usual, the place was bustling, with volunteers bumping into each other, trying to find a clear path around the dining room table. Piles of boxes containing campaign literature, plastic yard signs, and metal frames for the signs were stacked everywhere, making the space difficult to navigate.

"Hey guys," Avery said cheerfully. "I see some of our signs are going out."

Rosie's head popped up behind one of the stacks of boxes. She was removing metal frames and stacking them against a wall. She wore a serious look on her face.

"Yes, they're going out," she said curtly, "then they're walking away. That man who just left stopped by for a replacement."

Avery gave her a questioning look.

"He picked up a yard sign yesterday. Gave us a nice donation. Very nice man. But he came back today to get another because the one he put out yesterday afternoon vanished overnight."

"Somebody swiped a sign?"

"They did. And what's more, lots of them were stolen last night. He was the sixth person today to stop by for another."

"Tenth!" corrected the voice of a young man from the kitchen area.

Rosie's shoulders slumped. She corrected herself, "*Tenth* person to report thefts today. Somebody's been very busy putting a dent in our advertising."

"Where is this happening, all over town, or just in one neighborhood? Probably just some bad boys having a bit of fun at our expense," Avery said.

Rosie shrugged, but the attentive young volunteer piped up again. "The guy who just left lives near me, in the country. One of the other folks who came in earlier lives out that way, too. I can ask anyone else stopping to pick up a replacement where they live if you want. Maybe we can find out if the thefts are localized. Or maybe it's widespread."

"Will you do that?" Avery asked him.

"Can do, boss."

The thefts puzzled Avery. She was also curious about the young volunteer. He looked familiar. She tried to recall his name but couldn't.

"Excuse me," she said, "I apologize, but I can't remember your name, yet I'm sure we've met somewhere other than here.

"Oh, I used to work for you. Well, for the county engineer's office, anyway. I'm Frank Westfall."

Still, the name did not mean anything to Avery.

"I was one of your unpaid summer interns," he explained. Jasper stuck me on a crew with a shovel so I could dig out plugged culverts. I overheard you tell him I'd be better utilized on something more cerebral. He didn't like your idea, so I got to spend my summer sweating a lot and knee-deep in mud alongside jailhouse trustees."

Finally, Avery remembered seeing him at the garage before he'd left with the crew. She hated wasting his talents. Disliked Hollister for causing the waste. Westfall had a four-point GPA and was interested in and trained in GIS/GPS. He could have been a big help with mapping, but Jasper insisted he go out and get dirty. "Take that look of superiority off his face," were the words Jasper used to justify his assignment.

"Oh, I remember you now. So you've been promoted from ditches to data volunteer. I'd say you're moving up."

Frank grinned. "You bet. I figure if I help you win this election, maybe next time I apply for an internship with the county, I might get a crack at mapping or something better than digging ditches."

"Next internship? Weren't you a graduating senior when you came to us?"

"I was. Now I'm working on my master's."

"Well, Frank, if I win this election and you want an internship again, I can promise that you will not end up digging out culverts. And you'll get paid."

Frank's smile broadened with anticipation.

Avery's thoughts turned back to the loss of yard signs. "Ten gone missing, huh?"

"So far," said Frank.

Rosie, still unpacking boxes, joined in. "Ten signs is no big deal. But if more go missing, I'd say we do have a problem. They cost money. Money we don't have to throw away."

"We don't have much to spare, do we?" Avery asked, remembering the gas credit card in her wallet and thinking about her truck's low gas mileage. "Maybe I should drive less and walk more."

"No, no," Rosie said. "You keep driving wherever you need to. I can make last-minute pleas to donors as the campaign nears a close or even after it concludes. I promise this little annoyance will not put us in debt."

The words *in debt* had never occurred to Avery. Without a job, those words unnerved her.

The front door to Rosie's opened, admitting two supporters. They were pleased to meet Avery and shook her hand. They offered verbal support and good wishes in the approaching election. The reason they stopped by, one explained, was because their yard signs had been stolen in the night, and they wondered if they could pick up replacements. Free if possible.

Avery looked to Frank. Frank looked at Rosie. Yes, they had a problem.

"Where do you live?" Frank asked, pen in hand, to take notes.

Simone closed the door as Avery's truck disappeared down the road. She felt weak. She pressed her forehead against the back of the door and stifled a sob.

Why did I ever make that call to Ximi? Foolish! I was foolish to question Kyle, to make him angry, so angry he broke my beloved Rothschild. No. They don't know I did that. I'm just paranoid. They can't possibly know. What would happen if I told them how I always make him angry? So angry he broke their china? I'd lose their friendship. That's what. I can't tell them. He's Kyle Beck, Coach Beck. I can't let them see me sniveling. Weak. Stupid. No one understands the failure I am

He's successful. He's popular. Everybody knows Coach Beck. Nobody knows me. Everyone says just how amazing he is and how lucky I am to have him. Yes. Kyle is amazing. Popular. Well-liked. He knows what's best for me. Always will. Kyle loves me. They don't know how stupid I've been.

Simone examined the ring on her trembling hand as her thoughts kept replaying the same questions and swirling around to offer up the same answers.

See? What kind of man would shower his wife with such a beautiful object? A good man. That's right. A good man. Kyle is a good man. I am the problem. Why can't I please him? What's wrong with me? I've tried. I've altered my schedule. I've quit my job. I'm home for him every day. I gave up my car. I've even given up my friends. What more must I do to prove my love?

Failure. That's what I am. Nothing but a stupid failure, a scatterbrained failure. Kyle says I'm crazy. Maybe I am. But I'm better than that crazy former fiancé of his, aren't I? She jilted him at the altar. I won't give up on him. I won't hurt him like she did. But how? How can I fix what's wrong?

17

Avery needed a moment to seek inner peace. She withdrew mentally from the world of bad news. She disliked this feeling of frustration. Losing yard signs to a petty thief was costing her campaign, however small. Still, it was an expense. Her war chest didn't have money to throw away. Instead of blowing off steam at campaign headquarters, she left Rosie's to continue her canvassing for votes but drove to the guild hall first for one of Nora's coffees and a bit of friendly counsel. She knew Nora would be a calming influence, like the kindly grandmother she imagined Nora to be, a grandmother Avery never had as a child.

Nora was bustling about, as usual, in the kitchenette when Avery walked through the doorway. The aroma of roasted coffee beans greeted her. Immediately, she felt better about the human race.

"Coffee ready?" Avery asked, walking toward Nora and retrieving a cup from the cupboard without waiting for an answer.

"Just in time, Avery," Nora said. "What brings you here so soon after last night's visit?"

"Your coffee, of course. And I could use your wisdom on a problem I have."

Nora looked pleased, then puzzled. The two pulled out chairs facing each other and sat down at one of the work tables. The room had been set up for a class with several tables and chairs scattered about the hall.

"Yard signs are disappearing after supporters put them out. Nearly a dozen people stopped today alone to get replacements. They all told the same story. They'd put out signs one day. Then, the signs were gone by morning. I'm upset about it." She drew a long breath, then took a sip of Nora's perfect hot coffee.

Nora was always available to offer free advice with a cup of coffee to anyone who came through the door of the Tea Basket Quilters Hall. She liked Avery and knew the woman was serious about needing her opinion. Nora rarely thought ill of anyone. Stealing signs seemed like a dirty little political trick. There was obviously no financial benefit to the thieves to take them. No money to be gained. "Oh dear. Sounds to me like some neighborhood kids pulling pranks. Probably boys. Girls would never do something like that."

Avery sipped Nora's hot coffee and nodded. That had been her first guess.

"Could it be your competitor?" Nora then asked.

That thought had never occurred to Avery. *Jasper? Hollister yanking up yard signs? What a silly, juvenile stunt to pull. Surely not.* "You think Hollister would stoop so low?"

"There's but one advantage to taking your signs," Nora suggested. "Stealing yard signs isn't for profit."

Lois entered the hall just then, catching Nora's words. Her arms were burdened with objects. She dropped a pillow encased in bright pink fabric on the table beside the door.

Blue prairie points finished off the hem. Beside it, she deposited a new package of paper towels into the laundry basket. That left her holding only her purse and a tote bag over her shoulder.

"Is that Jasper up to shenanigans?" asked Lois, joining the pair and taking a seat beside Nora. She had prepared an agenda and program for an upcoming meeting. The draft was stuffed into her purse. She had come to the hall to seek Nora's input before she printed copies for her members. She had also picked up take-out for herself on the way to the hall. The food was stored in the tote slung over her shoulder. She pulled a plastic bag out, a twelve-inch sub with extra cheese. She withdrew a bag of chips and a soda next. She then noticed Avery's troubled expression. She opened the bag of chips and offered some to Avery.

Avery accepted. "Isn't it kinda early for lunch?"

"Early?" Lois snorted. "I've been up since dawn doin' chores. I'm famished. Jasper pilferin' your signs? That a problem? Expensive, are they?"

"They are," said Avery. "Or can be if the thefts continue. My campaign doesn't have money to burn. That's really why it's annoying. I need to catch these little snatchers in the act. Make them stop. I can't keep replacing 'em. I need what few we've put out to keep my name out there before the election. The more signs, the more it appears I have major support."

"OK. I can do that," Lois responded immediately. "I know some farmers who can help out, maybe even donate, too. I'll make some calls, ask them to send you a check. How much should I ask for?"

"You've done too much already, Lois," Avery said. "You've let us use your place for the roast, donated the steer… "

Lois waved off her comment like a pesky fly in the face. "That steer was a nuisance. You needed a place, and I had one. But the money…" Lois paused. She knew several well-to-do farmers, as well as many more with small bank accounts like hers. She was positive they'd listen to her when she told them Avery was capable of the job and was the right choice for the office. *It wasn't neighborhood kids. Sounds like Jasper to me. Maybe one of Jasper's crew is ripping off Avery's signs. Ol' Jasper's getting' back at Avery for stoppin' him from crashin' her fund raiser.*

"Do you know where these signs were placed that went missin'?" she asked, munching on a chip while unwrapping her sub.

"There's a young man at Rosie's named Frank. He's tracking the losses," Avery said as she snatched more chips from Lois' bag in absent-minded frustration.

"I'm goin' over to Rosie's with my little checkbook soon. I'll ask this Frank when I get there."

"I'm going to report the theft to the sheriff. Probably nothing he can do since nobody saw who swiped them," Avery said, then sipped her coffee. "It's hardly grand theft. Still, replacing those little signs costs money, and I can' keep replacing them forever."

"Well then, you just tell the sheriff. Won't do no good, but you make your report," Lois said. She dipped her hand into the bag for a chip only to discover they were gone. Avery had hoovered them up in her frustration.

Avery noticed the disappointed look on her friend's face. "Those were really good, Lois. I'm afraid I ate them. Sorry."

Lois smiled. "Bar-B-Q's addictive, ain't they? I love taters."

Nora stood up. "I agree with Lois. You have to report the thefts. But there's probably nothing that will come of the effort. But somehow, you need to find out who's stealing from you."

Avery was disappointed. There was no easy solution to her problem. But at least she had shared the burden with friends. That alone seemed to ease her concerns a little.

Lois drove to Rosie's after Nora had wholeheartedly approved her agenda items and congratulated her on her work. Her planned demo on mitered binding was apropos for her beginners. At Rosie's house, Lois wrote a check for a modest sum and took two-yard signs. The young man who gave her a receipt for her contribution was Frank, whom she wanted to talk to about the disappearing signs.

"So, sounds like they're all walkin' off places with rural road frontage."

"Seems that way," Frank said. "Guess the culprits can get away easier out in the boonies. Plus, they all vanish during the night."

"S'pose somebody cared to lay a trap of sorts?"

"A trap? Like a leg-hold trap?" Frank said with a bit of horror in his eyes.

"Nah, nuthin' dangerous like. Somethin' harmless, painless too, but foolproof. You tell Avery when you see her that her friend, Lois, has a plan to catch her sign bandit. You know what a wildlife camera is, Frankie?"

Back at the farm, Lois set out on her golf cart, going up the dirt road that ran past her farmhouse and barn. She had Avery's signs strapped to the back of the cart and her wildlife camera in a little wire basket behind the bench. She drove just far enough that the signs would be hidden from view from her house but still located within reach to offer temptation to the thief. Along the edge of a hay field where cars had recently parked for the ox roast, she found just the spot. She steered off the road and drove up a gentle bank into the field. She parked, picked up her signs and the camera, and walked back along the edge of the bank. As she walked away from her golf cart, the bank gradually became steeper, offering the kind of spot she required.

Her helpers had taken the first cutting of hay off this field in May. The grass had grown back over the summer months to the height of two feet nearer the bank. They'd missed a swath inside the barbed wire fence when they cut it once again in preparation for Avery's fundraiser. But for now, this long stretch of tall grass offered the perfect location to conceal her approach by foot. Should the thieves actually look for a trail, which she seriously doubted they were smart enough to do, they'd not notice her camera. Still, she took every precaution not to leave any trail to mark her efforts.

She stepped in the signs at the top of the bank, placing them in such a way that they appeared vulnerable for the taking, yet not exactly easy to reach. To take them, the thieves would have to approach from the road and scramble up the bank. The fence above would prevent them from approaching from any other direction. She reckoned the incline would slow them down on the way up. Just what she needed. They would pull up the sign, then turn and scoot back down the bank to the road. Their escape would look easy, and her signs would be an easy target, she hoped.

Along the top of the bank, amid a large clump of redbud and sassafras saplings in the fence line, Lois knelt to set up the camera. The thicket grew too far up the embankment for the county road crew to trim with their brush hog. There, it was also too steep even for Lois to cut with her weed whacker from above. It provided the perfect spot to hide the camera.

She strapped the green box near the base of a sassafra. The camera was elevated barely above the tops of the grass. She checked the lens orientation, making a small adjustment so that the camera was pointed directly toward her signs with the incline beyond. If she was accurate in her placement, she would catch the face of the thief or thieves as they climbed up the hill toward her sign. Satisfied she had arranged it properly, she opened the front panel, pushed one small switch to the infrared setting and another switch to activate the camera's motion sensor. Anything that moved past the sensor would trigger the devise to snap a photo. The longer movement occurred in the camera's line of sight, the more photographs it would take. With the setting on infrared, the subject wouldn't know they were being filmed. She would have a face as the culprit approached and his back as he departed.

Satisfied, she walked casually back to the golf cart with a lighthearted step. She was careful not to follow the same path she had travelled on her way to the thicket of sassafras. All that remained was to wait for the signs to vanish. Then she'd have all the proof her friend Avery needed.

Lois paused and sat a moment behind the wheel of the golf cart, taking in the view of her hay field and the surrounding hills covered in trees. The hay was good this year. She'd gotten several hundred bales from the first cutting and almost as many from the second. Now, all was stored inside the barn, waiting for late fall when the pastures no longer produced enough forage for her little herd. She probably had enough hay this year to see her through the coming winter all the way to April, when the pastures would once again sprout and grow enough forage to sustain the cattle. There were many moments in her life when Lois felt very content and happy to work and live in the country. Today was one of those moments. If only her daughter could have seen and felt that sense of contentment. Lois sighed. She wished her daughter would call, write, or visit. It had been years since she had seen her. Years.

Lois turned the key and pressed her foot to the golf cart pedal, and the engine rattled to life for the drive back home.

Tensions were increasing in the Beck household. Simone felt edgy, confused, and frustrated. If she dared speak her mind, she knew he'd knock her down again. He told her she was childish.

"Only children complain as much as you," he'd yelled. Any frustrations she felt, he told her, were her own doing. She needed to "stop being so self-centered. Your place is in the home. Running a household. That should offer you all the challenges you need. If not, then you have only your own unimaginative self to blame." At least, that's what Kyle said.

But her best efforts to please him still weren't going well. He wasn't satisfied that the house was perfect, a hot meal waited for him on the table when he got home, and that she was present for him. He was more often grumpy and short with her than he was kind like he had been in those days when she'd first met him. Sometimes, he would come home and instantly burst into a rage. That would be followed by a show of being wounded. He'd spill his own feelings of pain and disappointment onto her. He expected her to listen and sympathize. Perhaps a member of the university had insulted his ego. Perhaps he felt his reputation was under attack. At those moments, Kyle seemed so vulnerable to her. He needed all the comfort she could offer. And she was willing and eager to offer support.

Of course, Simone gave him comfort. She lavished him with caresses. She was tender; her body was what he required. She gave him all her love and devotion willingly. He was her husband. And yet, the next day, he would once again be short with her. He'd cut off her own feelings with criticism. And if she apologized for her behavior, he would always make a point to blame her for having triggered his anger.

Kyle's hot and cold mood swings left Simone reeling. She dared not bring up his behavior unless she was prepared for a lashing from his tongue. Or worse. He might accuse her of planning to leave, "just like that bitch before!" That would remind Simone of the pathetic picture he had painted for her so early in their relationship: poor Kyle, standing alone at the altar, pieces of his heart held like a shattered crystal goblet falling apart in his open hand. The parallel he drew worked every single time. Simone would stop wondering about Kyle and begin to doubt herself for being uncaring.

No matter what she tried to do to please him, she failed more and more, or so it seemed to her. Her meals weren't hearty enough, or they were served too cold, or they did not contain the correct balance of protein to carbs. The floor might be spotless, but she had neglected to dust some pieces of furniture, or one window did not gleam in the morning's sun. Her attire was also a target of his disapproval. That outfit was too passé for a coach's wife. This one made her look like a whore. One color was OK on Monday, but the next week, it made her look sickly. She should wear slacks more. She shouldn't wear slacks at all. They made her butt look big. Her hair looked fine. Her hair looked old.

There were evenings when Simone quietly curled up in her favorite chair with a piece of embroidery, trying to blend into the fabric like a chameleon. She learned to be exceptionally alert when Kyle was acting withdrawn. Over dinner, he would begin telling her all about his day, to which she was always attentive. But as the evening progressed, he'd become more and more removed. Simone had learned over the months that this remoteness was a sign that he was about to erupt like a volcano. He'd spew a stream of angry criticisms at her. Her solution was to make every effort not to engage him in any form of conversation. She would pray that whatever she had done was insignificant enough that his irritation at her would wane before they retired for the night. She had learned that any conversation with Kyle might be construed as a challenge, a conflict to be swiftly resolved by hurtful accusations or by his fist.

That evening, shortly after dinner, their doorbell rang. Simone jumped and ran to answer it, sensing the need to keep the home quiet. Outside the door stood a group of neighborhood children gathering orders for candy bars for a school fundraiser. They were raising money for the band. Simone's first instinct was to turn them away with a simple "no thank you." But they were so cute and earnest in reciting their sales pitch that she made the mistake of asking them to wait while she went to get a checkbook for an order.

She returned to the living room to ask Kyle for their checkbook. As soon as she addressed him, she saw his eyes squint suspiciously. He got up abruptly, retrieved the checkbook from his briefcase where he always kept it, and returned with a look of resentment. Simone knew at once she had violated another unwritten rule. Thinking that she should be conservative with her donation, Simone signed the children's paper and ordered only one box of chocolates. She made out the check for a small sum and sent the children on their way down the street toward the next house. She had no sooner closed the door behind them when Kyle was in her face.

"What is it with you?" he demanded. "Every urchin in this city comes to you for a handout, and you give them what they want. Do you know how hard money is to come by? Of course not. You don't work. You think I'm made of money. Well, I'm not. Why do you have to order every piece of junk that every school kid peddles? What's wrong with you?"

Simone could only blink with confusion. Which rapid-fire question was she to answer? She attempted to explain, tried to reason.

"They were just little kids going door to door to make money for the school band, Kyle. We'll have a chocolate bar to enjoy. It didn't cost much at all, see? Just ten dollars. I thought we had plenty of money. You're the one who wanted me to quit my job. You said you made enough for both of us. Was that not true?"

Kyle backhanded Simone, sending her to the floor of their entryway, down to the floor she had just that morning waxed and polished.

Simone felt the sting against her cheek, then her head struck the floor. She squeezed her eyes shut, reeling in pain.

"How many more times do I have to tell you not to argue with me?" he screamed at her. "Don't you ever, ever, accuse me of lying. Do you hear me?"

Kyle shoved Simone's crumpled body aside using their front door, pushing her out of his way as he stormed out of their house in anger.

Simone could hear the familiar sound of his car's ignition in spite of the ringing in her ears. She heard the tires on the gravel as he backed out of the drive. Then, she could hear the engine fading away as he drove off into the distance. She gathered herself up as best she could. Her face and head throbbed painfully. She checked her image in the hall mirror. No blood. But she could see a knot beginning to form where her head had come into contact with the floor.

Simone stumbled to the kitchen. There, she rummaged through her purse and withdrew her wallet. Kyle had forgotten to take away her credit cards. She removed one bank card, then turned and retreated to the front door. She opened the door but left it unlocked as she closed it behind her. She walked shakily down their drive, holding her hand against her cheek, which was now growing hot and still stinging. On the sidewalk, she turned in the opposite direction where she thought she'd heard Kyle travel. She had one destination in mind at that moment. She had no other thoughts at all. She just walked away.

Slowly, as the stinging in her face seemed to lessen, a series of new questions formed in her mind. *How long? How much longer can I take this?*

Beck returned home an hour later, carrying with him a small conciliatory bouquet of roses from a flower shop. He came through the door, dropped his keys on the side table, and called out for Simone in a pleasant voice.

He received only silence in reply.

He went from room to room, calling, "Simone, Simone, honey?" He felt his heart beginning to pound and clutched the bouquet tightly. Surely she hadn't left, he thought. When finally convinced that Simone was nowhere inside the house, he thought of looking for her phone. He found it—shattered in pieces but gathered in a heap near her purse, where she always kept both. Her purse was still there, which was a good sign.

Not until that moment did he recall that he had deleted all her contacts and that he had been the one to destroy her phone. He pulled out his own phone. But Kyle didn't know any of Simone's friends' phone numbers. He'd never asked, never paid any interest. In this moment, he regretted his mistake. From now on, he would be sure to learn their numbers. He'd keep them in his own phone. She didn't need a phone.

As he wondered who might know her whereabouts, Kyle remembered the recent visitors. There was that lesbian candidate for county engineer and the two women with her, that tiny Asian slut, Ximi, and that linebacker woman. He didn't remember the large woman's name, but using Google, he searched "Athens County elections" and scrolled to the Underwood for Engineer campaign website. A phone number gave him the number he would start with. He punched in the campaign number. To his surprise, a male voice answered, not a woman.

"Underwood for engineer, how can I help you?"

"Coach Beck here. I need to reach your candidate, Underwood. Is she around?"

"I'm sorry, sir, Avery's out soliciting votes at the moment. Can I take a message? Have her call you back when she returns?"

"This is an emergency. Give me her number, and I'll call her myself."

The volunteer, Frank Westfall, knew coach Beck from his undergrad days. He was just about to give the popular coach Avery's private number when he remembered Rosie's instructions. "Absolutely nobody, *nobody,* was to receive Avery's private cell phone number under *any* circumstances. Anything that's important should come to me." Her number, as a real estate agent, was public knowledge, plastered on the side of her car, and posted in newspaper ads and on For Sale signs all over the county. But under no circumstances was a volunteer ever to hand over the candidate's private number to *anyone.*

"Uh, sorry, coach. No can do. I can give you Rosie Dyer's number. She's the campaign treasurer. Would that be OK?"

Beck was about to go off on the guy but thought better. "Fine. Give me that number. But mark my word, you'll come to regret this."

Frank was momentarily taken aback. Then he rolled his eyes in mock distaste and recited Rosie's number politely. After Beck hung up, Frank spoke into the dead phone. "I can't be fired, jerk. Slaves have to be sold!" Frank sneered and flipped the phone a one-finger salute.

18

Rosie's phone buzzed. She reached into the pocket of her blue jacket and pulled it out to answer. She was used to calls coming at all hours, dinner time being no exception. It was probably a client looking for property.

She heard Beck's voice. The man seemed distressed.

"I need your help. Simone's gone missing… She's quite ill, you know… takes a lot of medications. I'm afraid something may have happened to her. She's not at home. Her purse is still here, butI have no idea where she's gone. Can you help? Do you have her friend, the Asian's phone number so I can call to see if she's seen her?"

Rosie's heart skipped a beat, but she listened skeptically. She assured the coach that she would do everything in her power to help locate Simone.

"No, I have no idea where Simone is. Nor do I have Ximi's number. Sorry. But I'll call you back as soon as I find out anything, anything at all. You've already checked with the sheriff and the hospital, I assume? Good. I'll phone if I, you know, if I have news."

Rosie returned the cell phone to her pocket, then looked across the table at her evening dinner companions, Joe O'Feeny and Avery Underwood.

Lois discovered her new Underwood campaign signs missing. She checked that evening right after feeding her cattle and driving her golf cart around the perimeter fence to ensure no heifer had escaped. With that pesky steer butchered she had one less thing to worry about. For that, she was grateful. But chores around the farm still required much of her time, and her days were long. After checking on the perimeter fence, she drove her golf cart up the road toward the hay field, turning around beyond the point where she had posted the signs the day before. As she had hoped, she couldn't spot them anywhere from the roadway where they should have been visible to passing cars. She smiled, knowing what had happened.

Lois opened the gate to the pasture, then drove into the field and veered back along the road bank. She drove to the sassafra trees, not caring this time that she was crushing down grass, leaving a clear trail behind the cart. No matter. She now had proof and would soon know the identity of the political sign thief, caught in the act of petty larceny frame after frame.

She removed the tiny card from the camera back and slipped it into her bib overalls. She removed the camera from the trees and tossed it into the basket behind the seat of the golf cart. Once home, Lois changed out of her dungarees and struggled into one of her floral dresses for a trip into town. After she dabbed away a bit of sweat from her forehead, she checked her hair and image in the hall mirror. Satisfied she was presentable to the public, she picked up her purse and image card and headed outside to her truck for a quick drive to the sheriff's office to make a report in person.

"That was Beck," Rosie said, looking at her dinner companions. "Seems the coach can't find Simone anywhere. Purse is still in their house, he says. He sounds worried. Said she's on medication. Like I believe that! Simone's one of the healthiest people I know, next to Ximi Ling. He says he's afraid something may have happened to her. Maybe she's lying in a ditch somewhere."

Joe's muscles tensed as if prepared for a fight. *Could Beck have done something to his wife? Might he's creating an alibi?* "Did he say he called 911?" Joe asked.

"Said he did," she replied.

Joe pulled out his own phone, punched up a contact, and waited. "This is O'Feeny. Did you get a recent 911 call about a missing woman? A Simone Beck? Yeah, I'll hold."

Rosie and Avery watched Joe, waiting for the answer.

They didn't wait long.

"The dispatcher reported 'Negative.' Joe relized Beck had just lied. "He never made any call to 911 to report Simone missing or in danger."

Rosie looked at Joe in disbelief.

It was Avery's turn to feel uneasy and anxious. "Why would he lie about something like that? Is she ill?"

"No!" said Rosie. "Simone is not ill."

"Why indeed. I think he's playing you, Rosie. He's painting a picture of his wife as sick or maybe mentally disturbed. My guess is she's jumped in her car and left him."

Joe did not tell them his other thought, a gruesome one about the woman's possible whereabouts or condition. He knew that Rosie and Avery were Simone's friends. It would be insensitive of him to dump unfounded suspicions on them.

"But Simone doesn't have a car. She sold it," Avery said.

"Who's her best friend?" Joe asked.

Both Rosie and Avery spoke simultaneously. "Ximi Ling."

Joe looked at Rosie, arched his red eyebrows, and nodded toward her suit pocket where she stored her phone. "Call Ximi."

"Right." Rosie scrolled nervously through her addresses until she came to Ling, then punched the screen. "Ximi. Rosie here. Is Simone with you?"

The sun had barely set by the time Simone walked wearily back through her front door. She had seen Kyle's car parked in the drive. There was little doubt in her mind that she was about to face his wrath once again. She also had little doubt that this time, she would stand her ground no matter what the cost. At some point during her walk, the clouds of doubt vanished, and she began to think clearly. The bump on her head had knocked sense back into her mind. She stopped questioning herself and began to question him, particularly his motives. The answers she arrived at did much to bolster her courage and resolve. She realized she did have worth, had had it long before she met or married Kyle, and was determined to get all of it back. The thought of going up against him, however, made her fear what was to happen when she did confront him. She prepared herself mentally for the worst.

Kyle had been sulking alone in a chair in their darkened living room when he heard the front door open then close. Simone had come home to him. He rose quickly to confront her. He found her standing in their kitchen just as their house phone began to ring. He ignored the phone, letting the call go to voicemail. He was intent on punishing his wife for her behavior. Her back was toward him. She had picked up her purse. It dangled by her side, the strap slung over her left shoulder. He saw she was preparing to leave once again. He was determined she would never leave. Never!

Simone turned around, hearing his arrival. Her arms hung down by her sides, her trembling hands hidden behind the folds of her skirt. She looked tired, her eyes swollen from hours of crying. Her hair, usually not a strand out of place, wrapped neatly in a French twist, fell loosely about her head and shoulders. Her cheek was red and bore a developing bruise from his fist. Her forehead was swollen.

"Where the hell have you been?" he demanded.

Simone took a deep breath to steady her nerves before speaking. She held herself as tall as possible. "Out," was all she said.

"Out? Out where?"

"I went for a long walk."

"Ran out's more like it. Where did you run off to? To your *girlfriend*s, I suppose," he sneered mockingly.

"I went for a walk… a long walk… to think about you… to think about all the things you've done to me."

"*I've* done to *you*? Why, you ungrateful, self-centered fool." Kyle stepped closer, threateningly. "You're the one who's hurt me."

"Stop! Stop right there," Simone said, holding up a hand like a traffic cop. "Don't come any closer. I don't want you near me… not now… not ever again."

"You don't order me around, woman. I stand where I please," Kyle took another menacing step forward.

Simone was ready. Kyle had not noticed that she held one of their kitchen knives in her dominant hand, hanging it down by her side and hiding it behind her skirt. As he approached menacingly, she thrust the knife out in front of her, the long blade glistening before him.

Kyle stopped short.

"No, Kyle," Simone said, "Tonight you're going to listen to *me*. You've tried to make me feel like I was losing my mind. You've hit me. You've coerced me. You've demeaned me. You tried to make me feel worthless and nearly succeeded, too. But tonight I've decided, *no more*. No more intimidation. No more disrespect. No more abuse. You will no longer hurt me or my body. You've pushed, pulled, slapped, and kicked me down for the last time. Do you hear *me*?"

Kyle took a step back and raised both hands as if to surrender.

"Look, I'm sorry. Maybe I've been a jerk, but I love you. I only get angry when you make me angry. You push my buttons."

"Stop blaming me for how you behave! I'm leaving. This marriage is over. And don't try to stop me."

"And just where do you think you'll go, huh? You walk out of here, and I'll cut you off from everything—credit cards, bank account, everything. You'll come crawling back. Just you wait and see."

"No, Kyle. I won't come back, not after the pain you've caused. I don't care what you do. I'll sleep under an overpass while snow flies if I have to. Any place will be safer than being under the same roof with you."

Kyle suddenly lunged at her. He caught Simone off guard.

She was no match for him.

He rushed hard against Simone's chest with one hand outstretched like one of his running backs plowing through a defensive lineman.

Simone folded. She crumpled with the hit.

He struck her with his other forearm and knocked the knife from Simone's outstretched hand to send it flying. The knife plunged to the floor with a rattle, sliding beyond her reach. Kyle pinned Simone against the counter. One hand pinned her around her neck, preventing her from falling to the floor. He sneered at her, breathing hard, his breath hot with anger, gloating at his superior strength and quickness.

He noticed the other knives still parked in a block on the counter. He took one out and shoved the block away. Block and knives hit the floor on the far side of the island.

"You're stupid," he snarled. "I'm going to have to teach you a lesson."

Grabbing Simone's hair, he jerked her away from the counter and spun her around, striking her hard against the same cheek he had earlier hit.

As before, she fell to the floor limp, nearly unconscious. Her purse fell away, most of its contents scattering across the floor: a credit card, house keys, tissues, a small brush, and a new burner phone.

Kyle took no notice.

In his rage, he focused only on the source of his anger. If he had, he might have seen the cell phone was on and active. His rage was all-consuming. He fixated on obliterating the object of his wrath. Sweat dripped from his temple, and a bead ran down along his chin.

He paused to admire the handle of the knife he had taken from the block, then caressed the blade and smiled down at Simone with menace. He was in no hurry now that she was disarmed. There was nothing she could do to him. He approached Simone's limp form and bent down over her, experimentally choosing the best point of entry for the blade. He touched the tip of the knife to her throat then lowered it to her chest. Should she die slowly, or should she die quickly?

"I think I'm going to have fun, my dear, dear wife, watching you die a long, slow, painful death. You can never leave me. Never. I'll think of a way to keep your useless body right here near our happy little home, *forever*."

He reached for her auburn hair, grabbed a fistful, and yanked her head up off the floor. He moved the knife toward her ear.

Simone was petrified. There was indeed nothing she could do to stop him. In a haze, she wished for death. Her greatest overriding fear was not death but that he meant what he said. He would kill her slowly.

Kyle Beck suddenly felt the most excruciating pain in his spine. His knees buckled. A split second later, he felt a second blow. This one to his temple. His vision of Simone began to fade. Then everything went dark.

Ximi bent over Simone, reaching out to touch her neck, to check on her friend's condition. Ximi could see blood trickling down the side of Simone's bruised face. Her friend had a severe laceration above the eye. She felt a pulse along the woman's carotid artery. Simone was alive. Ximi turned back to the limp form of Beck sprawled on the floor where she had put him. She stood up, stepped over to him, and kicked the knife across the floor far from his grasp. For extra measure, arguing with herself that it was only to see if the beast still posed a threat, Ximi gave him another swift kick to his middle. Nothing. The man did not move. Satisfied she could safely turn her attention away, she returned to Simone's side.

Simone groaned.

"Don't move! You're injured. I'm calling 911 right now."

"My phone…" Simone whispered weakly. "My phone."

"Not now. We've got to get you to the hospital. I have my own phone. See?"

Ximi brandished her cell close to Simone's swollen face for the battered woman to see. But Simone was adamant and struggled to lift her hand to point toward her purse. The new phone lay on the floor nearby. "Recording," she whispered hoarsely.

The sheriff's small office was unusually crowded. Lois stood behind him, while he was seated in his chair at an oak desk that took up a large portion of the room. The sheriff was not a small man, himself. He and Lois were both staring at a computer screen, looking at a series of black and white photos taken off a memory card from her wildlife camera. The Caldwell woman had produced definitive images of the culprit who had been swiping yard signs from her field and probably from others. The signs belonged to the thief's competitor.

The sheriff knew the evidence was damning. He was a Democrat, too, like Hollister. Something like this looked very bad for the party. He immediately picked up his desk phone and dialed O'Feeny.

"Can you come to my office at once?" he asked. "There's something you've gotta see." He wouldn't have to wait long. O'Feeny was in town having dinner with friends.

O'Feeny arrived soon after the call, accompanied by a tall woman wearing tan Dockers and a pale blue Oxford shirt. The sheriff recognized Underwood, the very competitor whose signs Hollister had pilfered. Also in tow was the real-estate agent and chair for Underwood's campaign. The sheriff groaned.

Lois was surprised to see Avery. "How'd you know to come here?" Lois asked.

"I was with Joe," she replied.

The news caused Lois to grin mischievously.

"And Rosie," Avery added, seeing the look on her friend's face.

"We cannot have this sort of hooliganism going on by one of our own, O'Feeny," the sheriff began. He spun the computer screen around for Joe to see one black and white photo, obviously taken under infrared light. Hollister was clearly visible, clawing his way up an embankment. Another shot showed Hollister walking off with a yard sign under his arm that read, "Underwood for Engineer."

"This is outrageous. What do you suggest?" the sheriff asked. "At best, it's a misdemeanor. At its worst… if the press gets hold of this… "

Joe sighed heavily. "He's brought this on himself. Don't even entertain the idea of a cover-up. I say charge him with a misdemeanor based on this evidence. Publish the arrest just like any other arrest. Then, when the press gets wind and want proof, and they will, give them one of the shots. As a matter of fact, give them the best one you have."

Avery's cell phone rang. It was Ximi.

Joe drove fast with Avery seated beside him. Joe switched on an emergency light mounted on the dash. They followed two sheriff's cruisers and an ambulance responding to Ximi's earlier 911 call for help. Avery was tense and quiet, saying nothing about how fast Joe drove. What worried her most, what they might find once they reached Simone's house, was uppermost on her mind.

Joe brought his car to a hard stop in the street outside the Beck driveway. The EMS van occupied most of the drive, its red lights flashing. Both Joe and Avery jumped out quickly. Avery caught sight of Ximi Ling standing at Beck's open front door. She was waving, urging the EMS responders to hurry.

"Stay here," Joe ordered Avery. "It's a crime scene. You can't go in."

Avery understood and nodded, falling back reluctantly.

Joe followed two deputies through the doorway. On the floor of the kitchen lay two bodies. One was a woman, the other a man, Simone, and Kyle Beck, he guessed. The little Asian woman was talking firmly to one of the deputies who towered over her.

"Yes, *I* knocked him out," Joe overheard her say.

"My friend was about to be killed," Ximi said, pointing down at the man's form, then over to the knife she had kicked away. "He was enraged, intent on stabbing her. He didn't hear me come at him from behind. He threatened Simone. Said, 'I'm really going to teach you a lesson. I'm going to kill you.' Then he raised the knife like this. She demonstrated for the deputy. So I ran at him and got him from behind. He never heard me coming."

The deputy looked doubtful. Kyle outweighed Ximi by a hundred pounds or more.

"Don't look at me like that," she scolded the deputy. "I'm trained in all manner of martial arts. I had to defend myself against my brothers, who are also martial arts *experts*. I know the way of internal power, the way of foot and fist, of Tai Kwon Do and Sin Moo's Hapkido. I could put you on the floor right now if I wanted to, so don't patronize me with that scornful look on your face… officer."

Her tone alone convinced the cop that she spoke the truth. He began taking notes. The EMS crew, in the meantime, separated, with one paramedic attending to each victim. There were no visible signs of injury to Kyle Beck, who was beginning to moan and slowly regain consciousness. Simone, however, was bleeding badly from a head wound. Her face was bruised and swollen. She also groaned in pain.

Joe stepped over to the deputy, who nodded in recognition.

Still lying on the floor, dazed, Kyle slowly became aware that many people surrounded him. He rolled over on his back, grimacing.

Joe knelt down, put his face close to Beck's, and said, "I've been waiting for you to pull something like this, Beck. Been waiting a long time. I knew you'd eventually show your true self to another woman. Debbie Taylor knew you would, too. She's been waiting longer than I have. Debbie's going to tell the judge and a jury all about your past. I don't think Simone's going to hold back, either. And now I have an eyewitness that you can't bribe. Between them, I have a feeling the judge is going to regard you with nothing less than the contempt you deserve. I'll see to it that a jury will agree. Get yourself a good lawyer. You need one. This deputy will read you your rights now, which is more than you deserve. He's going to place you under arrest for assault with intent to kill."

Joe stood up, turned to the deputy, and said, "Haul his sorry ass out of here and charge him."

Ximi put a hand on Joe's arm. "Simone said something about a phone, a recording." she pointed to the mess scattered across the floor. "On her phone, maybe."

Joe looked first at Ximi and then to the floor. Among the items, he spotted a cell phone. It was still active.

"Deputy, can you bag that? Can you see it? Is it recording?"

The deputy, wearing gloves, picked up the phone, then looked questioningly toward Joe. "Sez, 'Home.' It's not recording. Just a cheap phone. "

"Bag it anyway. Then Joe noticed the light on Beck's home phone. "And take their home answering machine. It looks like evidence, too. Strong evidence. Thank you, Simone Beck."

Ximi was arguing with the EMS staff now, insisting she ride with her friend to the hospital. The paramedic remained firm. He refused her request and insisted she would have to follow in her own vehicle at a safe distance.

Joe returned to Avery, who stood waiting anxiously near his car, the light on the dash still flashing red and then white.

"Well?" Avery asked impatiently. "What happened? Is Simone OK?"

"They're taking Simone to the hospital. Her injuries look to me to be non-life threatening. Still, she's hurt. Seems your friend Ximi knocked Beck out cold. Did her Tai Kwon Do thing on him from behind. I'll be sure she gets a commendation for that. Beck will soon be on his way to jail with an appointment for an arraignment. He'll be charged with domestic violence and assault with attempt to kill if I can pin that on him. Your friend, Simone, I believe, recorded the whole thing on her home answering machine. I predict that Beck is going to spend some serious time in prison. Guess the university will have to find a new coach for next season."

The couple stepped back against Joe's car to make way for The EMS van and Ximi Ling to squeeze past. The van was taking Simone to the hospital. It turned and lumbered down the road, picking up speed in the distance, its siren fading away. Ximi Ling drove her car right on its bumper.

"Where's Beck?" Avery asked.

"They've called in a second ambulance to haul his sorry ass to the hospital. Should take a few minutes before it gets here. Don't want both perpetrator and victim riding in the same box. I think your friend, Ximi, busted a few of his ribs and maybe broke his back if we're lucky. Anyway, he's in no shape to move fast or far. I had no idea a bit of Tai Kwon Do could do that to such a fit jackass. Serves him right, though. Ximi gave him a little taste of what he likes to dish out."

Joe's mind began to work ahead to the arraignment. Then he recalled Jasper's escapade and their visit to the sheriff's office. "I assume by now our sheriff's told Hollister's he's got a fine to pay, and he'll be charged with a misdemeanor."

Avery withdrew her phone to check the locator app. "Um hm. Looks like he's downtown right now. At the sheriff's, I think. Maybe Donkey Coffee. It's next door. Can't tell exactly. But he's definitely downtown."

"Don't suppose you'd mind going with me to the newspaper's night desk, would you? Somebody should give them a scoop. Your other friend, Lois, she takes a mean surveillance photo."

Avery smiled. "After that," she asked, "Would you care to take in a movie? My treat."

"No, my treat. I hear there's a good revenge flick playing tonight. We can catch the late showing."

"Joe! You're mean."

"Am not. But I am a fan of the little guy or little woman."

Dark photographs appeared on the front page of the local newspaper the next day, which were quickly picked up by a few regional papers. One gritty image showed incumbent candidate for county engineer, Jasper Hollister, making off with a campaign yard sign. The sign was not his. Next to that photo was a clear and prominent image of his competitor, Avery Underwood, the one whose sign he had pilfered. One of the TV stations in the capitol even sent a camera crew the eighty miles down to Athens to interview the sheriff and victim.

The news article under both photographs identified Hollister's offense as a misdemeanor. However, later that night, the local sheriff unearthed a number of Underwood signs stashed in the back of Hollister's pickup truck parked in his garage. That discovery proved to be fodder for the paper's Sunday editorial cartoonist. The drawing depicted a naughty little boy, whose face remarkably resembled that of Jasper Hollister, getting caned by the sheriff out behind a police station.

The television station interviewed Avery. She told the reporter on camera that she was not surprised Hollister had failed to destroy any of her signs. She was filmed saying, "His general approach to work, particularly paperwork, has always been to let somebody else do the job."

While Avery was giving her television interview outside the sheriff's office, Joe O'Feeny looked out his office window and watched. He had his phone to his ear, waiting for his call to be answered.

"Yes, hi. Debbie Tayler? Joe O'Feeny here. I've got some news for you."

Simone Beck was treated and released from the hospital the same evening she had been assaulted by her husband. Ximi Ling was there to take her home.

Beck didn't fare quite as well. Xim's forceful kick had indeed fractured a vertebrae in the coach's back. The Sheriff charged him with assault with intent to kill and instructed his deputies to keep him handcuffed to his hospital bed. If he was too ill to be incarcerated in the regional jail, then he'd be confined to his bed until such time as he could be moved.

University officials scrambled to take steps to terminate his contract. But first, they had adverse publicity to address. They announced that an official press release would be forthcoming related to their disapproval of the incident in question and their governing board's decision as to the coach's contract.

The camera crew that came down to cover the pilfered election signs got the scent of a much bigger story, one of spousal abuse by the university's very popular football coach. They interviewed the prosecutor for the county, who said he planned to bring charges before a grand jury as soon as possible. Then they interviewed one Brigitta Johansson, a young director of a local shelter for abused women, to get a bit of background for their story.

The drive home for Simone in Ximi's car was a short one but just long enough to let her make a few plans for her future. First, she would hire an attorney and begin the process of filing for divorce. That news greatly pleased her friend. Then, she planned to sell their house. She guessed her husband wouldn't object. He'd probably need funds to cover legal fees for his crime. If she was guessing wrong, then she'd fight to take the property in her divorce settlement. Ximi offered to be a character witness.

Simone also wanted to buy herself a car, or perhaps she'd take the one Kyle owned should Kyle put up any fuss about the sale of their house. He wasn't going to be going anywhere too soon. That thought seemed to lift her spirits. Once home, she'd ask her friend and savior, Ximi Ling, to help her tidy up the mess left in her kitchen. And then the two of them could visit the Thimble and Chatelaine together the next day. She'd ask Molly for her old job back, and maybe she and Ximi would pick out fabric for a quilt. They could work on the quilt together. Ximi eagerly agreed to design the blocks they'd make.

She felt guilty for not having done anything to support the women's shelter since the first day that Robin Prescott had told the Tea Baskets about Harbor House. It was past time she did something about that.

For the first time in a long while, Simone Beck felt like her old, independent self, useful, worthy, and appreciated.

As Election Day neared, it was the Democratic Party chair, Joe O'Feeny, who was quoted in the paper as saying he knew Underwood personally and thought "she'd make a fine engineer for the county, even as an independent." That statement seemed to many Democrats as permission and an invitation to break with the party and cast a vote for her.

On Election Day, Jasper Hollister, excommunicated by his own party and licking his wounds at home, lost to his former assistant by a landslide. By Christmas, the party chair, O'Feeny, had publicly welcomed Underwood back into the fold of the Democratic Party. On December thirty-first, county officials held a brief swearing-in ceremony for all newly elected officeholders in the courthouse. Avery Underwood put her hand on a bible and swore to accept and execute her duties as the new county engineer.

The next morning, New Year's Day dawned overcast and cold. Avery arrived early for her first day back on the job. She nosed her big Ford in the spot once reserved for Hollister's county vehicle. A big snow was forecast for the region starting in the afternoon, and she wanted everything prepared. She knew the roads would be a mess if crews weren't on alert, the plows gassed up, and dump beds full of cinders and salt. As she turned off the engine, she noticed many other cars and trucks already parked around the building.

Sheila Harper greeted her as she came through the door. She, too, had voluntarily come into work. Sheila's countertop was a buffet of food. There were several large boxes of pizza and cartons of soda pop donated by Joe and Avery's favorite pizza shop. The crew had brought in an assortment of hors d'oeuvres from home. Avery saw plates of deviled eggs, a bowl of gazpacho dip and chips, sausage wraps, nuts, sheet cakes, and even pies. Nobody was going to starve this New Year's Day. Several of the road crew had already arrived without any call from their new boss. All seemed eager to give up their holiday. Four of the men were mounting a big screen TV on one of the walls in the outer office. It seemed they were planning to catch the games while waiting for snow to fall. Other crew members busied themselves arranging benches repurposed from old trucks long-destined for the junkyard. Avery smiled. Not lost on her, this atmosphere felt remarkably different than when Hollister was in charge. She turned her attention to Hollister's old office, now her office.

Sheila followed her back through the door. "You want me to go through file cabinets searching for anything that might be important, left undone?"

"Sounds good. Thanks," Avery said. "But later. It's New Year's Day. Shouldn't you be home with your family?"

Sheila shrugged. "I can ignore football right here just as easily as I can ignore it at home. My role as chief cook is finished. My guys are well-stocked. While the games are on, they won't miss me. So, if it's OK with you, I'll just stay and answer calls. In the meantime… " She nodded toward the file cabinets across the room.

Avery nodded appreciatively. "If you need help, I know a kid named Frank Westfall who'd probably come in. He was an intern a while back. Hollister had him out digging ditches last summer. He'd be better served working on files for the moment. I think we can afford a temporary hire. Don't you? Pull Hollister's budget, Sheila. I want to see if we can afford an interim hire to take over mapping changes this year."

"Oh," Sheila said. "I almost forgot." She went to Hollister's old desk and pulled open the center drawer to produce a set of keys. "Someone told me you had a special key fob just for these." She smiled and handed Avery all the keys to the highway department's buildings.

Avery smiled back, thinking of Joe. She reached deep into the pocket of her jeans for the fob he had given her.

Avery's cell phone rang. She glanced at the display. Nora Radnor was calling.

"I'll bet you're already on the job," Nora said with mock frustration.

"That would be a yes, Nora."

"That's what I figured. Well, I just called to warn you I am not opening up the hall today. None of the ladies will be in. It's a holiday. Lots of snow forecast. I didn't want you to make a trip for nothing on your break."

"Thanks, Nora. I'll be at the office for some time with that snowstorm on its way. Will you be OK if we do get several inches?"

"Oh, sure. I won't venture out. I'd tell you to do the same, but I know you won't listen to me. Sometimes, you don't take my advice, no matter how good it is. However, should your travels bring you anywhere near my house, you know, I can make a good cup of coffee in my own kitchen as well as at the Tea Basket hall.

"I'm sure you can, Nora. I'm sure you can."

Sheila located the budget in one of the file cabinets and handed the folder over to Avery.

Avery said goodbye to Nora on the phone and took the file to Hollister's old desk. There, she dropped it on the desk just as the big TV in the outer room boomed into life with the sounds of a parade clearly audible. The aroma of pepperoni and possibly fried chicken drifted in, making Avery suddenly hungry. The budget, she decided, could wait an hour or two. She joined her crew and Sheila, eating slices of pizza for their breakfast, drinking sodas, and watching the New Year's Day parade on the big screen.

She thought she might call Joe later to find out what his plans were for the day. He'd probably be at his apartment, not cooking. Not much he could do with county offices closed; maybe having takeout. Her first day on the job, however, was going to be a long one. She wondered if maybe he might like to join her here in her new office if the approaching storm wasn't as bad as predicted.

Avery Underwood smiled, happy to be back at work.